THE NAMELESS DEAD

Inspector Patronas' mystery, Greek Island Mystery #5

Leta Serafim

coffeetownpress

Kenmore, WA

coffeetownpress

A Coffeetown Press book published by Epicenter Press

Epicenter Press
6524 NE 181st St. Suite 2
Kenmore, WA 98028.
www.Epicenterpress.com
www.Coffeetownpress.com
www.Camelpress.com

For more information go to: www.coffeetownpress.com
Author Website: Letaserafim.net

The Nameless Dead
Copyright © 2025 by Leta Serafim

ISBN: 9781684922512 (trade paper)
ISBN: 9781684922536 (ebook)
LOC: 2024952554

To all those seeking a new life and freedom on foreign shores

Acknowledgements

Many people aided me in the creation of this book, most notably my late husband, Philip Serafim, and my cherished friend, Nancy-Nickles Dawson.

Chapter 1

Chief Inspector Yiannis Patronas and his second-in-command, Giorgos Tembelos, were sitting at a cafe in Chora, the capital of the Greek island of Chios, when the call came in about the dead girl. They had been conducting a half-hearted stake-out of the area, hoping to nab a pair of shoplifters who had been plaguing the neighborhood. It had been a long fruitless day in the rain, a useless exercise. Unlike cops, apparently thieves didn't work in bad weather.

"A workman found her in Souda," the dispatcher told Patronas. "It's bad, sir. Someone slit her throat."

Holding the phone to his ear, Patronas threw some money down on the table and stood up. "Call forensics. We're on our way."

Now abandoned, the Souda refugee camp had once occupied a ravine near the center of town. Overshadowed by a crumbling medieval castle, it remained a dank and claustrophobic place, a vast, garbage-choked slum.

Souda had a troubled history. In 2016, the residents of the camp had been attacked, unknown men raining Molotov cocktails down on them from the castle walls. Fortunately, no one was killed, although a Syrian man was seriously injured.

The attacks had occurred over a three-day period; and on the second day, the refugees had broken into a store and stolen fireworks to defend themselves.

Patronas had once seen a photograph of a man attacking a tank with a rock. It might have been in Budapest or the Warsaw Ghetto, he couldn't remember; and in his opinion, the situation in Souda had been similar, desperate people seeking to defend themselves with nothing.

After the theft of the fireworks, the police had been called and forty-seven migrants had been arrested.

Deeply frightened, the refugees then fled, preferring to sleep outside in a parking lot rather than return; and, subsequently, the camp had been closed, its eight hundred residents transferred to Vial, a much bigger camp in the interior of the island.

"The Molotov cocktails set their tents on fire," Patronas had told his superiors, seeking to get the migrants released. "The fireworks were the only way they could find to protect themselves."

No one had listened; and the refugees had remained in jail.

Although the men who'd thrown the Molotov cocktails were never caught, Patronas was sure they were members of the right-wing party, Golden Dawn. It stood to reason. Virulent racists, they'd been targeting immigrants all over Greece. On the nearby island of Lesbos, they had taken to patrolling the streets with wooden clubs, seeking migrants to beat up. They'd also orchestrated 'Greeks-only' food banks and blood-donation drives and muscled their way into hospitals to check the residence permits of immigrant nurses.

Seeking to appeal to voters, a politician from Golden Dawn had promised to 'turn on the ovens' and make lampshades from the skins of the migrants.

The government had barely lifted a finger when they killed a Pakistan fruit worker or attempted to murder three Egyptian fishermen. However, when one of their operatives stabbed Pavlos Fyssas, a Greek rapper, to death, it had set off a firestorm and made headlines around the world, culminating in the trial of sixty-eight of Golden Dawn members, the largest trial of fascists since Nuremberg.

Golden Dawn was still out there; Patronas was sure of it; lurking in the shadows like a nest of vipers. Given the location of the dead girl—in an abandoned refugee camp—this killing might well have been their handiwork.

A pair of German tourists had found her. They'd been strolling beneath the castle walls, walking sticks in hand, and noticed birds attacking what appeared to be a pile of rags. Curious, they'd walked over to see and stumbled across the body.

Not exactly what they'd been expecting, it had taken some time to calm them down, the dispatcher said.

"Wife is hysterical. They'll have a field day with this back in Hamburg."

"Do what you can to contain it," Patronas said. "No press. Nothing on the scanner. Call the coroner and the forensic team and tell them to hurry. Rain is washing away the evidence."

• • •

No one had bothered to clean up Souda after the camp was closed; and remnants of the white plastic tents were still there, flapping in the wind. Stamped with the insignia of the United Nations refugee agency, UNHCR, they were a ghostly presence in the rain. Before departing, the migrants had written farewell messages on some of them. 'I am alone,' one read. 'Love all people,' another.

Patronas could still see where the fire had ripped through the camp, the blackened plastic a mute witness to the attack.

He wondered what had become of the people he'd interviewed at the time, the boy from the Central African Republic, who'd drawn Africa surrounded by a heart on his t-shirt, or Fezma and Ahmet, the two brothers, who had journeyed here from Pakistan.

They'd had so little—a copy of the Koran, an extra pair of shoes—and then someone had fire-bombed them and they'd lost even that. It still troubled him.

One of Patronas' officers, Melissa Costas, was struggling to string yellow crime scene tape around the body, but it kept getting away from her, snapping and fluttering in the wind like a macabre party decoration.

She was soaked to the skin, her dark hair plastered to her face. He grabbed one end of the tape and helped her to anchor it.

"Coroner is on his way," he told her.

Pulling the hood of his jacket up, Patronas walked around the dead girl, inspecting her from all angles.

Dressed in a faded velvet caftan, she was lying face down on the damp ground. Her dress had wide bands of gold embroidery along the sleeves and hem and was caked with mud. Her long black hair was loose; and she was barefoot. Patronas could see tiny abrasions on the soles of her feet, inflamed areas that looked like the beginning of blisters.

"Somebody do that to her, you think?" He pointed to the girl's feet.

"Hard to tell," Costas said. "Could have happened from going around barefoot."

"Was she wearing a hijab?"

"No, not that I could see."

"You find any identification?"

"No. Nothing."

He looked around the camp. It had rained all night and water was pooling everywhere. "Where are the people who found her?"

Costas gestured to one of the tents. "I put them in there."

Ducking his head, Patronas entered the tent. It was very dark inside; and he left the flap of the tent open so he'd be able to see. He could hear the rain beating against the canvas, the howling wind tugging at the ropes that held it down.

Hearty, strapping specimens, the Germans was dressed in black ponchos the size of tents, pants with zippers on all sides and matching Tyrolean hats with feathers. In addition, the man was had a wide leather belt with a hammer and what looked like a pickaxe hanging from it, a length of coiled rope. Odd garb for the beach, Patronas thought, taking them in, but then they were Germans; and Germans often did things the rest of the world didn't understand.

Actually, in the past, Germans had done a lot of things the world didn't understand. Just ask Poland.

They were both enormous people, well over six feet tall. Nearly a foot shorter, Patronas felt this keenly. He began to bluster and shout, seeking to attain the high ground in volume if not in size.

"Start at the beginning," he bellowed. "Your names please."

"I am Hannah Reichmann," the woman said. "My husband, he is Ernst Reichmann."

"Address?"

"Maximilianstrasse 25, Munich."

Her glasses sat awkwardly on her face, tilting slightly forward; and she stared down at him from on high, rather like an eagle eyeing dinner.

"Describe what you found."

"The gulls, they were pecking at something. Peck, peck, peck. We thought it must be an animal and we walked over to see. That is when we saw her. Soaked in blood, she was. So much blood, it made the sand black."

All in all, this took some time to get said. She was speaking English which meant Patronas had to use the app on his phone; and he wasn't fluent in apps.

Getting out his notebook, Patronas carefully wrote down the date, November second, and time. 11:40 a.m., the Germans had found the body. He then drew a crude map of Souda, marking the location of the dead girl. He'd start a murder book when he returned to the station and re-enter the information there.

"You see anyone nearby?"

"No. There was no one. Only the birds."

Understandably distraught, the couple had little else to report. Once they'd realized it was a body the seagulls were attacking, they'd stayed well away, knowing enough not to contaminate a crime scene.

"We called the emergency and waited."

After taking down their contact information, Patronas ordered Costas to drive them back to their hotel. "Get their passports while you're at it. For the time being, they cannot leave Greece."

"They want to go home. They're not going to like that."

"Tough. Tell them there's nothing you can do. You're only obeying orders. They're Bavarians. They should understand."

The Germans left a few minutes later. Rain dripping off their wet ponchos, they hurried to where Costas was waiting with the car, carefully avoiding the police activity on the beach.

The forensic team had arrived. The police photographer was on his knees, taking photos of the scene, the flashing of his camera bright in the gloom. Inching around, he kept shooting, the camera making a small pinging noise from time to time as it recharged. The coroner was next to him, going over the girl's body centimeter by centimeter with his gloved hands.

After he finished, he and the photographer gently rolled her over. Patronas gasped when he saw her. Even in death, she was extraordinarily beautiful, her face reminiscent of a Raphael Madonna.

He was sure her beauty had led to her death. She was probably Syrian; and somewhere on her journey, she must have attracted the attention of the wrong kind of man.

The front of her dress was soaked in blood, the wound in her throat, jagged and raw.

"Any idea what they used?" Patronas asked the coroner, a thin, bespectacled man named Dimitri Constantinou.

"An axe or a hatchet would be my guess," Constantinou said. "Something with a big blade."

He continued to examine her, gently trying to move the limbs back and forth.

In the past, the staff at the local hospital had determined cause of death and filled out the necessary paperwork, but there had been an upsurge in drug overdoses recently and they hadn't been able to keep up. A retired gynecologist, Constantinou had been hired to assist them on a case-by-case basis.

At first Patronas had kept his distance, thinking no one in their right mind would willingly spend their lives plumbing the depths of the female anatomy, going where no man should ever go; but as time went by, he'd come to rely on Constantinou and trust his opinion.

"Advanced rigor," the coroner announced. "Given the chill in the air, she's probably been dead for at least eight hours."

"Anything else?"

"Whoever did this put these clothes on her. You see that caftan she's wearing? It's way too long. She wouldn't have been able to walk in it."

"Was she interfered with?" Patronas couldn't bring himself to say the word, 'raped.'

"Couldn't say. I'll know more after the autopsy."

Standing up, he pulled off his latex gloves. "I've done all I can do here. I'll finish the rest at the hospital."

He and Patronas loaded the girl's body onto the gurney and wheeled it out to the waiting ambulance.

"After I perform the autopsy, I'll call you with the results," the coroner said. "Butchering a young girl like that…Let's hope this isn't the start of something."

"A serial killer?"

The coroner nodded. "This level of violence…it wouldn't surprise me."

• • •

Murder was exceedingly rare in Greece; and, consequently, most local policemen had little experience dealing with it. Chios was no exception; and Patronas spent the next three hours yelling at his staff, trying to keep them from trampling all over the crime scene and destroying evidence.

"Scour the area," he instructed. "Collect what you find, put it in evidence bags and label it with your name and the time and place it was found. We must preserve the chain of evidence."

It wasn't much, but it was all he had. That bit about 'chain of evidence,' had come from an American movie he'd seen. It was what you did in lieu of talent, he told himself. You channeled your counterparts on the silver screen.

He'd solved his share of homicide cases--seven over the last ten years, a record in Greece—but the truth was he still didn't know how he'd cleared those cases. Luck had certainly played a role; as for the rest, it was a mystery. He hadn't known what he was doing then, didn't know what he was doing now. He'd do his best to catch the girl's killer—he always did his best—but in his heart he knew his best didn't amount to much.

He was no Sherlock Holmes or Hercules Poirot, although he was about the same size as the latter. He wasn't even a very good cop, just a dumpy, pigeon-toed little man with a moustache, the Charlie Chaplin of Greek law enforcement.

Another member of the force, Papa Michalis, joined him around noon. A retired priest, he worked part-time for the department, counseling violent drunks and wife beaters, a job he was ill-suited for—having been a teetotaler and celibate his entire life—and had failed at spectacularly. One offender told Patronas just the thought of Papa Michalis made him want to slug somebody.

He had, however, proven indispensable during interrogations, which was why Patronas kept him around. One moment a suspect would be sitting there, scowling, then after a word or two or three—-Papa Michalis never shut up—- that same person would be signing a confession. How this miracle occurred, Patronas couldn't say, but he suspected it was the endless talking.

"Hell, I'd confess, too," he told Giorgos Tembelos. "Anything to shut him up."

And talk he did that afternoon and on into evening, "I see we have no *corpus delecti*," he declared at one point. "In layman's terms, that is the body of the crime."

This time it was Patronas who wanted to slug him.

The priest was addicted to American detective shows, especially those featuring lab work, the bloodier the better, and fervently believed the hours he spent watching them made him an expert in forensics—that a kind of knowledge transfer had taken place. It hadn't so far as Patronas was concerned. He fervently wished Papa Michalis would go back to his holy books and lay off the TV.

He did say one thing that had merit, however, and that was that the origins of the murder might lie elsewhere. In Syria or perhaps Turkey. A situation the girl had come to Greece to escape from.

Chapter 2

Patronas spent the next two days attempting to identify the dead girl. He went through every database he could think of, including the massive one maintained by the United Nations Refugee Agency, but found no trace of her.

He worried that if he didn't learn her identity and learn it soon, the case would stall and she would be forgotten, the evidence of her death—what little there was of it—put in a box and shelved in the back of the police station.

The coroner had called with the autopsy report. "Maximum liver mortis occurs twelve hours after death, I'd say that's what we have here. She died last night around eight or nine o'clock."

"Are you sure?"

"Yes. The liver doesn't lie."

"You asked if she'd been interfered with," he added, "Surprisingly, the results came back negative. Her hymen was intact. She was a virgin."

"A girl like that? Why didn't he rape her?"

"Being a virgin would have increased her value. There are men willing to pay a lot of money to be the first."

"But instead, he killed her. It doesn't make sense."

"You're the homicide detective, Patronas, not I. I only deal with its bloody aftermath, never with the events leading up to it."

"We don't even know her name."

"One more lost migrant. What can I say? The world is full of them. I've worked with women all my life, Chief Inspector, and you won't believe the things they've told me, the way some of my patients have suffered at the hands of men."

• • •

That afternoon Patronas drove to Vial, the largest refugee camp on the island. He kept thinking if he only had the dead girl's name, he'd be able to trace her movements and reconstruct what might have happened to her.

There'd been a riot in the camp, residents protesting the appalling living conditions and setting fire to the place. A canteen had been lost during the uprising, along with the facilities of the European Asylum Service and countless housing units.

A miasma of smoke hung over the facility; and the air was rank and had a greasy feel. A high wire fence, topped with razor wire, marked the entrance. A cattle chute for humans, Patronas thought, taking it in. Run the people through it and do with them what you will. Children's clothing was hanging from the fence, worn-out t-shirts and pajamas with cartoon characters, Spiderman, Ilsa and Anna from *Frozen*.

A group of men were waiting to use the latrines; and they eyed him warily. Not Syrians—Afghans or Iraqis—men who'd known nothing, but war. He took care as he made his way around them. As Chief of Police on the island. he was all too familiar with what these men were capable of; and they terrified him.

Robbery was common in the camp—one group strong arming another and taking their life savings—as were violent confrontations and rape. For the most part, the victims were reluctant to talk to the police; and he'd gotten nowhere when he had questioned them.

He stopped by the administrative offices and spoke to the person in charge, Dimitri Liadis. Liadis' wife was also there, leaning over her husband's shoulder and reading something on his computer. She straightened up when she saw Patronas and quickly shut down whatever she'd been looking at.

'Yiannis Patronas.' he said.

"Ah, yes. The Chief Inspector," she said. "My husband told me about you."

Although she tried hard to sound like she was from Kolonaki, an exclusive area in Athens, she hadn't quite mastered it; and the port of Piraeus kept breaking through.

Much younger than her husband, she was dressed in a silk shirtwaist, printed with some Frenchman's initials. Her designer handbag—Yves

Saint Laurent, judging by the name engraved on the clasp—must have cost thousands as did the gold necklace with the lion heads she wore around her neck. Patronas recognized the design. His wife, Lydia had sighed over it when they'd visited the Lalalounis' store in Athens. Each lion had a ruby eye and diamond encrusted mane; and the whole thing had weighed a ton. How much was it? Ten, twenty thousand euros? He couldn't remember.

A woman like that could run up a big tab, Patronas thought. Way beyond Liadis' pay scale.

If he'd seen her in a restaurant, he would have assumed she was the wife of a shipowner. She had the same gloss, the same imperious air those women did, the ones who divided their time between London and Monaco.

But she wasn't in a restaurant, she was here in her husband's office in Vial. Idly, he wondered what the residents of the camp made of her, the refugees who counted themselves lucky if they had a coat.

Liadis had been away when they'd first discovered the girl's body which was the reason why Patronas hadn't approached him sooner. A Greek civil servant of the old school, he was dressed in a three-piece suit and driving moccasins of the softest leather. Inappropriate footwear, given where he worked, a place where raw sewage ran in the street.

Patronas handed him the photo of the dead girl. "Do you recognize her?"

Putting on his glasses, Liadis studied the photo. "Yes, she was here. Why? What happened to her?"

"Someone killed her and dumped her body at Souda."

"I don't remember exactly when she was here. It was some time ago. If she's who I think she is, she was deeply traumatized. Something happened to her, something horrific; and she was terrified. Couldn't sleep at night and kept the others awake with her screaming."

"Do you know what it was?"

"Could be anything. These people have been through hell, Chief Inspector. There are children in Vial who witnessed beheadings, women who saw their husbands get burned alive. People don't leave their homes because they want to. They leave because they have no choice."

"Do you remember her name?"

Liadis shook his head. "Thousands of people pass through here; and I don't know the names of all of them. We do our best to keep a record of who stays here, but it's hardly complete. We're always behind."

He handed the photo back to him. "Do you think it was a random attack?"

"No. It felt personal to me. I think she was targeted."

"An honor killing?"

"I don't know. Maybe."

The killing of one's child was anathema in Greece, unthinkable, but Patronas wasn't sure it was the same for the refugees in the camp, especially those from Jihadist countries, where men valued purity above all else in their women.

"She was staying with some Syrian women on the western side of the camp," Liadis said.

"Are they still here?"

"Yes. I'll introduce you to them. They don't speak Greek. Only Arabic. If you want, I can translate for you. I'm fluent in Arabic."

"Where'd you learn Arabic?"

"Alexandria, Egypt. I grew up there, but then Nasser came and forced us to leave. That's why I took this job. I've made the same journey these people have, Chief Inspector. I, too, am a refugee."

After saying good-bye to his wife, Liadis led Patronas out into the vast labyrinth of tents, many of the stamped with the logo of the United Nations Refugee Agency. There were five Syrian women crowded into the one where the victim had lived, along with a handful of children. A little girl was playing outside with a doll in a red dress. She was tending to it lovingly, tucking a square of cloth around it like a blanket and humming a tuneless song. Her face darkened when she saw them; and she got up and scampered into the tent, leaving her doll behind.

"*Omm!*" she cried. "*Omm!*" Mommy. .

• • •

Liadis handed the women the picture of the dead girl and asked in Arabic if they'd seen her. The oldest in the group nodded. Half crippled with arthritis; she caressed the picture with her gnarled hands.

"Raina," she whispered. "Raina."

None of the women knew the girl's last name, where she was from or what had happened to her. They weren't even sure she was from Damascus. She'd been traveling alone. 'Hiding,' one of them said in Arabic.

Pantomiming fear, she pretended to tremble, backing away and holding her hands in front of her face.

"When did she arrive here?" Liadis asked.

"Before summer," the woman said and started to cry.

And that was as far as they got.

The women didn't know what to make of them and were obviously uncomfortable having foreign men in their midst. And the children were terrified, the little girl with the doll, hiding her face in her mother's skirt.

Patronas opened the language app on his phone and asked her what her name was in Arabic.

The technology obviously impressed her—a talking phone—and she answered him, smiling shyly. *"Dalia,"* she whispered.

Nodding respectfully, Patronas and Liadis retreated, calling out *Alleh akbar,* God is great, to her and her mother as they walked away.

• • •

"Do you know how many migrants there are named 'Raina?" Patronas asked his wife, Lydia Pappas, that night. "According to the United Nations, well over a hundred thousand."

Sitting outside on the terrace, they were wrapped up in blankets, drinking wine and discussing the case. High above the trees, a full moon was rising, its light illuminating the sea in front of them and making the water shimmer.

The area where they lived was deserted now that summer was over, the only sound the murmuring of the waves in the distance. The cove at the front of their house was enclosed on three sides, a small rockbound island at its center. When it was warmer, they sometimes swam out to it at night, lay on their backs in the water and watched for falling stars.

"What do you wish for?" Lydia had asked him one night.

"This," Patronas had answered, reaching for her hand. "Only this."

They'd met on the Greek island of Sifnos two years before during a murder investigation. She'd been a professor then, teaching ceramics at a design school in Boston and had come to Sifnos to run a summer study and research local pottery.

"I'm an artist," she'd explained the day they met. "Clay is my medium."

"A potter?"

"I prefer the term, 'ceramicist.'"

Patronas knew things were strange in America, but this was the first time he'd heard you could get a degree in pot-making at a university. He hadn't taken her seriously at first—clay, mud, it was all the same to him—but she'd gradually won him over; and he had proposed not long after,

He still considered her presence in his life a kind of miracle. God knows, he was nothing to look at, two-thirds the size of a normal man and shaped like a penguin. And then there was his moustache, as thick as a paintbrush.

She'd been after him recently to cut if off—it had been one of the few things they'd argued about—but so far, he'd refused. His father had had a similar moustache as had his grandfather before him. How could he shave it off? Abandon a family tradition?

Out of date, she called it. But then so was he.

Other than that, they got along well. He'd come roaring home on his moped, eager to discuss the events of the day with her; and they would sit outside and talk. Lydia was an avid listener—no one had ever listened to Patronas the way she did—then when they were done talking, they would go inside and eat dinner.

Ah, yes, dinner. The only fly in the ointment.

Lydia believed recipes limited her creativity and liked to 'wing it,' her term, not his; and the results—carrying the 'winging it' to its inevitable conclusion—was most often a plane crash.

Sometimes fiery and sometimes not, but nearly always inedible.

He'd bought her a cookbook for Christmas and inscribed it, 'where there is life, there is hope,' but so far, she hadn't used it.

• • •

"Have you thought about offering a reward?" Lydia asked. "They do it all the time in the states. You put up posters with the missing person's photo, the amount of money you're offering and the phone number they should call."

"How much of a reward?" asked Patronas. America had money. Greece didn't. A fact Lydia often overlooked. .

"A hundred euros maybe. You need to catch this man, Yiannis."

He looked over at her. "What makes you so sure it's a man?"

"A woman would never do something like this."

She was right. Women didn't use knives when they wanted to hurt someone. No, judging by Patronas' experience with his first wife, Dimitra, they used words. He'd never forget the day she'd told him she'd been to the doctor; and it wasn't her. She wasn't the reason they had no kids. It was him. Her delight in the pain she'd caused him.

But that was Dimitra; Lydia was different. She was a true innocent, his second wife, incapable of hurting anyone. Killing mosquitos gave her trouble.

When he and Dimitra got divorced, she'd taken possession of the house, leaving him homeless and adrift for close for eighteen months, all his earthly possessions stowed in a cardboard box under his desk at the office. Given the economic situation, he couldn't afford to buy another place or even rent one, not if he wanted to eat; and he'd still be homeless, camping out at the police station if fate hadn't intervened and he'd met Lydia on Sifnos.

Turned out Lydia had money and after they returned to Chios, she'd bought the cottage for them. It was on a beach; and at night, they'd leave the windows open; and he'd lay there in bed and watch her sleep, her auburn hair like a cloud on the pillow, so overcome with tenderness he could barely breathe.

• • •

Early the next day Patronas ordered his staff to print up reward posters and distribute them throughout the island.

"We will set up a hotline," he told them. "Someone calls, you record it and get as much information from them as you can. Perpetrators have been known to call in and taunt the police, so be vigilant. We will be working in shifts, monitoring the phone line twenty-four hours a day. Officer Costas, you're on duty from now until three, after that Giorgos Tembelos will take over; and I will do the night shift."

There were no calls that day or the next; and by the end of the week, the posters had all been defaced, graffiti scribbled all over them, spray painted with initials and the strange hieroglyphics the young favored. Patronas thought about tearing them down, but he decided against it. He hadn't given up hope that someone would see the photo and recognize the dead girl.

• • •

The case had stalled; and time hung heavy on Patronas' hands. According to local merchants, the shoplifters were still active in the area; and he decided to head back to the café with Tembelos and make one last effort to apprehend them.

"We've got a couple hours before you take over for Costas," he told Tembelos. "Might as well make use of them."

Mid-November, a strong wind was blowing as they walked to the cafe; and it stirred the ancient plane trees in the square and sent leaves scuttling across the stone pavement.

"θρόισμα," he said aloud. Greek for the rustling of the wind in the trees. An ancient language, his native tongue had many such words, covering nearly every aspect of life. He especially loved the ones pertaining to the sea, φουρτούνα, a tempest, *kyma, kýmata,* waves, large and small.

Once he'd tried to purify his Greek and rid his speech of all foreign words, but his marriage to Lydia had put an end to that. Although she did her best, her Greek was not for the faint-hearted.

Once she'd ordered '*katralou*,' little girl peeing,' at a taverna instead of *yiaouptlou,* 'with yogurt.' Patronas would never forget the look on the waiter's face.

He'd shelved his quest for purity after that and never went back to it; and at home, he spoke a hybrid of English and Greek. '*Congolesika*,' he called it. What people spoke in the Congo.

He felt like he'd lost a piece of himself; and it grieved him, but then so much did now. His homeland had been transformed—the Greece of his childhood irrevocably gone. As a boy, he and his friends had biked down to a bar by harbor and stood outside in the dark, listening to the *rebetiko* singers, a genre brought to Greece by refugees from Asia Minor. The bartender would give them orange juice and check up on them as the night wore on. All was safe then, all was good.

He still remembered the lyrics of one of those songs.

You don't want to marry me.

You're afraid of being poor.

But I have a dowry which is honor

Which is worth much, much more.

Once everyone in Greece had shared the same history, the same expectations for themselves and others, but not anymore. Who spoke of φιλότιμον now? The love of honor Plato had written about. A concept that had no equivalent in English or any other language as far as he knew, it meant the honoring one's responsibilities and duties and the preservation of one's dignity and pride at all costs. It was the code Patronas lived by as had his father before him.

They didn't speak of Plato anymore, the kids. Φιλότιμον was a foreign concept to them. They didn't talk of dignity either or nobility, all the old words.

No, Narcissus was king now and the selfie ruled the day.

America was worse, what with their guns and the buffoons, who were running things, but he didn't care about it or the rest of the world. All that mattered to him was Greece, his precious homeland, with its miraculous light and endless sea; and he felt like Greece had lost its way.

A group of children were playing a game of tag; and he watched them for a moment. They were Syrians from the look of them, probably from a nearby camp. Somehow, they'd survived the journey from Damascus to Greece, and unless things changed, would probably grow up here. Shouting in Arabic, they continued to chase one another across the square, their voices growing fainter and fainter as they ran.

A homicide detective, catching shoplifters had never been one of Patronas' priorities, but eliminating petty crime had worked wonders for the city of New York; and, as head of the police department on Chios, he had decided to give it a try. His subordinates had objected, but he had gone ahead anyway and ordered them to arrest drivers all over the island for speeding which had caused no end of ill will. Worse were the drunks who'd been booked for disturbing the peace and threatened to kill him.

The mayor had eventually called and begged him to call off the campaign, saying the local population was up in arms, but Patronas had dismissed his concerns. "The law is the law," he'd told him. "My job is to uphold it."

"Old leather ass," they called him at the station and not without cause.

Admittedly, this attitude had caused him no end of trouble with the mayor and with the women in his life.

"You are as stubborn as the day is long," Lydia often said.

The first Mrs. Patronas had been less charitable. "You know what I say, Yiannis? I say you chew shit and spit it out. You are nothing, but a shit machine."

Ah, yes. Dimitra. The ancient Greeks said it best, 'the tongue serves some, the teeth, others;' and his ex-wife was all about teeth, fangs, actually.

The sidewalk was littered with rotting fruit no one had bothered to pick up, clouds of wasps hovering above the festering oranges and lemons. A legacy of Greece's entry into the European Union. The Union controlled the export of citrus fruit—-once the lifeblood of Chios— and had set the prices so low it had killed off the entire industry.

A naked mannequin lay in front of the window of an empty building, its arms raised as if in supplication. "Bare-assed and begging." Tembelos laughed, pointing to the mannequin. "That's us now, that's Greece."

Wads of gum were stuck to the lamp posts and a car, long abandoned, had been stripped of its tires, its metallic blue color bleached to a leprous gray by the sun. On all sides, buildings stood deserted, red signs plastered across their windows. *'Enoikiazetai,'* for rent

An abandoned mosque stood in one corner of the square. Built by the Ottomans centuries before, it was one of the loveliest buildings on the island; and there'd been talk of turning it into a museum, but the Turkish government in Ankara had objected and the plan had been scrapped. No one on Chios wanted that kind of trouble, not now with the Turks on the move, their president, Recep Tayyip Erdogan, seeking to reclaim the Greek islands in the Aegean. Like everything else in the area, the mosque had a forlorn air, its portico padlocked and full of dead leaves.

They didn't catch the shoplifters that day, nor the next, in part because Papa Michalis kept turning up. The old man had a nose like a bloodhound when it came to free food, could smell it from across the ocean.

He'd eaten his way through a mountain of pastries—baklava and tarts mostly, the expensive ones with the nuts—none of which he paid for. He kept asking them loudly—in his eighties, he was quite deaf—and repeatedly—again, the hearing—why they were here and not at the police station. Apparently, discretion was not part of the coursework at the seminary. But then again, perhaps Papa Michalis had skipped that class and gone straight for the one on freeloading.

If the shoplifters were nearby, now they were undoubtedly aware of the stake-out. Papa Michalis had seen to that. He might as well have used a bull horn.

"Go away, Father," Patronas finally said. "Go back to the station. You are impeding our investigation."

"I am doing no such thing," the priest said, drawing himself up. "I am just sitting here quietly, having a snack."

"Quiet, you will never be."

Papa Michalis continued to eat. He'd gotten crumbs stuck in his beard and more than a few nuts which he fished out now and chewed on.

"I mean it, Father. Get out of here."

The old man walked off in a huff, muttering to himself.

"He can't even dress himself anymore," Tembelos said. "He's got his robe on backwards."

"I've been thinking about retiring him."

"You can't, Yiannis. We are all he's got. Where would he sleep? Where would he go?"

Along with the deafness and the gluttony, the old man also had difficulty with authority which is why he worked for Patronas and not for the bishop. The bishop had kicked him out, as had the faithful in every parish he'd ever served in. He'd eaten them out of house and home and had made a half-day out of the liturgy which usually took ninety minutes. If he was the father of anything, it was chaos.

Patronas once asked him why it took him so long to recite the liturgy.

"I've always been a bit of a tortoise," he'd answered. "Never could finish a test in school. I'd write down one answer, then start fretting and cross it all out and start over again. Over-thinking, I believe it's called. That's one of the reasons I became a priest. No guesswork, only ready-made-answers."

"What were the other reasons you became a priest?"

"Love of God, oh, my, yes. Love of God. Also love of man, although lately that one has been giving me trouble."

For the time being, the priest was living in the police department, sleeping in a closet or on occasion in an unoccupied cell. It wasn't an ideal solution—he had taken to undressing and bathing in the sink in the washroom which upset everyone, especially the women, who called it sexual harassment and threatened to quit.

"It's not harassment," Patronas told them. "He's just taking a bath."

"He's exposing himself, Chief Inspector," one of the women had said. "Here in the station. You should see him. All his equipment is out on display."

After this discussion, Patronas took it up with Papa Michalis, explaining that he couldn't stand there naked in the bathroom of the police station and sponge himself off. It was unseemly, unsightly and very likely illegal.

Consequently, Papa Michalis now bathed at Patronas' house every Saturday night.

Not that the rest of Patronas' staff was much better. Giorgos Tembelos was the classic, 'don't stand if you can sit,' kind of civil servant; and as for Melissa Costas, his most recent hire, the less said about her the better.

She had seriously bungled a murder investigation on the island of Spetses and been fired as a result for 'gross incompetence.' Patronas had taken pity on her and hired her on a provisional basis, but she'd been a liability since day one, reeking of alcohol and given to fits of uncontrollable weeping.

"What'd you do?" the other members of the force would ask him. "What'd you say to her?"

And the answer was nothing. The waterworks just came out of nowhere.

When he'd discussed the situation with his wife, she'd nodded sagely and said, 'menopause.'

He had immediately changed the subject and never brought it up again.

Tembelos, Costas and himself.

Larry, Curly and Moe.

Then there was his boss, Stathis, who never wanted to pay for anything during an investigation—the boats, hotels and meals involved—and they had taken to packing a suitcase full of food whenever they went somewhere.

A problematic solution as Papa Michalis always ate more than his share, taking a foot-long salami and whittling it down to nothing in a matter of minutes. Just yesterday, Tembelos had spotted teeth marks on a chunk of cheese in the department refrigerator and threatened to beat him up.

Patronas sighed. A flock of magpies would have made better cops.

• • •

In the end, Patronas' stake-out netted two migrant children, Syrians who'd been pilfering a pair of pajamas and a blanket for their little sister. The tent at the camp where they lived was cold—they mimed shivering—and she was coughing. They acted this out, too, hacking and wheezing.

Deeply discouraged, Patronas paid off the store owner and gave fifty additional euros to the children. "Tell your mother to come here and buy whatever she needs," he told them, indicating to the man that he'd foot the bill. "And if your sister is still coughing, bring her to the police station on Polemidi Street and I'll get her to a doctor."

The conversation with the children took over an hour—he'd needed to consult the translation application on his phone for every word—and he was exhausted by the time he got back to the station.

Like most of the people on Chios, Patronas was deeply ambivalent about the migrants—tourism had ceased to exist on the island since they'd come pouring—but the fact that children were stealing to keep warm horrified him. It wasn't even that cold yet. How would they survive come winter?

"They can't stay in those tents" he told Tembelos. "You saw them. They're desperate."

"Hell, Yiannis, so are we," Tembelos said.

Chapter 3

"A boat full of migrants capsized in the channel near Karfas," the dispatcher told Patronas on the phone. "Storm's coming and the Coast Guard's worried they won't be able to rescue all of them."

Starting up his moped, Patronas raced to the site of the rescue operation on the beach of Karfas. The channel between Chios and Turkey was very narrow there—less than five kilometers—making it an ideal entry point for migrants seeking to enter Europe. This was not the first time a boat had capsized near Karfas and Patronas had been summoned to pull people out of the water, but never on a night like this.

The storm broke a few minutes later, rain coming down in sheets as he drove. Worse was the wind, so strong it whipped the trees around and sent branches scuttling across the road.

He parked along the road and headed down to the sea. Huge klieg lights had been set up on the sand; and there was a row of cars idling with their headlights on, the drivers seeking to help the rescuers and illuminate the people struggling in the water.

A Coast Guard cruiser was anchored halfway across the channel; and Patronas could see people clinging to its hull. Shedding his shoes, he dove in and began to swim toward them.

He reached one of the men first, grabbed his life jacket and pushed him up the ladder of the cruiser, then went after another and did the same. A group of women were floundering nearby, their wet dresses weighing them down; and he rescued them, too, treading water and helping them climb onboard.

A bolt of lightning flashed across the sky; and it sent a ripple of fear through him. The dispatcher had been right. They didn't have much time.

The wind was increasing, and it was whipping the sea into a frenzy, the swells so high now, they threatened to overturn the cruiser. A Coast Guard officer was moving a searchlight back and forth across the channel. searching for stragglers.

"Over there," he shouted to Patronas.

Patronas looked where he was pointing and saw a tiny shape in the distance. Plummeted by the waves, it was a child in a life vest, struggling to stay afloat.

But when Patronas grabbed him, he wrenched himself free, yelling something in Arabic and pointing at a woman, floating in the distance.

She was strapped into a red life preserver, but something was wrong with it; and, instead of holding her up, it appeared to be pulling her under.

Cradling the boy in his arms, Patronas struggled to get to her; but she kept drifting out of his reach, borne away by the fast-moving current. A beacon had been attached to her vest; and it was blinking faintly, the light barely visible in the heaving surf.

She was lying face down in the water, her arms dangling limply at her sides. She didn't stir when Patronas turned her over, didn't move or cry out.

Pulling the woman by her life vest, Patronas swam as fast as he could to the cruiser with the boy. The boy kept trying to reach her; and Patronas struggled to keep their heads above water, afraid they'd both drown.

Crew members scrambled down the ladder, grabbed the woman and carried her up to the deck, laid her out; and one of them immediately started mouth to mouth resuscitation. Patronas followed them onboard with the boy a few minutes later.

The officer continued breathing air into her lungs and pounding her chest.

"Μην πεθάνεις!" he kept saying. "Μην πεθάνεις!" Don't die.

The little boy never took his eyes off them.

Twenty minutes later, the captain called a halt. "Stop, Christos," he told the officer. "Can't you see she's gone. Leave her."

Nodding, the man doing the CPR gently released the woman. He straightened her dress and closed her eyes, then crossed her hands over her chest and left her. He appeared badly shaken.

The other migrants began to keen then. Patronas didn't know who the dead woman was to them, wasn't sure it mattered. Although he didn't understand Arabic, he knew what he was hearing. It was good-bye. They were saying good-bye. A dirge, a lament—there were a thousand words for it—she was one of them and she was dead; and they were mourning her.

The little boy began to wail. Crawling across the deck on his hands and knees, he put the dead woman's arms around him and tried to get her to hug him. When she didn't respond, he tried again, yelling desperately at her in Arabic, struggling to bring her back to life.

It was one of the saddest things Patronas had ever seen.

Picking the child up, he held him to him, smoothing down his wet hair with his hand. The child fought him at first, but eventually Patronas succeeded in quieting him down, singing a lullaby his mother had once sung to him about a child from Babylon.

"*Ola kala,*" he whispered. "*Ola kala.*" Everything's okay.

The cruiser got underway a few minutes later. The trip went quickly and as soon as the boat docked, the coast guard led the migrants down the gangplank and over to the waiting vans. They had no luggage, only backpacks and an assortment of clothing. Nothing of value. A representative of the Red Cross was standing by with shiny thermal blankets which she indicated they should wrap around themselves.

The migrants then boarded the vans, a strange alien procession packaged in foil. Patronas had no idea where they came from or what their story was. It was obvious they'd been on the road for months, probably moving through a progression of camps, first in Syria, then in Turkey. All to get a foothold in a new world, a world that had no use for them.

Seeing them there, waiting so patiently with their pitiful belongings, he felt a wave of sympathy.

Not quite like those trainloads bound for Auschwitz, he thought, but close. The only differences were here was the destruction was self-inflicted—unlike the Jews, these people had willingly embarked on this journey—and it would take longer,

They'd all end up at the Registration and Identification Center at the Vial detention center where aid workers would process them and where a lucky few would find shelter in one-room containers without heat, light or electricity, the rest in canvas tents like the Syrian women he'd spoken to or outside in the pouring rain. A migrant had recently died there, his body consumed by rats before it was found.

They'd spend years there most probably, years in that hellish place that reeked of feces and despair.

Thirty-three people had been onboard that night and—save for the woman—all had survived. November, winter was fast approaching; and the next time a boat went down, far more people would die.

Patronas looked out at the dark water. At least Noah had had the ear of God when he set off. Who did these people have? Where the fuck had God been tonight when that child's mother had drowned? Or any night in his young life?

• • •

It was close to midnight when he started home on the moped, the child sitting on his lap. Their clothes were drenched; and they were both shivering uncontrollably. The storm had grown in intensity. Cursing, Patronas splashed through the pools of water, praying his moped wouldn't stall and they'd be able to get to the cottage in one piece.

Across the channel he could see the vast landmass of Turkey, a dark sinister shadow stretching as far as the eye could see. 30,000 Ottoman soldiers had come ashore not far from here on Easter Sunday in 1822 with orders to kill all Greek males twelve years and older. In the ensuing carnage, they'd murdered or enslaved nearly 60,000 people, four-fifths of the total population of the island. The skulls of the dead could still be seen in churches all over Chios, dusty piles of them stacked up in the corners.

"You wonder why we have problems with Turkey," he'd once told an American tourist in the church of Aghios Minos, pointing to the stack of skulls, many of which were small. "This is why."

But that was old history. Now it was a different kind of invasion, a more poignant one. Hordes of desperate people coming ashore every day, not to kill, but to live.

Unlike them, at least he had a home to go to, he told himself. At least he had that.

Hiding the boy from the officials at the harbor, he'd taken off with him. He had no idea what he was going to do with him. All he knew was he couldn't let him go to Vial—an unprotected four-year-old? The child wouldn't stand a chance.

At the very least, people would steal his food and he'd go hungry. At the very least.

Hearing the motorbike, his wife, Lydia, threw open the door. "Yiannis, thank God. I've been so worried. Come in, come in."

He carried the boy into the house. "Get some blankets," he said.

Lydia fussed over the child, pulling off his wet clothes and redressing him in a sweater of hers. "There you go, that's better."

The boy wandered around the house for a few minutes, obviously confused. He kept searching, opening doors and calling out in Arabic, seeking his mother. Eventually, he returned to the living room, climbed up into Lydia's lap and went to sleep.

Lydia didn't ask where the child had come from or why Patronas had brought him here. She was good that way, Lydia. Did what needed to be done always.

He wanted to tell her what happened, but he couldn't stop trembling, couldn't seem to form words.

Opening the walnut buffet in the dining room, he got out a bottle of scotch, filled a tumbler and drank it down, surprised at how much better the scotch made him feel, numbing both the cold and the rage.

"Boat capsized and his mother drowned." He gestured to the sleeping child with his glass.

"They set off in this weather?"

Patronas nodded. "The person in charge probably thought tonight was as good a time as any. No one would see them in the rain; and they could slip ashore undetected. Thirty-three people were onboard, Lydia, thirty-three people on a boat designed for eight.

"I didn't know what to do, Lydia. That's why I brought him here. I couldn't let him go to Vial, not by himself. A little kid like that? He'd get eaten alive in that place."

"It's okay, Yiannis. You're exhausted. Go to bed."

"He likes to be sung to."

"You sang to him?"

"Yes, an old song of my mother's about a child from Babylon."

Lydia looked down at the boy. "A child from Babylon. Yes, yes. That's what he is. A child from Babylon."

• • •

Pulling off his sodden clothes, Patronas left them where they fell and staggered into the bedroom. Remembering the boy's mother, he was afraid he might cry; and he didn't want to, not in front of Lydia. They hadn't been married long, less than a year. Let her think he was strong a little while longer.

Although he was physically exhausted, he found it impossible to sleep. Every time he closed his eyes, he saw the dead woman in her red life jacket, her skin as gray as the storm-lashed sea around them, heard the boy's anguished screams. At some point, he managed to doze off, but he woke up with a start not long after, his heart pounding.

He got out of bed, pulled on a sweater, and headed down to the beach. The storm had abated; and all was quiet. The ground was littered with debris, pine needles and branches the wind had shaken loose from the trees, so thick on the ground, the sand was covered. The streetlights were shrouded with mist; and the air was cold against his skin, saturated and heavy with moisture.

Picking up a rock, he threw it into the sea. The physical activity gave him a sense of relief and he repeated the gesture, grabbing another stone and hurling it as far out into the water as he could. He continued for a long time. Working with a kind of dogged persistence, he'd raise a rock over his head and slam it down into the sea. There was nothing playful or lighthearted about what he was doing; he wasn't skipping the stones or trying for the loudest splash. It was as if he was trying to fill in the cove and render it safe. He continued lobbing rocks for a long time, working faster and faster in a kind of frenzy.

It was growing light when he stopped; and his body was aching. He spotted something snagged on a rock on the far side of the cove and walked toward it, only to discover it was a life jacket. From the looks of it, it had been in the water a long time and could no longer float. Standing there holding it, he began to cry, whether from fatigue or grief, he couldn't say. All he knew was he couldn't keep doing what he'd done today, standing by and watching women drown.

He'd joined the police force twenty-three years ago. He'd been young then, driven by the desire to be of service. But that had all changed. What service had he provided those people tonight? That woman, dead in his arms?

Chapter 4

Patronas and his second-in-command, Giorgos Tembelos, met with a group of Frontex officers the next morning to discuss what had happened. The men were all members of the European Border and Coast Guard, assigned to Chios by the European Union.

They had been patrolling the channel for weeks, they told Patronas, intercepting migrants and sending them back to Turkey. There'd been a recent upsurge in such people—five hundred in the last two weeks alone—and they were struggling to keep up with the traffic.

They were well prepared and handed out piles of papers. There was map of Greece on display with pins on it, each pin representing one hundred people. The man in charge, a muscular young German with a shaved head, used a laser pointer to trace the route the migrants were following. He said Chios was fast becoming one of the most popular entry points which was why they'd been dispatched there. Deeply pessimistic, he said the European Union might be better able to manage the problem in the future, but they would never be able to solve it.

"Where were you last night?" Patronas demanded.

"Given the weather, we assumed no migrants would be crossing."

'You assumed, you assumed…" Patronas fought to keep his voice down. "You could have stopped them; and you didn't."

"Our orders are not venture forth in inclement weather."

"One of them died…" Patronas was screaming now. "A woman, you worthless bastards."

Holding up his hand, he shoved it in their direction, giving them the *moutza*, the Greek equivalent of the finger, and stormed out, letting the door slam behind him.

Tembelos caught up with him a few minutes later. "You really have a gift, Yiannis. You go after trouble like a heat-seeking missile. It they complain to Stathis. you're done."

"I know. I know."

Patronas had only recently been reinstated as Chief Inspector of the Chios police force, and his superior, Haralambos Stathis, had warned him to tread lightly, 'No fuck-ups this time, no dead goats."

The last had been a dig, a reference to Patronas' first murder investigation. Thinking he had the killer in his sights, Patronas had mistakenly opened fire on a herd of goats, killing a goodly number of them. Goats which whinnied and soiled themselves as they died; goats which cost over six thousand euros to replace and took a week to bury; goats which were featured in newscasts throughout Greece, accompanied by much raucous laughter by commentators. In some countries, they joked about morons. In Greece, it was people from the island of Chios. And, thanks to Patronas, for a time, they joked about how the residents of Chios were unable to tell the difference between livestock and people. Night after night, there he'd been. A big photograph of him, a soundtrack of 'baa, baa, baa,' playing in the background. Patronas had wanted to kill himself.

• • •

Two days later, another boat went down; and again, Patronas drove to the beach, swam out to the capsized vessel, and dragged people to safety. The water was much colder this time; and he doubted he'd be able to do it again, as he was too old and too tired, the weariness, not just physical, but something far more profound, deep within him.

He was gratified to see the Frontex officers participating in the rescue. One of their motorboats was anchored alongside the capsized vessel; and they were out there in the water, helping people.

It felt good seeing them. At least he'd accomplished that if nothing else; he'd gotten that arrogant German wet.

No one died this time, but Patronas had no illusions about the future. If the migrants attempted to cross again in the coming months, many of them would perish.

He requested the boat be dragged ashore and inspected it. An old *caique*, fishing boat, the hull was damaged in places, the wood so rotten, it gave way when he scraped a nail across it.

It was a wonder the people onboard had survived.

He asked a Coast Guard officer to take some photos of the boat with his phone and send them to him, then walked back to the station.

He kept returning to the night of the storm, remembering the woman's life jacket and how light it had felt. He'd held onto it, stuffing it in a closet at the police station; and he got it out now. Using a pair of scissors, he opened it up and inspected it. It was full of newspapers.

"Murder," he said softly. "My God, it was murder."

• • •

"Nothing you can do about it," Tembelos said. "That boat came from Turkey which means whoever sold her that life jacket was a Turk."

"I don't care. We need to go after him."

"How? By invading turkey? The last time Greeks did that, it didn't go so well. They killed half of us and threw the rest of us in the sea."

"Maybe we could collaborate with the police in Istanbul, get to him that way."

"Forget it, Yiannis. Turks are Turks and Greeks are Greeks. A lot of water under that bridge. No, not water. Blood."

Chapter 5

The make-up of those crossing the channel had changed over the last year . It was now mostly Afghan, Iraqi and Pakistani men, traveling solo, instead of Syrian families. They didn't get along with the North Africans in the camp, had even stabbed one. Patronas had sent assailant back to Turkey, only to have him return and assault another man three days later.

His boss had ordered Patronas to write a report on the stabbing and its aftermath; and he was working on it at the station.

He had arrested the culprit and locked him up; and as soon as he finished his report, he would set about deporting him all over again.

The life jacket was still on his desk: and he shoved it aside. It had been over a month since they'd found the girl in Souda, a week since the boy's mother had put on that life vest and drowned.

The child was still living with Patronas and his wife at the cottage. He had warmed up to Lydia, but continued to back away whenever Patronas came near him.

"It's the trauma," Lydia said, seeking to console him. "You remind him of that night in the water, his mother's death."

"But I saved him."

"He doesn't see it that way. Maybe someday he will, but not now."

Using an English-Arabic dictionary, she'd succeeded in finding out his name.

"Ali," the boy had told her in Arabic. "My name is Ali."

The child didn't know how old he was and had just looked puzzled when she'd asked him.

Lydia was doing her best to make him feel at home and had bought him a whole new wardrobe and filled the house with toys. She fed him ice cream for breakfast and ice cream for dinner and let him watch cartoons all day. She'd even gone so far as to purchase audio-lingual tapes of Arabic and practiced with them every night so that she could communicate with him.

Sometimes Patronas and she practiced together, mouthing the words for 'home,' 'good morning' and 'good night.'

Still, the boy often wept at night, calling 'Omm, Omm!' which Patronas had sadly learned was the Syrian word for mother.

Patronas hadn't informed the authorities about the child, afraid he'd be taken from them and sent to an orphanage or worse, dispatched alone to a camp. Nor had he discussed the situation with anyone at work. He wanted to legitimize the relationship, maybe even adopt Ali; but he hadn't yet figured out how to go about it. He didn't know if the same rules governing adoption applied to orphaned migrant children or if there were different ones, what the adoptee's exact legal status was in such cases.

The law didn't appear to have kept up; and he'd been hopelessly confused when he'd read up on it. He hadn't even been able to establish what a migrant's legal status was, let alone that of an orphaned child.

For the time being, he decided to keep the boy's presence a secret. The location of their house would help. No one came near the cove in the winter, but Patronas worried what would happen to the child come spring. They couldn't keep him locked up inside then. Even if it was to protect him, it would be too cruel.

Recently, the boy had started running to the door when Patronas came home from work and welcoming him with a big smile. The two of them would make a fire together, Ali handing him pieces of kindling, and they'd spent the evening in front of it.

Against Patronas advice, Lydia had taken in a stray cat; and Ali would play with it on the rug, teasing it with a little mouse she'd crocheted out of yarn. It was the only time Patronas had ever heard the boy laugh.

The cat didn't like Patronas and scratched him whenever it got the opportunity. Patronas had complained about this to Lydia, even gone so far as to show her the scratch marks on his ankles, but she'd waved him off, saying it was good for Ali to have a pet.

Patronas also suspected the cat had mange, given the patches of fur missing on its coat; and the fact that it was always scratching itself when it wasn't scratching him.

"Oh, for God's sakes, Yiannis," Lydia said. "It hasn't got mange."

"Fleas then. It's got fleas."

He and the cat were now at a stand-off. He'd shoo it away whenever Lydia wasn't looking or throw a slipper at it; but if she or Ali were around, he'd cozy up to it and pet it. The cat wasn't fooled—Patronas' hands were covered with scratches from these encounters—nor, he suspected, was his wife, who handed him back his slipper with a frown.

Ali had named the beast 'Jinn' which meant 'demon' in Arabic, a totally suitable name in Patronas' opinion, given its evil nature. It was a whirling dervish of malicious energy. It would watch him at night sometimes, its golden eyes upon him, and he would remember the stories about how cats always knew when your days were numbered and kept you company as you died.

• • •

Patronas looked out the window at the police station and sighed. No way the situation with Ali was going to end well. God had never rained blessings down upon him; and Patronas was pretty sure He wasn't going to start now. He and Lydia would have a pleasant interlude with the child, a pretend family for a time; and then Ali would be taken from them. That's how these things went. Love and loss, in that order.

Sitting across from him, Tembelos was happily pinging away at Grand Theft Auto on his computer. Once it had been porn sites; and Patronas missed those days, the oohing and aahing over the naked women on display. Tembelos would never cheat on his wife—too dangerous, she'd disembowel him—but he could dream and dream he had, day after day after day.

Now he just raced a noisy car around and shot people.

Looking over at him, Tembelos paused his game. "What's the matter?"

"This case." He gestured to the murder book, open in front of him. "I thought at first Golden Dawn might be responsible, but it's not their style."

"A frustrated lover…?"

"They used a machete, Giorgos. A fucking machete."

"We don't know that. It might have been a knife."

"You saw her throat. Whatever it was, it was big."

"Sending a message, you think? Way the Mafia used to?"

"Could be. Stathis told me there are over two hundred mobs operating in Greece now. Most of them in Athens, but, who knows, maybe some of them found their way here."

"The godfathers of night." Tembelos kept his voice low. "I thought all those guys did was smuggle cigarettes."

"Not anymore. Stathis said they're into all kinds of things now—drugs, weapons, kidnapping."

They exchanged glances.

"Women," Patronas said. "I'd bet money on it."

Tembelos nodded. "As the coroner said, a girl like that would have been a valuable commodity."

"They usually operate out of nightclubs. It's their preferred locale."

"I got nothing on. I could pay them a visit tonight."

"Let me know what you find out, but be careful, Giorgos. Don't take any chances."

• • •

"I went to two of the most popular nightclubs on Chios, Plan B and En Plo," Tembelos reported the next morning. "Spent a fortune."

He shook his head. "Jesus, the price of beer in those places. Nothing criminal going on as far as I could see. No prostitutes, no dope, no gangsters. Just a bunch of kids looking to hook up."

"Any foreign women?"

"Nope. Both clubs were noisy and had a lot of neon lights, very visible places. Maybe shit goes down in those outfits along the beach, but it's winter now and they're all closed."

Patronas thought this over. "So, if the mob is trafficking, they're not doing it in nightclubs. They're doing it somewhere else."

Chapter 6

After Ali had joined them, Lydia had instituted a new set of roles at home—no cigarettes, no alcohol, no meat. She believed in the restorative power of vegetables and served them up in a variety of ways, all of them unspeakable. Cabbage cooked twice was death, the ancients said; and Patronas heartily agreed. Death, too, was okra and all its foul cousins, rooted in the earth.

To compensate, Patronas now drank and ate what he wanted on the job. It wasn't an ideal solution, but he was careful only to do it after hours; and never when Melissa Costas and Papa Michalis were around. His reasoning was simple: Costas would drink him under the table; and the priest would eat all the food.

Picking up the phone, he called the taverna next door, ordered suckling pig and had it delivered. When it arrived, he and Tembelos ate it with their fingers, their faces slick with grease.

Tembelos also had issues with his spouse, a fierce, raven-haired Cretan named Eleni. Worried about his health, she'd put him on a diet and was mystified when he didn't lose weight. Patronas thought the suckling pig, a favorite of theirs, might have something to do with it, but he'd never tell Eleni that. She'd bury those long red nails of hers in Giorgos' vitals and that would be that.

"I don't know if I told you," Patronas said. "I ran into Dimitra yesterday,"

Tembelos raised his eyebrows. "She's back?"

"Yup. Came back two months ago. There's something wrong with her; and they wants to run some tests. Her mother is too old to take her to the hospital; and she wants me to drive her."

Patronas still remembered her words. "You are all the family I've got, Yiannis. I don't have anybody else."

35

Family? Him? He supposed after twenty years of marriage it was true.

"I know you don't like me," she'd gone on to say, "and I'm sorry to be asking this of you. But there's no one else. I'm all alone."

Hearing the despair in her voice, Patronas had agreed to take her. He'd been shot once and woken up alone in the hospital. He knew how it went.

Tembelos was horrified. "You can't go running her around. You just got married."

"It's not like we're going on picnic. I'm taking her to the hospital."

"You be careful, Yiannis. As my father used to say, 'better to live with the devil than a mean woman;' and God knows Dimitra is one mean woman. If it had been me, I never would have married her. I would have gone with the devil."

In less than two weeks, she would be here. Fangs, cancer and all.

The smell of the food had awoken Papa Michalis and he stirred in his chair. "Come, come," he said, joining the discussion. "She can't be as bad as all that. For the most part, females are docile creatures, peaceable."

The priest often held forth on the nature of women, a subject he knew nothing about it, the only woman he was familiar being the Holy Mother, who was holy for a reason.

'A strand of her pubic hair could pull ships,' old timers had said of women. They could sink them, too, as Patronas had found out in his first marriage.

"Peaceable, Father?" he said. "In my experience, females are anything, but.."

"Amen," said Tembelos. "Amen to that. You know the saying, 'he made a bed of nettles and lay down on it?' That's marriage, my friend. That *is* marriage."

"Nettles?" Patronas repeated.

"At best."

"Shit, Giorgos."

"Shit is right. Morning, noon and night. Sometimes I dream about running away with a tourist, one of those tall Swedes with legs that go on forever, but then I think, no, she might have blonde hair, but underneath it all, she's still a woman, a woman like my Eleni. Which means snakes and spiders and never getting to do what I want."

Patronas also had problems with Lydia, but he kept them to himself. She was getting restless, staying at home all day with Ali, and wanted to take him to a playground and introduce him to other children, give him the semblance of a normal life.

"People will notice," Patronas said. "You don't match. Ali is much darker than you are."

"It'll be all right" she'd said. "Ali and me, we'll set an example, show people what brotherhood means."

"Are you kidding?"

"No. I mean it."

"It won't work, Lydia, this brotherhood of man of yours. At best, people will clean their glasses and stare at you. At worst, they'll summon the authorities."

• • •

After Lydia and he put Ali to bed that night, Patronas poured her a glass of wine and told her about Dimitra. She listened attentively and kissed him hard after he'd finished. A long, lingering soulful kiss. He held on to her, afraid Dimitra's resurfacing would cause problems between them.

But Lydia surprised him. "I'm glad you said you'd drive her to the hospital. I'll come, too. Some of these tests are tough. They can be hard on people."

"Dimitra's my problem, Lydia. No need for you to get involved."

Ignoring him, Lydia continued to talk about what they'd do for Dimitra. Special foods and new pajamas, maybe an iPad to distract her. Patronas listened with growing alarm.

A flaw in Lydia, he believed, this foolish trusting of people. She might have started out Greek, but her years in America had ruined her. Sartre wrote 'hell was other people,' and so it was in his experience.

Lydia refused to accept this; and they'd argued about it. She'd quoted Ann Frank, insisting that 'people were basically good at heart.' When Patronas pointed out things hadn't gone so well for Ann Frank, Lydia had burst into tears, saying he was a heartless man. Sometimes it was like being married to a child.

"You don't know her, Lydia. She's not a nice person."

"It doesn't matter. Kindness is everything."

Patronas looked out at the night. He'd been a policeman his entire adult life and, in his opinion, kindness wasn't everything. It wasn't even on the list. Other qualities—greed, fear, lust, to name a few—inevitably ruled the day. Forewarned was forearmed. And forearmed he intended to be with Dimitra.

"The Delphic Oracle said, 'an old enemy cannot become a friend,' And that's what Dimitra is, an enemy."

Lydia reached over and took his hand. "No harm will come to us if we help her. You said she's sick. She might not have that long to live."

"You don't know her," Patronas said again. "Tembelos says she's like Rasputin."

"Kindness," Lydia repeated softly.

"Rasputin," Patronas repeated.

• • •

"It was worse than I expected," Patronas told Tembelos when he got to work the next day. "Lydia wants to take care of her."

"Ach, Yiannis. This is what comes from living with Americans. Your good sense…. What can I say, it commits suicide."

"She says it's the right thing to do. 'We have so much,' she says. 'It's the least we can do, usher her peacefully into the hereafter."

"Usher her into the hereafter? It's you who will be heading there if you're not careful."

Patronas smiled. "I have to say, the older I get, the more appealing I find the idea of a hereafter. Angels beating their wings when my time comes, bearing me off…"

"Depends on where they take you, Yiannis. Up or down. And from the sounds of it, you are going down."

• • •

And go down he did. Dimitra duly arrived with five suitcases and her mother in tow. The latter, a quarrelsome old crone, had grown even more fearsome with age, having lost most of her teeth, hair and mind since Patronas had last seen her.

She scowled when she saw Patronas, would have spat on him if she could—and he would have happily spat right back. Spit, spat.

The three of them had a fight at the airport and then again on the way to the hotel. Both fights came out of nowhere and ended with Dimitra screaming at him. For someone so sick, she still had a powerful set of lungs.

"As cantankerous as ever," he told Tembelos.

Nor did the rides back and forth to the hospital go well. His ex-wife was nauseous and vomited frequently, a catastrophe given that it was a rental car.

Patronas did his best, but the stress was taking a toll. He was drinking more and had invested in a box of cigars.

Lydia had accompanied him once or twice on these rides to the hospital; and even she was wavering in her resolve. "All she does is complain. I am beginning to think there is nothing we can do for her. "

No surprise there. Patronas had come to that conclusion on his honeymoon. None of his efforts had paid off; they'd had a huge argument. Words with a lot of I's—impotent, inadequate, idiot—had been bandied about; and he'd ended up sleeping on the floor.

He'd tried to talk to Dimitra once, had even told her about the Syrian girl who'd been murdered. Her response, "I see you haven't changed, Yiannis. You always did care more for strangers than your own kind."

She'd lost some of her hair and had taken to wearing a wig. Jet black and straight as a pin, it looked a little like the hairpiece Elizabeth Taylor had worn in Cleopatra. The day she bought it was the only time he'd seen her cry.

He'd done nothing, not even offered her a Kleenex. He'd just looked on in silence.

How do you take care of someone you despise? he wondered. Do right by them in their time of trouble? He didn't know. It seemed impossible—like Sisyphus pushing the rock up the hill, only to have it come crashing back down again, and Dimitra was his rock.

Just the thought of another ride in the car with her a made him want to die. The doctor had taken him aside during the last visit and told him it was serious, that what she had might kill her. Although he hadn't spelled it out—in Greece, no one ever said the word 'cancer'—Patronas was pretty sure that was what was wrong with her.

It didn't grieve him, the thought of her dying. All he felt was pity, animal pity.

Chapter 7

"Mr. Police! Mr. Police!"

Using hand gestures and snippets of Greek, the woman told Patronas she'd seen the poster. "I know her. I know Raina."

She was standing in the street in front of the police station, half-hidden behind one of the vans used to transport migrants. A Syrian, Patronas judged, seeing the hijab and floor-length caftan she was wearing. Even when addressing him, she kept her eyes averted, unwilling to look at him.

Getting out his cell phone, he called Liadis. "Get here as fast as you can. A witness has come forward and I need you to translate."

The camp administrator arrived fifteen minutes later. He was wearing a belted trench coat, a Burberry from the looks of it and a silly-looking fedora with a feather. Again, Patronas wondered where Liadis got the money. Coat like that cost over 2500 euros, nearly twice most civil servants' monthly salaries.

Liadis smiled at the woman. "Salam aleykum", he said, greeting her warmly, peace be with you.

Visibly relieved, the woman repeated the phrase back to him. "Salam Aleykum."

The two of them spoke Arabic for a few minutes. "She says the girl's name is Raina Mustafa," Liadis reported.

"Get her background. Where's she from?"

"Damascus, she says, but then they bombed it and she fled to Turkey. Stayed in the Elbeyli Camp on the border before making her way to Chesme on the coast."

"How did she get to Chesme?"

The woman's smile was grim. "Walked," she said in English. "Walked long time, many days."

Patronas took over the questioning. "Did you meet Raina in Syria?" he asked in English.

"No, on boat to Chios. Raina, she comes and stands next to me, says please, please pretend to be my mother. Very scared, even then. I think will be better in Greece, but no. Even in Greece, she is afraid."

"Do you know why?"

Another blast of Arabic.

"Someone was killed, another girl," Liadis translated. "She doesn't know where it happened, whether it was here or in Turkey. As for Raina Mustafa, one day she was there and then she wasn't. The weather had changed; and it was getting cold when it happened."

"November maybe." Patronas nodded, thinking it fit. The girl's body had been discovered at the start of that month.

"Chesme?" he repeated. "Chesme is where you met?"

The woman nodded.

Patronas wrote this down in his notebook and underlined it. A town on the western coast of Turkey, it was located directly across the channel from Chios.

"Raina, good girl," the woman said, addressing him again in English. "Others bad. In camp. Bad, bad." She then lapsed back into Arabic.

"Ask her to explain."

The woman refused. "No names. Bad for me, names. No say, no say."

"Do you have any idea who Raina was afraid of?"

"Yes," the woman said. "Man in Chesme. Hard man. Very hard."

Patronas entered the woman's name, Amira Al-Bashir, and her address in his notebook in case he needed to get in touch with her again. Third row in from the main gate of the Vial refugee camp, the white tent on the left—near the one with the toys, the doll with the red dress.

After thanking her for her help, he arranged for one of his men to drive her back to Vial.

"Be careful, Mr. Police," she said. "*Al-shitan, al-shitan.*"

"*Al-shitan* is Arabic for Satan," Liadis whispered to Patronas. "She's warning you to beware of Satan."

After the woman left, the two of them stood there, talking.

"Anything like this happen before?" Patronas asked him. "Women go missing from the camp?"

"No, none that I'm aware of."

• • •

"Victim's name is Raina Mustafa," Patronas told Tembelos when he got back to the station. "Arrived here from Chesme and was living in Vial the week before she died. We need to go back to that camp again and question the residents. Bring a propane lantern, flashlight. Whatever you've got. We'll probably be there all night."

"What about me?" asked Melissa Costas.

"I want you stay here."

"Why?"

"You're going into Vial undercover; and I don't want the residents there to know you're a cop."

Taking an unmarked car, Patronas and Tembelos exited Chora and turned onto the narrow road that led to the village of Chalkis, near where the camp was. Initially, the area was full of olive trees, their silver leaves flickering like flecks of mica in the afternoon sun, but as they drew closer to Vial, the land grew more barren.

Further to the south were the most picturesque villages on Chios, the Μαστιχοχώρια, some of which dated from the Middle Ages, where farmers grew *mastica*, a plant prized for its resin. It only grew in the southern part of Chios—no place else in the world—and it had been so greatly prized by Ottomans, they'd given the islanders special privileges. Chios had grown rich on the trade, but all that had ended in 1822 when the Turkish soldiers came ashore and slaughtered more than half of the population.

Mastica was still grown on the island; and a consortium of local farmers produced a vast number of products from it—liquors, gum, face creams, soap, even toothpaste. The list was endless. Extracting the resin was a torturous process; one tree only produced three hundred grams per year; and wildfires were a constant danger.

The resin oozed out of tiny, man-made cuts in the bark, one glistening drop of liquid at a time. At first, it was clear, but later it solidified and turned white. People called mastica, "the tears of Chios," and the name was apt.

No mastica grew near Vial. The area around the camp was a wasteland, only a few scrub-covered hills; That was the main reason the camp had been built here. The ground beneath it was worthless, real estate no one wanted.

"You're about to enter one of the circles of hell," Patronas warned Tembelos. "The last one maybe, where Satan lives and devours all comers."

Tembelos raised his eyebrows. "You been reading Dante?"

Patronas nodded. "Lydia has me on a regime, a book a week and this week it was the *Inferno*."

"Shit, Yiannis. That woman has whacked your balls off."

"She says it's for my own good."

"They all say that. You need to put a stop to this eunuch-fication and put a stop to it now. You don't, pretty soon you'll be singing soprano."

• • •

"Look around, Giorgos," Patronas said. "This is as close to hell as I ever want to get."

They were in the barbed wire corridor that led into Vial. Hostile signs were posted along the fence; and Tembelos was reading them. "Καταστρέψατε τα νησιά" You have destroyed the islands. Μην ξεπουλάτε πια την Ελλάδα. Don't sell out Greece.

"My sentiments exactly," he said. "Send these people back where they came from."

"They're trapped, Giorgos. Trapped with no place to go. They cannot go back even if they wanted to. Their countries no longer exist; and no place else on earth wants them."

"Let them be trapped in Germany. Merkel made this mess, let her deal with it."

"Germany has taken its share."

"'You give a peasant his freedom, he will take over your bed,' my father used to say. Only now, it's not your bed, it's your whole fucking country."

"You sound like Golden Dawn."

"Just saying, Yiannis, just saying, not throwing Molotov cocktails."

• • •

Patronas and Tembelos slowly worked their way through the camp, showing the girl's photograph and asking about her by name this time.

Liadis had prepared a page of Arabic for them; and they handed it out as well. The questions were simple:

-Who did Raina Mustafa spend time with?

-What did she like to do?

-Was anyone bothering her in the camp?

-If someone was bothering her, who was he and what did he look like?

Papa Michalis joined them that evening, doggedly going from tent to tent in his long black robe and sandals, splashing absent-mindedly through the runnels of filthy water.

Dalia, the little girl with the doll, ran up to the old man as he approached her tent, all smiles. Holding the toy up, she showed him the doll's new clothes, a frilly red dress and matching pair of red crocheted shoes someone had sewn for it. Jabbering in Arabic, she explained how she'd combed the doll's hair and braided it, picked wildflowers and woven them through it.

"What gives, Father? Patronas asked the priest after the girl left. "How come she knows you? You take up residence in one of these tents?"

"No, no, nothing like that. She's one of my students. I come here three days a week to instruct her and the other children in Greek. Their parents all have cell phones; and there's an app on it for language. We go back and forth on it. I take the bus here in the afternoon and walk up the road to the camp."

"Why didn't you tell me? I could have driven you."

"Mustn't speak of such things. The bible is also very specific on this point. 'Do not to perform your righteous acts in front of others.' Matthew 6:1. In other words, do good, but be silent about it."

Patronas grinned. "Must be hard for you, the silence."

"Oh, my, yes. Makes me exceedingly nervous, silence. I could never have been a Trappist."

"Not many priests would do what you're doing."

"Jesus said, 'truly, I say to you, as you did to one of the least of these my brothers, you did it to me.'

"And that means teaching migrants Greek?"

The old man nodded. "Love God is one of the tenets of my faith as is love of man, although as I told you before this last has been giving me trouble, human beings what they are."

"You proselytize, too?"

"Of course, not. I merely teach them Greek. They need so much, but at least it's a start."

His black robe was filthy, the hem caked with mud; and he moved slower and slower as the night wore on. Still, he pushed on and continued to interview people, making his way up and down the alleyways and calling out 'massa' al kheir' as he approached, good evening in Arabic.

Patronas told Tembelos about Papa Michalis' make-shift school. "He says if someone had welcomed Attila the Hun and taught him Latin, it would have gone differently."

Tembelos chuckled. "Man's an idiot."

"I like what he's doing."

"I don't."

"Why?"

"It's a foot in the door. You familiar with the 'sea people,' Yiannis? The group that came out of nowhere and destroyed everything in their path, upended civilizations all over the Mediterranean. That's what we're up against here. The very same. The third world is coming to take what's ours and it's coming fast."

"Come on, Giorgos. You saw those shoplifters. What harm can they do?"

Tembelos shook his head. "Those kids and their damned pajamas."

• • •

"This might well be nothing," a middle-aged migrant told Patronas in English. "An Afghan wanting a bride perhaps. Nothing the police need be involved in."

It seemed a curious thing to say.

Patronas took down the man's contact information before he left Vial and took a photo of him with his phone. He had a greasy way about him that Patronas didn't like; and he made a note to run his name through the database when he got back at the station.

He showed the photo to Liadis on his way out. "You know him?"

"Yes. An unsavory character. The women here avoid him."

Patronas nodded. He'd bring the man in. See what his problem was with women, see how deep it went.

Huge floodlights came on a few minutes later, turning the grounds of the camp as bright as day. The migrants began to retreat into their tents and close the flaps, making it even harder to speak to them.

"Explain what we are doing," Patronas told Liadis. "Ask if anyone's seen her."

Using the camp's broadcast system, he did as Patronas asked, but as the night wore on, not a single person came forward.

After they left Vial, Patronas broadened the effort to include the surrounding countryside; and he and his men visited the village of Chalkis and questioned the inhabitants there. Although it was relief to speak Greek, they learned nothing.

Flashlights in hand, they explored the nearby orchards and walked the entire length of the road leading into the camp, pawing through the debris on either side of the asphalt, searching for some evidence the girl had passed this way. Once again, they came up empty-handed

• • •

Patronas' cell phone rang exactly at nine a.m. the next morning. "Sympathy for the Devil," the ringtone he'd picked out for his boss, liking the devil part, if not the sympathy. Stathis kept a tight schedule. In at nine, out at five with a two-hour lunch break in between. Not that Stathis ever did much work when he *was* in the office.

A savage infighter, his boss didn't care about protecting the public or arresting criminals. His only interest was advancing his career, and woe unto those who got in his way. He didn't just cut them down to size, he eviscerated them. Patronas had suffered this on more than one occasion, leaving Stathis' office with his ego in tatters and his entrails on display.

"You're stupid with a helmet on," was one of his boss' favorite sayings. Also, "Do that again and I will castrate you," accompanied by a snipping motion.

The minute Patronas answered, Stathis started right in. "You find out who she is? What happened to her?"

"Yes, sir. We have a name, Raina Mustafa."

He described how they'd gotten the tip from the woman, returned to Vial the previous night and interviewed the residents.

"We didn't learn much," he said.

"They might have been afraid and with good reason. There are criminal gangs operating in those places now. Men, who will do anything for money. Snatch people and harvest their organs, sell kids to pedophiles. They even drained one man of his blood and tried to sell it. Women, children. It doesn't matter. They are just commodities to them."

"Do they kill, sir?"

"What do you think happened to that man, they drained the blood out of, Patronas? Those kids who lost their livers? Of course, they kill."

Patronas was surprised by Stathis' vehemence. Normally, his boss had little use for migrants. They were a swarm of locusts, as far as his boss was concerned, intent on devouring his homeland. If he could have walled off Greece, he would have, checked a person's DNA before letting them enter. If their lineage went back to Sparta, so much the better.

'Got the job done, the Spartans did,' he often said. 'Can't keep up, off you go. Wish we could do the same.' Eugenics in other words.

Maybe the Spartans had practiced it, but so had the Nazis.

Stathis had missed his calling; he would have made a fine storm trooper.

• • •

Patronas questioned the man who had made the remark about the Afghan seeking bride, but nothing came of it. According to the man's entry papers, he'd arrived on Chios at the end of November, long after Raina Mustafa had been killed.

Another dead end.

Patronas doubted there was anything more to be learned at the camp; and he returned to the station. He had other plans, big ones. Turkey figured into them; and he was eager to get started.

As soon as he arrived at the station, he ordered Costas and Tembelos to come into the conference room and shut the door.

"Here is the plan: our mission is twofold. First, we go to Chesme, then, we infiltrate Vial."

Coffee cup in hand, Melissa Costas studied him. "Vial, I can see, but why Chesme?"

"A Syrian woman came forward and told me she and Raina Mustafa were in Chesme together. She says Raina was frightened of a man there."

"She say this man was Turkish?" asked Tembelos.

"'No, all she said was he was a 'hard man.'"

"'How are we going to find anyone based on that description? There must be 50,000 people in Chesme. What, we just go there, hand out Raina Mustafa's picture and say—in Turkish, I'm assuming, as we will be in Turkey—'excuse me, folks, have you seen this girl?"

"It's our only lead."

"Lot of problems with this, Yiannis. A whole lot of problems. Say we *do* succeed and we find this man, what are we going to do with him? We're Greek. We got no authority in Turkey."

"We put him on a boat and bring him back here."

Costas choked on her coffee. "What do you mean 'bring him back here'?"

"We kidnap him, exactly the way the Israelis did Adolf Eichman, the man in charge of the death camps. They searched for him for over fifteen years, but in the end, they got him."

"We are hardly Israelis," Tembelos said drily. "Those Israelis you're talking about, the Mossad agents, they know what they're doing. Us, not so much."

Patronas was beginning to feel like a piece of bread in a flock of geese. "It's our only lead," he repeated.

"You discuss any of this with Stathis?" Tembelos asked.

"No. I wanted to talk to you first."

"Out a limb, Yiannis. He finds out, he'll fire you for sure."

"Not if I'm successful."

"That's a mighty big 'if.'"

"I'm thinking of reaching out to a colleague in Turkey—the man who helped us on a previous case—and asking for his help, make this a collaborative effort. But even if the Turks *do* get involved, going to Chesme will still be very dangerous. If either of you want to back out, now is the time to tell me."

"Hell, Yiannis," Tembelos said. "I'll go with you. If only to keep your sorry ass alive."

Costas nodded. "I think you're right, sir. We should go to Chesme. As you said, it's our only lead."

• • •

"Raina Mustafa was sighted in Chesme, Turkey," Patronas told Stathis. "I want to go there and see if anyone remembers her."

"Go to Turkey? Have you lost your mind?"

"It's all we've got."

"But Turkey, Patronas, Turkey… I don't know if you this, but my family was from there originally." He then went on in great detail the tragic turn of events that had driven his Greek ancestors out of Asia Minor, the 'slaughter of the innocents,' as he termed it.

"Greeks owned everything in those days," he said. "Out of 391 factories in Smyrna, 322 were Greek. But in 1922, the Turks set fire to the city and burned us out. Three thousand years of history gone in an instant. One million people displaced, and God knows how many dead. Over 100,000, they say."

"It wasn't an instant, sir. It was nine days. The fire burned for nine days."

"It was like the Apocalypse," Stathis continued. "Like God had cursed the Greeks."

Patronas listened impatiently. As a policeman, he'd seen plenty of violence and God hadn't played a hand in any of it. It had always been human beings, human beings who'd been to blame.

He continued to plead his case with Stathis. "What I envision is an operation like the ones Interpol used to nab child pornographers. They were very successful, those operations. Rolled up whole networks."

"That's Interpol, not you, Patronas. Roll up a network? You must be kidding. From what I've seen of you, you couldn't roll a cigarette."

Ignoring the jibe, Patronas plowed on. "Those busts generated a tremendous amount of publicity, sir. If we succeed, we would be setting a precedent for the whole world. It would put us on the map, sir, I don't know if you realize that. Television reporters would be fighting to talk to you. CNN, all the networks."

His only card, he was playing it. He knew Stathis loved to see images of himself plastered on the front page of newspapers and held weekly press conferences to that effect, courting the reporters from the major Greek dailies, *Kathimerini* and *Ta Nea*, assiduously. He hadn't quite mastered television—too much make-up and hesitation—but he was working on it.

"Hmmm," said Stathis. "I don't know, Patronas. You would be taking a terrible risk." "I went to Turkey on another case, remember?"

"Yes, but you were chasing known fugitives that time, a pair if murderers. Here, you have no idea who you are after."

He then spoke at length about the sanctity of borders and the perils of being a law enforcement officer operating on foreign soil. Stathis fancied himself a dispenser of wisdom, but he was no Socrates in Patronas' opinion. If his boss was anyone from ancient times, it was Caligula.

"If you think there's even a remote chance of solving this crime, you have my permission to go, but bear in mind: first, you will have no authority inn Turkey, absolutely none; and if you run into trouble, I will claim to have no knowledge of you or your activities. I will publicly disown you." Stathis droned on. "Second, don't even think about mounting this operation on your own. You will need back-up. Take that team of yours with you."

Orders were orders and he would comply, although the people serving under him hardly qualified as a 'team' in Patronas' opinion. Hopefully, no shots would be fired this time, no dead goats on the hillside. But, given who he had to work with, anything was possible. Once they got to Turkey, dead goats might be the least of their problems.

"We'll find him, sir."

"There is no 'we,' here, Patronas.

"None whatsoever. I repeat: you go to Turkey? You are on your own."

Chapter 8

"What do you mean, 'you're going to Turkey?'" Lydia's voice went up an octave. "What about Dimitra? Who's going to take her to the hospital?"

"I'll only be away a couple of days. She can take a taxi."

"A taxi? She's going for chemotherapy."

"We're divorced, Lydia. Have been for a long time. If it were you, it would be different."

The fight continued for well into the evening. Lydia brought out the heavy artillery at dinner, serving up sausage-flavored tempeh which looked like dirty, boiled shoelaces and was very hard to get down.

Spite, Patronas told himself, sawing away at it. Pure spite.

They ate in silence or rather Lydia ate while Patronas watched. No tempeh for him. Not tonight, not ever. He'd rather eat scorpions.

Ali got to eat hot dogs. Seeing the way Patronas eyed them, the child moved his plate away.

"Come along, Ali," Lydia said after the boy finished. "It's time for bed."

• • •

Returning to the table, Lydia sat down and picked up her wine glass. She studied Patronas. "You need to rethink your priorities."

Again, with the priorities. It was better than his emotional 'constipation,' another a favorite of hers. It had stopped him cold when she'd first said it. How does one defecate emotion? Sadness or grief? Or hold back the same which was what happens when you're constipated. You get blocked up.

Faulty plumbing, he decided it meant. Some kind of faulty plumbing when it came to feelings.

She continued to speak eloquently on the priority theme. Work versus home, work versus personal obligations, work versus her. His sins were many and Lydia kept track.

"Ali is just starting to warm-up to you and now you're leaving."

"I'm not his father. "

"I know and he needs one."

"Lydia, I am a homicide detective. You know that. That's how we met. I was investigating that murder on Sifnos. And this case is a thousand times worse. The man who killed that girl nearly took her head off. The coroner thinks he was trying to behead her."

"But Turkey. Yiannis!? Turkey?! I saw *The Midnight Express!* I saw how they locked up that kid and beat him half to death. I know what goes on there."

Be patient, Patronas told himself. She's American and Americans always confuse what they see in the movies with reality. It's a national failing.

"The person in that movie was a drug dealer, Lydia, not a cop."

"Why can't those border people do it?"

"Frontex? They're talking about suspending operations in Greece because of human rights abuses. It's up to me, Lydia. There's no one else. I want to find the man who killed her. I want justice for her."

"There's no justice in this life, Yiannis. You're a policeman, surely you know that."

"What happened to you? To the person who believed 'people were basically good at heart,' and happily after?"

"I've changed. Now I think most people in the world only want one thing in life and that is to live to see tomorrow."

She stood up and gathered up the dishes. "You need to find someone to drive Dimitra."

"I was hoping you'd do it."

A test, this.

Lydia didn't hesitate. "Yes, yes. Of course, I will."

"It'll be rough."

"I don't care, Yiannis. How many times do I have to tell you? Kindness is everything."

Oh, Lydia, Lydia. A week with Dimitra and you'll be singing a different tune.

He followed her into the kitchen, "I have been wrestling with this, Lydia. Don't think I haven't. In the 1930's, it was the Jews; and we failed them. And now it's the migrants; and we're failing them, too. That's why I want to go to Turkey. Somewhere along the line we failed that girl and I want to make it right."

That night he woke up and found the bed empty, Lydia gone. He thought she might be with Ali, but the boy was alone in his room, sleeping peacefully.

He found her outside on the terrace. Her hair was loose, a wild nimbus of red from the humidity; and she was shivering from the cold.

"Come back to bed," he said gently.

She looked up at him. "When are you leaving?"

"The day after tomorrow."

"I didn't mean what I said at dinner, Yiannis. I still believe in 'happily ever after.' She grabbed his hand. "Maybe not for everyone, but for us."

• • •

Dimitra and her mother had rented an apartment near the harbor. In the past it had been used as student housing for the University of the Aegean; and the remnants of its previous occupants were still visible on the walls, graffiti and old campaign posters of Andreas Papandreou when he was running for prime minister, his face silhouetted against a rising sun along with $A\lambda\lambda\alpha\gamma\dot{\eta}!$ in bold letters. Change. Patronas well remembered that time, the day when the men he thought of as 'the moustaches' took over.

Greece had indeed changed under Papandreou. All the old values had been washed away; the economy had collapsed; and much of what Patronas loved about his homeland had disappeared. Looking now at the socialist's beaming face, Patronas wanted to scratch his eyes out.

The apartment consisted of a living room, galley kitchen and a single bedroom where the two of them slept. Patronas couldn't imagine bedding down next to the old woman, what with her whiskers and scent of decay. It would be like being in Alfred Hitchcock movie.

A small balcony overlooked the street below, trucks thundering beneath it heading to the harbor. Dimitra was sitting outside in the sun—no wig, no make-up. She looked relaxed, better than she had in some time.

She started when she saw him. "Yiannis, what are you doing here?"

"I stopped by to tell you I have to go to Turkey; and Lydia will be driving you to the hospital next week."

"Bah. I don't like it. That wife of yours? She drives like a turtle."

"It's important. People's lives are at stake."

She glared at him. "In case you've forgotten, so is *mine*."

"I know, I know."

"No, you don't. No one does." Her voice caught. "My mother doesn't know who I am half the time. She's gone just like me only in a different kind of way. It's hard to be alone when you're sick and I can't stop thinking about what's going to happen after I die, if there'll be anybody at my funeral or if I'll be alone there, too."

Patronas didn't know what to say. The Dimitra he knew had been a warrior, a woman who took on all comers and never faltered.

"Come on, Dimitra. You're not going to die."

"You know what they say, 'dust to dust. Well, I'm dust now, Yiannis. I'm living dust."

"I will be back by the end of the week. You have my word of honor."

Then, just for an instant, the old Dimitra showed herself. "I don't want your fucking 'honor," she hissed. "I'm dying. Can't you see? What good is your honor to me now?"

Chapter 9

Patronas drew a map of Turkey on the blackboard at the police station. He'd barricaded the door of the conference room and was doing his best to keep his voice down. If someone overheard him and spoke of it, Costas wouldn't last a minute undercover.

"I've arranged for the Frontex people to drop you off here," he told Costas, tapping the blackboard with a piece of chalk. "You will come ashore and start walking. Walking is important. You're posing as a migrant and that's what migrants do—they walk. There will be others on the road, so with any luck, you'll be able to blend in. Tembelos and I will follow in a second boat."

"'A second boat?'" Tembelos asked. "We're cops, Yiannis. We don't have a boat."

"A shipowner I know has agreed to loan us one. His family came from Asia Minor; and he feels strongly about what happened to the girl. It's a pleasure craft, a Stingray. Small, but with a big 220 horsepower engine. There are hundreds of boats like it along the coast, so it's a good way to go. We will slip in quietly, do our work and leave. No need to draw attention to ourselves."

He returned to Costas. "Once you leave Chios, you will have no direct physical contact with us. I want you to take photos with your phone of the men who are smuggling people into Greece and send it to me. I spoke to the Turkish authorities in Chesme; and once they have the photos in hand, they will go after the smugglers and inspect the life jackets they're selling, make sure they're legitimate."

"No more fake life jackets?" asked Costas.

Patronas nodded. "No more fake life jackets."

Costas looked down at her phone, checking to make sure it was charged. "I'm good," she said a minute later.

"Take as many photos as you want, but make sure the smugglers don't see. Then after you forward the pictures, erase them. Someone sees them on your phone, they'll ask questions."

"Got it."

"After you're done photographing the smugglers, I want you to approach one of them and ask him to take you to Chios. Pay him whatever he asks and climb onboard his boat. Once you arrive back on the island, get yourself processed and dispatched to Vial. Keep in mind you'll be working undercover the whole time, posing as a migrant woman of indeterminate origins, traveling alone and unprotected. This last is very important. I can't stress it enough. The man we're after is a predator; and predators always go after the isolated and the weak."

"Once I am in place at the camp, how do we communicate?"

"You text me. Every day at 4 p.m. Every single day. And if something happens and you need to run, you call. Day or night. You call."

"Have her text me, too," Tembelos said.

After Patronas gave Costas the number of Tembelos' cell phone, she ran a test, texting Patronas and waiting for him to respond, and then doing the same with Tembelos.

"Does the camp administrator know I'm coming?" she asked. "The staff?"

Patronas shook his head. "I wasn't sure I could trust them."

A lengthy silence followed, Costas looking first at him, then at Tembelos.

"No gun, no badge?"

"No, nothing. Just a backpack and your cell phone."

He handed her a wad of bills. "Here's two thousand euros in cash. Might be a good idea to scuff it up a little, make the bills look like they've been around for a while."

She crumbled the bills up and smoothed them out; then, satisfied with the results, stuffed them into her backpack. "Anything else?"

"Yes. Don't take notes or leave anything around that might identify you. And trust no one. You hear me? Absolutely, no one."

"Don't look so worried, sir," she said. "I can handle this. I bought a *hijab* and a robe at the *laiki*, the outdoor market, in Chora, exactly like the ones the Syrian women wear. I'll change into them before I go and disguise myself. I won't need to talk much. Women from that part of the world don't, as far as I can tell."

"Be very careful." Patronas fought to keep the fear out of his voice. "You're taking an enormous risk."

"I know sir,"

She was holding a mug of coffee like her life depended on it. Judging by the look on her face, it wasn't her first and was of the Irish variety.

Another plus for his mission, Patronas thought. The camp was overwhelmingly Muslim, and as such, totally dry. For Costas at least, the stake-out would be a form of rehab.

Patronas studied her. "Are you sure you want to do this? You can't drink, you know, not while you're there. If you do, it could cost you your life."

"All the more reason to go."

Her voice rose. "Sir, please. Raina Mustafa came to Chios seeking a better life; and some man butchered her. I want to correct the terrible wrong that was done to her. To get justice for her. That's why I became a cop, why I joined the force."

"Watch your step is all that I'm saying. Make sure you find this man before he finds you."

"I will, sir. I promise."

Chapter 10

Initially, all went smoothly. Melissa Costas boarded the Frontex cruiser and left; Patronas and Tembelos followed in the speedboat a short time after.

Like most Chiots, Patronas knew his way around boats and easily steered the Stingray across the channel and into Turkish waters without incident. He cut the engine as they approached and slowly drifted into a large marina near Chesme. There were hundreds of boats there; and he and Tembelos quickly tied up the Stingray and came ashore.

Patronas had expected Chesme, a harbor town, to be a kind of wild west by the sea; and he was surprised by how peaceful it was. A fortress of bone-colored limestone dominated the center of the city; and beyond it was a mosque, a delicate minaret with a blue steeple next to it.

"Not exactly Chicago under Al Capone." Tembelos said.

"It's naptime," Patronas said. "Maybe the people we're after will come out later."

But they didn't. Only hordes of well-dressed young people far more polite, Patronas noted sourly, than their counterparts in his homeland, all of them falling respectfully silent when the imam called them to prayer.

Although they wandered around for hours, they never located the place where Syrian migrants gathered and departed for Chios.

"I give up," Patronas said. "Let's eat."

They ordered lunch at a small restaurant by the sea— cheese borek and *iskender kabob,* a specialty of Bursa, a town to the north. The kabob was unlike any Patronas had ever eaten before—a mountain of succulent lamb piled onto squares of toasted pita bread and doused with a tomato-brown butter sauce and fresh yogurt.

Gobbling it down, he moaned in pleasure.

Tembelos waved a fork at him. "Stop making those sex sounds. People are looking at you."

The waiter, a dignified, elderly man, stopped by their table after they'd finished. "*Ακόμα τρως*?" he asked politely in Greek. Are you still eating?

Patronas didn't ask how the man had come to know Greek. This close to Smyrna, anything was possible. Perhaps a relative of his had gotten a foot caught in the door during the exchange of populations and stayed on, a grandmother maybe, and she'd taught him the language in secret. The Greek people had kept their language alive that way for centuries during the Ottoman occupation. Maybe this man's family had done the same.

Jews in Spain had gone into hiding during the Inquisition, so why not here? 'Conversos,' Patronas remembered they were called. Perhaps such people were hiding out in Turkey now, too; and the waiter was one of them—closeted Armenians, closeted Greeks. People would do anything to survive.

When they told the waiter what they were doing—Greek cops tracing a murdered girl—he suggested they go to Alacati, a picturesque village known for its windsurfing.

"There are clubs there, Assyria and The Electric Lounge. They have girls there, girls who do other things."

After paying the bill, the two of them flagged down a taxi, went to Assyria and spent the rest of the night nursing drinks and studying a bunch of kids gyrating under a strobe light. Foreigners mostly with a sprinkling of Turkish men.

Patronas showed the bartender the photo of Raina Mustafa. "We're Greek cops," he said in English. "This girl been in here?"

The bartender studied the photo for a moment, then handed it back to him. "Too young. They would never have let her in. They're strict about that here."

"If you were us, where would you look for her? Patronas asked.

Not meeting his eye, the man concentrated on wiping down the counter. "There's an area behind the airport in Izmir, a row of dumpsters. I've never been there, but I've heard you can buy anything you want there."

"Women?"

"Yes." He hesitated. "Of all ages."

• • •

After much discussion, Patronas and Tembeloa rented car, a modest, grey Korean sedan, their reasoning being if they succeeded, they couldn't very well transport the man who'd killed Raina Mustafa in a taxi. The handcuffs and yelling, all hell would break loose. No question, the trunk of a car would be the best place to put him.

Idly, Patronas wondered how the Israelis had spirited Eichmann out of the country. Maybe he should look it up.

The waters of the channel were calm today, the light so bright on the surface, it seared the eye. Remembering the night of the storm, Patronas couldn't believe it was the same body of water. He could still see the people struggling in their life jackets, waves crashing over them as they tried to climb onboard the Coast Guard cruiser, still hear the wind whistling like a weapon of war

Faithful earth, unfaithful sea.

• • •

A soaring, glass-enclosed edifice, the airport in Izmir was located twelve kilometers to the south of the city.

"According to the internet," Tembelos informed Patronas, "this airport serves over twelve million people a year. In other words, a million a month, which translates into roughly 35,000 per day. And if even a handful make it to those dumpsters the bartender told us about, that's at least a couple hundred people."

"Shut up, Giorgos."

After parking the rental car in a lot, they got out and walked around the perimeter of the airport, following the barbed wire fence that enclosed it. The dumpsters were lined up behind the last runway, the yellowing grass around them littered with used condoms.

A long line of cars was parked alongside the dumpsters, all of them with their engines running, a single man behind the wheel.

Off to the left, a Slavic-looking man was directing women one by one to the waiting cars.

A kind of unholy parking lot attendant.

"We'd better go get the rental," Patronas said. "This isn't going to work on foot."

After they retrieved the car, they joined the queue and waited their turn.

"We want a young girl," Patronas told the man when they got to the front of the line. "She must be fresh. New to this."

"Fresh will cost you."

Patronas shrugged. "We have money."

Grabbing a girl by the arm, the man pushed her toward the car..

"Here you go. Meet Sofia. Whatever you want, she will do. You don't like? Come back later. More coming. A 'fresh' supply." His laugh was ugly.

After pocketing Patronas' money—one hundred euros—he returned to dispatching the rest of the women to the idling cars. "You, Tanya, that red Toyota. Alicia, the silver one behind it."

The girl was wearing a sequined halter top and low-cut shorts. Her gold platform shoes were so high, she could barely walk; and she teetered awkwardly as she came toward them. Her make-up was smeared; and she appeared to have been crying.

She balked when Patronas opened the car door; and she saw Tembelos. "No, no!"

Patronas motioned for her to be quiet. "No customers. Police, *polis.*"

"You no want?" She pointed to his pants.

He shook his head.

"Him?" She nodded Tembelos.

"No."

He showed her the photo of Raina Mustafa and asked if she'd seen her. The girl shook her head. "What happened to this girl?" she asked in English.

"Someone killed her."

"Sometimes happens. The girls, they die."

"Here in Turkey?"

"Everywhere. Is everywhere the same."

They put her in the backseat and drove her to the police station in Izmir where they turned her over to the officer in charge. It wasn't much, but Patronas didn't know what else to do.

"You know she'll be back turning tricks tomorrow," Tembelos whispered. "You see her arms? She's a junkie."

"I don't care. I couldn't walk away and leave her there."

"I wish I knew what you were doing. What does any of this have to do with Raina Mustafa?"

"The coroner said we should look for a man that trades in flesh," Patronas said. "And she's flesh."

Before leaving the station, he spoke at length to the Turkish officer he'd met on another case. s case, a courtly man named Hazmas Arsian. The two of them had chased a pair of murderers across Turkey and, during the investigation, developed an uneasy friendship.

Patronas handed Arsian the photo. "You seen her?"

The Turk gave the photo a cursory glance and handed it back to him. "I have not seen her," he said in English. "Dead or alive."

Arsian's voice was flat. "All the time now, we find bodies, dead bodies on a beach, dead bodies in the water. Every day. Dehydration kills some, exhaustion, many others."

"Any of them murdered?" Patronas asked.

"Who knows? All we do is bury them. We don't have the resources to investigate. There are too many, Chief Inspector. Just too many dead migrants. We cannot even identify most of them. They remain nameless, nameless in life , nameless in death. . They're just corpses to us, corpses which need to be disposed of."

"Her name was Raina Mustafa; and she was seen in Chesme before she died."

"So why come here and trouble me with little hooker girls? This is Izmir."

"We are trying to trace her. You can call Athens if you don't believe me."

"Oh, I believe you. I just don't understand why all this fuss over one dead migrant."

"He cut her throat with an axe."

The Turk paused, processing this. "Very well. I will tell you what I think. I think this girl of yours, someone noticed how pretty she was and thought to himself, 'this one, she will bring me money.'"

"They wanted sell her?"

"Sell her, yes. To a brothel in the Near East perhaps. Or maybe it was a private sale. A man saw her and commissioned it."

"A man on Chios?"

"That's where it happened, so yes. Doesn't mean it was a Greek, could have been a tourist. These men find a way to get what they want. The dark web is full of sites catering to them."

"We're trying to retrace the route she took to Chios, visit the camps she stayed in along the way."

"Most of the refugee camps are located on the border with Syria. You cannot go there. It's a war zone. You'll get yourself killed."

"Can you give me a phone number at least? A way to contact the people who run those places?"

"I see you are new at this, Chief Inspector. What makes you think they will answer the phone? And even if they did, how are you going to talk to them? You are Greek. You don't speak Turkish."

He gazed at him sorrowfully. "Go back to Chios, Chief Inspector. This quest of yours..." He made a helpless gesture. "It's hopeless. More than three million Syrians live in Turkey now, most of them in those camps you wish to visit. You'll never find what you're seeking. The numbers alone will defeat you."

"What about the smugglers? The ones that put these people on the boat to Chios. Maybe one of them will remember her."

"Again, the numbers. Do you know how many people are involved in smuggling migrants into Europe, Chief Inspector? Tens of thousands. It's a huge business and very well organized. There are entire networks operating in Turkey now with hotels and fleets of trucks, secret print shops to produce fake passports."

"Do most of the migrants leave from Chesme?"

"No. They go from everywhere, up and down the coast. My guess is someone approached this Raina Mustafa—they're easy to spot, the migrants, their fear and their backpacks give them away—and offered to smuggle her into Chios."

"Then what happened?"

"She paid, a truck moved her to the point of departure; and she boarded a cheap inflatable raft. Sometimes the smuggler gives the migrants a course in seamanship, sometimes not. 'Head toward the flashing lighthouse,' they tell them and 'puncture the boat after you come ashore. That way no one can send you back.'"

"How many people are you talking about?"

"It's a tsunami, Chief Inspector. A tsunami for us, a tsunami for you."

"Can't you keep watch along the coast?" Tembelos asked. "Keep people from doing this?"

"We could if they always left from the same place, but they don't. The location keeps changing. Every day it's different. The smugglers partner with the people who live by the water and there are a lot of them. The owner of the land gets fifteen percent. Fifteen percent of six thousand dollars, that's a lot of money here."

"How much do the smugglers make per person?"

"It varies. $1000 to $1500 usually."

"Russians involved?"

"In this, no. But in everything else, yes. No doubt that little girl in the gold sandals came in on a Russian train."

Chapter 11

"I fear I have bad news, Yiannis," Papa Michalis said on the phone. "Your witness, the woman, who claimed she was in Chesme with Raina Mustafa, called the station and said she needed to speak with you. I suggested she come in, but she never showed up. She gave me her number and I called and called, but she's not picking up."

"She gave me an address in the camp. Have someone drive out there and do a welfare check."

Papa Michalis called back a half hour later. "Her stuff is there, but she's disappeared."

"This is on me," Patronas told Tembelos as they raced back to Chesme. "I should have assigned someone to keep an eye on her."

Abandoning Turkey, they boarded the Stingray and returned to Chios. If Raina Mustafa had passed through Chesme, she'd left no trace. Just another of the nameless dead the Turk had spoken of. It had been a mistake coming here.

"Good chance she's dead," Tembelos said.

"I know."

"What do we do with this man once we find him?"

"The one who killed her? We put him in jail, I guess."

"It's not enough."

"There are laws, Giorgos. Laws governing crime and punishment."

Again, Patronas flashed on Eichmann in his glass cage in Jerusalem, thinking the German's fate had been far better than he deserved. If it had been up to him, he would have cut off a knuckle for every thousand people Eichmann killed, a limb for every million.

He never would have done it, of course. As a law enforcement officer, he was sworn to uphold the law, but, more importantly, he believed in it, in due process and the rest. Tembelos was a different story.

His colleague could have walked right out of the Old Testament. In his mind, revenge was the natural order of things. Someone does unto me or mine. I will do unto them. Cretans had followed this rule after World War II; the vendettas against collaborators had gone on for years— traitors tracked down and killed in countries as far away as Australia for their misdeeds during the war.

Tembelos never would have done what the Israelis did with Eichmann, transported that man halfway around the world to stand trial. No, he would have cut out Eichmann's heart, stuck it on a stick and danced gleefully around with it. Such was his way.

• • •

A pair of boys were parasailing in the channel; and Patronas carefully steered around them. They looked exhilarated as they rose and fell with the wind, laughing as they sought to be one with it.

Patronas tied up in front of the Chandris Hotel. Stepping ashore, he and Tembelos pushed their way through the throng of young men and women milling around on the quay, the so-called 'bazaar' and headed to the station. Once it had been a kind of mating ritual, the 'bazaar'— girls parading chastely with their mothers and fathers in tow, the boys eyeing them, but keeping their distance. Not that the old system had worked all that well. Patronas had first seen Dimitra at one of those gatherings and approached her. He grimaced, recalling how that had gone—the stilted conversation, her mother ever watchful, overseeing everything.

How had Raina Mustafa spent her evenings, he wondered. Maybe she wasn't as pure as those women in the camp had alleged and had come here at night. Painted her face and sashayed around. Maybe it wasn't Chesme at all, but here that the killer had spotted her.

When he got to the police station, he retrieved his notebook and quickly jotted down all the items he wanted to follow up on. Tembelos joined him a few minutes later; and they divided up the work.

"First and foremost, we need to put out an all-points bulletin for Amira Al-Bashir. Send some officers to Vial and have them speak to the women who lived on the same corridor she did. See if anyone was hanging around her and get a description."

"Second, we need to check with the phone company and trace the calls on her phone, also on Raina Mustafa's. The girl had one. Those women said they heard it ring once or twice. Maybe she set up an appointment with her killer."

They kept throwing things at each other, writing feverishly. Melissa Costas was due to text them in an hour; and they wanted to be finished before then.

Tembelos folded up the list and put it in his pocket. "You know what puzzles me about Raina Mustafa, the motive. According to the coroner, a young virgin is a very valuable asset; and that Turk in Izmir, Hazmas Arsian, he said the same. So why kill her?"

"I don't know, Giorgos."

Pulling out the bottle of ouzo he kept for emergencies, Patronas poured them each a shot. "I keep thinking about all those people in the camps. Hazmas Arsian said there were three million people in Turkey alone, and there are close to a million here in Greece. What's going to happen to them? What's going to become of them?"

"You got something with the migrants, Yiannis. I saw it with those kids, the ones we caught shoplifting. You wanted to save them—it's a fucking crusade with you—and you can't. You just can't."

"Lydia says the same."

"Normally, I would not advocate listening to one's womenfolk, but in this case, maybe you should. Your personal life is a catastrophe. That harem of yours...."

Holding up his hand, Tembelos counted off his fingers "First, there's Dimitra, your ex-wife, who's on her last legs, second, there's Dimitra's mother, your erstwhile mother-in-law, who's not that far behind and last, but not least, there's your present wife, the lovely Lydia Pappas, who wants to turn you into an American. Reshape you like one of her pots.'"

Patronas contemplated the bottle of ouzo. "Your point being?"

"Forget the migrants. You don't have the bandwidth."

Patronas grimaced. "Bandwidth?"

Another one gone. Not even Tembelos spoke his language anymore.

Night had fallen and he could see the lights coming on in the distance, the flashing red and green beacons at the entrance to the harbor. The neoclassical buildings along the waterfront were barely visible in the growing darkness. 'The melancholy hour,' his mother had always called it, that interval between day and night.

Pulling on his coat, Tembelos made ready to leave. "One final thing, Yiannis. You know, my family started out on the other side of the Aegean, same as these people. They crossed that same body of water out there, but at least they were going to a place where they worshipped in the same place, spoke the same language."

"What are you saying, Giorgos?"

"I'm saying these people are different. They don't speak our language. They aren't *us*. And there are so many of them, they're swamping the fucking boat. Do the math. Forty million tourists in any given year and at least a million migrants. And you know how many of us there are: eight, eight million and that's on a good day. This keeps up, Greeks are going to become extinct, a vanishing breed like the wooly mammoth."

"We must help them, Giorgos. It's who we are, who we have always been. We might lose our identity to a degree, but if we don't, it will be worse. We will lose our soul.'

"Fuck our souls. It's a different world, Yiannis, a world we don't know."

"And us? We're cops. Where do we fit in this 'different world'? Where's our place?"

"I don't know."

"It sounds like you are thinking of quitting."

"I admit it's crossed my mind. I became a cop to catch criminals, not arrest kids for stealing pajamas."

"That's not the focus of the job. Solving homicides is."

"Let's say we *do* catch this man, what comes after? We go back to catching shoplifters or worse, patrolling that hell hole of a refugee camp? Is that who we are, Yiannis? Is that why you joined the force, who you want to be?"

• • •

Melissa Costas texted Patronas exactly on time. "Vial w/2 women."

"Stay with them for now," he texted back, his fingers fumbling as he typed the letters on his cellphone. "Let people get used to seeing you. Chesme was a dead end. The answer lies in the camp. Be vigilant and take no risks."

It took him over twenty minutes to type the message. Tembelos had explained the nuances of texting to him—LOLs and the rest—but he hadn't gotten the hang of it and continued to write in complete sentences, subject, verb, subject, verb. Auto fill also gave him grief. Urinate instead of enunciate...piss for pass.

A moment later, Costas texted back, a thumbs up.

With that, she was gone.

• • •

Patronas sat there in the dark for a long time, thinking over what Tembelos had said and trying to figure out what his next move should be. They needed to trace Amira Al-Bashir's movements. See if they could find out where she might have gone. After he did that, he'd check the registries at the hotels and run the names on the passports the guests had submitted through the databases—Interpol, the United Nations Office of Drugs and Crime. See if the man they sought had been flagged someplace else.

The list kept growing. He also should speak with the harbormaster and air traffic controllers, see if they'd noticed anything unusual around the time of the murder, yachts from abroad, for example—which were rare at this time of year—or a private plane, that requested permission to land.

If the Turk was right and the killer had planned to sell Raina Mustafa, he would have needed a way to get her off the island.

It all had to be done. They'd spoken of the 'godfathers of night,' but he wasn't convinced a criminal conspiracy was involved. The island was a backwater. It wasn't Bangkok or Amsterdam. No one would go to such lengths for a lone, Syrian girl. There had to be something else driving this man.

In the morning he'd organize a search party and try to find Amira Al-Bashir. He'd hit the airport and the harbor later.

That was the most important thing, finding Amira Al-Bashir and finding her alive.

He poured out more ouzo, drank it and slammed the glass down.

"Shit! I should have known she was at risk and protected her. What the hell was I thinking?"

Time to go, he told himself, but still he lingered on, wracked with guilt.

He was in no hurry to go home, to pick up where he'd left off. Dimitra had called five or six times, no doubt to make sure he was back and would take her to the hospital tomorrow, but so far, he hadn't responded. No point in rushing into trouble. He had enough already.

Amira Al-Bashir had three children. She wouldn't have gone off and left them for this long. She was dead and he was responsible. It was as simple as that.

He finished off the bottle and threw it across the room. It shattered as it hit the wall, the air suddenly heavy with the smell of liquor.

Getting up from his chair, Patronas surveyed the wreckage and kicked the shards of glass aside.

Broken and useless just like him.

Chapter 12

"They found the body of another woman," the police dispatcher reported.

Patronas closed his eyes. "Where?"

"Souda, same as the other woman."

Thankfully, Patronas had set the phone on vibrate; and Lydia and the boy had slept through the call.

Ali had crawled into bed with them around three a.m., crying for his mother. They hadn't known how to comfort him—the language barrier had proven insurmountable—and eventually, they'd quit trying. Near dawn, the boy had finally fallen asleep, his face wet with tears.

To an extent, Patronas understood what the boy was going through. He had witnessed unspeakable things as a policeman; and the memory of those blood-soaked events had stayed with him and often haunted his dreams. With Ali, it must be a thousand times worse.

The child's trauma showed itself in strange ways. For one thing, he couldn't bear to be near the sea. Couldn't stand the sight of water. Boats also gave him trouble as did uniforms. As a result, Patronas now dressed in civilian clothes when he went to work.

Patronas pulled the blanket up over the sleeping boy. "Oh, child, child, may one day the sight of the sea bring you joy, not pain," he whispered as he tucked him in. And then for good measure, he made the sign of the cross over him, an old remedy of his mother's.

He then dressed and slipped out of the house. The sun was rising as he crested the hill on his moped, the waters of the channel gleaming in the early morning light. A lone workman was hosing down the pavement in front of a shuttered café; and he looked up as Patronas raced by.

Amira Al-Bashir was dressed in the same caftan and headscarf she'd worn when she'd accosted him in the parking lot. Unlike Raina Mustafa, there were no visible wounds on her body, no blood pooling beneath her.

A man in coveralls had found her. "She was just lying there," he told Patronas. "I thought she was sleeping. They do that, the migrants, sleep outside. But then I saw she wasn't breathing."

He was very thin, his face hollowed out and pale. His clothes were splattered with paint as were his wretched shoes, held together with duct tape.

"You the person who phoned it in?"

"Yes. I come to work at the hotel there." He pointed to a building under construction in the distance. "I see her there on beach; and I call 112, the emergency number."

Patronas took down his name and contact information, then turned him over to one of the forensic technicians and ordered him to fingerprint him.

"Run his prints. We might get lucky. You never know."

"Just the police database?"

"No. You heard his accent. He's Albanian. Run him through Interpol and Europol, too."

The coroner was bent over the dead woman, delicately swabbing the inside of her right arm. "Death and more death. Usually, it's old age takes them on the island, but lately it's been murder."

"Any chance she died of natural causes?" Patronas asked.

The coroner pointed to her arm. "See the bruising there. Somebody held her down and gave her a shot. My guess is it was heroin, but I'll know more after I run a toxicology screen."

"How long will that take?"

"How many times do I have to tell you? It takes as long as it takes."

Patronas waited while the coroner and the forensic staff processed the scene, then helped them load the woman's body into the ambulance.

"I'll call you as soon as I have anything." The coroner peeled off his gloves. "Toxicology takes some time. At least a week, a week at the earliest."

"Get it to me as soon as you can."

• • •

The priest was snoring peacefully when Patronas came into the station, sprawled on a cot in the back.

"What?!" he gasped when Patronas shook him awake.

"Amira Al-Bashir's dead. I need to know exactly what she told you. Her exact words."

The old man hesitated. "She said she'd seen the man in Vial, the one Raina Mustafa was afraid of."

"Are you sure?"

"As you know, my hearing is not the best and she was speaking English, a language I am not conversant in, but, yes, that was my impression. 'The man was in Vial.'"

"Anything else?"

"Yes, as a matter of fact. Something curious. 'Al-wahshi.' She must have said it twenty times. 'Al-wahsh, al-wahsh.' It means 'savage' in Arabic. I looked it up."

Patronas nodded. It was consistent with the warning she'd given him in the parking lot.

"I told her to meet with the police artist and work up a sketch of this man for us. But, as I told you on the phone, she never showed up."

"Do you know where she was calling from?"

"Vial would be my guess. I could hear people in the background speaking Arabic. But then there were also people speaking Greek, so it could have been anywhere."

• • •

Two women had been killed, one hacked to death, the other with a syringe full of heroin.

Patronas flipped through the murder book, rereading his notes. He'd foregone his nightly ouzo so that he could concentrate, but so far nothing had jumped out.

He'd had a long talk with Stathis earlier, who'd insisted, given that both victims were migrants and not citizens of Greece, that Patronas drop the case.

"They're not your responsibility, Patronas. They don't vote. They don't pay taxes. And quite frankly, we don't have the resources to deal with them."

"Sir, I don't care where they came from or what they were. Those women died a terrible death. We need to find the man who killed them and bring him to justice."

"Justice, Patronas?"

"Yes. I'm sure you've seen statues of her. She's holding up a scale, the one wearing a blindfold."

"Your point being?"

"Justice is blind, sir. It must be—for migrant and Greek alike. We can't ignore a homicide because the victim came from abroad. It's not right. It's just not right."

And with that, he slammed down the phone. There'd be hell to pay, but he didn't care.

He had always believed everyone was the same when it came to the law. Greek, migrant, it didn't matter. The origins of the people involved were irrelevant. He'd dedicated his life to that principle. He couldn't abandon it now. If he did, he'd be lost both as a man and as a cop.

The Turk had said they didn't investigate the death of migrants. 'We just bury them. They are nameless, these people, nameless in death as they were in life."

Not here, he told himself. There would be no nameless dead on his watch. Even if it cost him his job, he'd find the person responsible for killing those Syrian women, find him if it was the last thing he did.

Honor, he told himself. It was a matter of honor.

Φιλότιμον.

And if there wasn't enough evidence to bring that person to trial, he'd find a way to take care of it on his own, dispense justice the way the Cretans did to those who'd betrayed them during the war. He wanted that man's blood on his hands. Wanted him to feel the terror Raina and Amira had felt.

• • •

It was too early to go Vial and tell Amira Al-Bashir's family the news. Let them sleep a little longer, Patronas decided.

While he waited, Patronas researched Ali's situation on his computer. From what he could see, there were special judges now in Greece, who heard only requests for asylum; but he worried going to court might be too risky: the child could be taken from him and sent off to one of the homes funded by the United Nations for migrant children. They weren't bad, those places. Patronas had visited a couple of them the last time he was in Athens. Ali would get educated there and learn to speak Greek. He'd have other children to play with.

Still an orphanage was an orphanage; and he took a dim view of orphanages.

'The wounded old horse sees the saddle and trembles.'

That was him. He could feel the weight of the saddle pressing down on his shoulders.

He wanted to start over again in the Greece of his youth, to the days when he'd first joined the force, to listen to the old songs and feel the way he once had as a young man—that sense of promise. Oh, God, to feel just once more, that sense of promise, the promise of tomorrow.

Chapter 13

Although Patronas spoke in code to the husband of Amira Al-Bashir—using words like 'unfortunate incident' and the like—her three children somehow understood and began to sob. The migrants in the adjoining tents did what they could for them, but it was the stuff of nightmares.

Leaving the tent, Patronas set about interviewing everyone connected to the family, but over the course of the day, learned very little. The previous morning Amira Al-Bashir had gone to Chora to buy fresh vegetables at the *laiki*, and, at some point during the outing, had simply vanished.

When she didn't return, the husband had gone in search of her.

"I call her name," he told Patronas. "Call and call. Other people, too. But nothing. All the time, many hours, I look."

• • •

Stymied, Patronas reviewed what he knew. The killer must have followed Amira Al-Bashir to the market, but how was the question. If he'd been on foot, she would have seen him. If he'd been in a car, he would have had to park it, a difficult feat given that it was a market day. So how had he managed it? How the hell had he gotten to her?

Patronas had bought a new bottle of ouzo on his way into the office and was finishing it in solitude, drinking steadily as the evening wore on and the shadows lengthened. Not yet drunk, he was well on his way.

Putting on his reading glass, he read the text under the photos of Interpol's ten most wanted criminals he had posted on his wall. One was of a woman, who allegedly adopted an orphan in India, insured him for a lot of money and then murdered him.

"*Panagia*," he muttered. Mother of God. What people were capable of.

Once he'd viewed such people as alien life forms, these dead-eyed individuals from the far corners of the globe, but no longer. They were everywhere now; evil was on the move. And he was pretty sure one of them had washed ashore on Chios.

How could anyone knowingly choose evil? The woman on the poster had had a choice—you always have a choice—so why had she chosen to torment and butcher an innocent child?"

As a homicide detective, he'd often asked convicted murderers the same question. Most had just shrugged. "What can I tell you?" one of them had said ""I didn't think about it. I just did it."

Something dark in the human species. A little touch of Satan in the DNA.

He studied the woman's photograph again. There was something here he needed to remember. Something to do with the case...a woman. Maybe it was a woman, a woman, who was involved.

The migrants would be more apt to trust a woman, to get in a car with one. Still, he doubted it. Most probably she was an accomplice, the sister of one of the godfathers or perhaps his wife.

• • •

"I'm pulling you out," Patronas texted Melissa Costas. "There's been another murder; and I'm worried about your safety."

"Give me two more days," Costas texted back. "I'm on to something. Greek, not migrant.."

"Leave now." He kept pounding the keys on his phone, texting her the same message again and again: 'Exit Vial!!! Exit Vial!!!"

But Costas had gone silent.

"Come on, Melissa! Answer me! Damnit!"

"I got distracted."   "Costas is not answering. I tried calling her, but she isn't picking up."

He handed Tembelos his phone. "Here. Read her texts."

"'Greek, not migrant. She thinks a Greek is the killer?" Tembelos nodded, thinking it through.

"It's possible. You remember that case on Kos, the woman who was smuggling migrants into Europe? She was Greek."

"She didn't take an axe to her customers," Patronas said.

"Hear me out. She set up a whole network—safe houses, a printing press. Could be that's all Costas meant, someone doing the same thing here. Fake passports, asylum papers, that kind of thing. You sell those... you'd make some serious money."

"But would it be worth killing for?"

"I don't know. It's either that or sex trafficking. Either way, it's greed."

"I doubt it's documents. Sex trafficking is a lot more lucrative, a never-ending stream. Not just prostitution. You could make videos of the women and post them on the dark web. The possibilities are endless."

He opened the murder book. "Okay, say we go with sex trafficking, where do we begin?"

"There's that prostitute down by the harbor. Let's go talk to her. Find out what goes on in Chios at night, what our fellow Greeks are capable of."

Chapter 14

The prostitute was a tall, heavyset woman from Africa. Dressed in a low-cut jumpsuit and flip flops, she had no customers and was leaning against a metallic gold BMW, smoking a cigarette. Her hair was streaked with blonde; and she was heavily made up with long, false eyelashes and sparkly blue eye shadow.

She barely acknowledged Patronas and Tembelos when they got out of the police car and came towards her. Her movements jerky and unsteady, she continued to smoke. A junkie? Patronas wondered, seeing her agitation, how nervy she was. He tried to see the insides of her arms, but she kept them pinned to her sides.

Opening his wallet, he flashed his badge.

The woman laughed. "*Polis*, huh? *Polis*, shorty?"

"Yes," Patronas said, drawing himself up. "I am Chief Inspector Yiannis Patronas of the Hellenic Police Force; and this is my second-in-command, Giorgos Tembelos. We need to talk to you about the murder of Raina Mustafa."

"What's that girl got to do with me?"

"Did you know her?"

"No. Only what happened to her. Girl gets chopped up like that? Word gets around."

"Were you trafficked? Brought here to..." Patronas hesitated, not knowing how to frame the question.

"What? To walk the streets?" She gave a mirthless laugh. "Go ahead and say it, Chief. There are lots of names for what I do, what I am—whore, hooker, call girl." She gave a sad little wiggle. "Lady of the night. Lots of names. It's the way of the world. Wherever men look to buy, there be women willing to sell." Her African accent became more pronounced the longer she spoke.

"Were you willing to sell yourself or were you forced into it?"

She gave him a long, searching look. "You got here too late, Chief Inspector. Nothing you can do know about it now. Nothing anybody can do."

It had rained earlier; and the black asphalt was shiny with damp. A lone streetlight illuminated the area where she was standing, an island of light in the surrounding darkness. The entire scene—the garishly painted woman leaning against the shiny yellow car—embodied loneliness to Patronas, loneliness without end.

To stand out here night after night, soliciting strangers...

A wave of pity washed over him. Seeing her shiver, he took off his coat and draped her around her shoulders.

Surprised, she stroked the fabric with her hand. "Well, I'll be damned, a gentleman cop."

"What's your name?"

"Tariro," she said softly. "And, yes, I was brought here to do this. Had no say in the matter. Had to pay off my passage from Nigeria, the man said."

"What man?"

"The man who runs us. I'm not the only one. There are others. At the beach in Karfas in the summer. Here in town in the winter. I'm supposed to service the crews coming off the boats. We all have our assignments."

"I need a name."

"He'll beat me up. That's what he does. Got a real mean fist, that man. Real mean."

Although he kept after her for more than fifteen minutes, she refused to give up the man's name. "No way. He broke my jaw once. I had to use a straw to eat for two months."

"He ever film you?"

"Not much market in Greece for someone looks like me. But, yeah, he filmed some of the other girls. Other stuff, too. He's real imaginative."

"Where can I find him?"

"I can't say. He has ways of knowing and he'd kill me, sure."

"We can protect you."

"For how long, Chief? A couple of days? A week? I'm an African hooker, here illegally. I got no value. Only value I have is to the man I work for, money I make for him on my back."

"Does he have any associates that you know of?"

"Yes, there's Greek comes around sometimes. Not ordinary, him. No, that man's got *presence*."

"What do you mean?"

"Fine clothes, fine, fine clothes. Fancy way of talking. You know...all grand-like."

"Anything else?"

"No. He's not in business with the man I work for. I don't know what he does, but he's not a pimp. I would have heard about it if he was running girls. Drugs maybe. Something else."

"You be careful, Tariro. Someone comes at you with a knife, you run, you call us."

"A knife? I thought he used a hatchet."

Patronas and Tembelos exchanged glances. They hadn't released this information to the press which meant she knew something.

"He's on a rampage," Patronas said, pressing her. "There's been another death."

"Not my problem, Chief Inspector. Tariro means hope in my language. And that's what I am hoping to do...stay alive."

Giving her his card, he told her to call him day or night.

"You can call me, too," she said and winked at him. "I like 'em petite."

• • •

"Why didn't you ask her where that man came from?" Tembelos asked when they got back to the cruiser. "What his nationality was?"

"No need. He's Greek, Giorgos. As Greek as you or me. Women in Chora, women in Karfas? Not only is he Greek, he's from Chios. I'd stake my life on it."

"Should I follow her tonight? See where she goes?"

"No. She'll stay in that parking lot until after the bars close, then head off to sleep. This man is clever. He's not going to show himself. We'll have to find another way."

Looking out at the night, he mentally reviewed what the prostitute had told them. "She said that he hit her so hard, she had to drink out of straw which means he broke her jaw; and she had to get it wired up. That's something only a doctor can do. Go to the hospital and check the records, see if you can find the name of the person who brought her in."

"How am I going to do that? We don't know her last name."

"Shit, you're right. I forgot to ask."

But when they approached the woman again, she refused to give it to them. "Just call me Sexy," she said.

"Sexy what?" Patronas insisted.

"Fuck off, little man. Go bother someone else."

Chapter 15

Patronas had spoken to Costas on facetime once and still remembered the background of the call, the battered white tent with the UN logo and a rip along the bottom; and he searched Vial until he found it. Costas' backpack was still there, neatly stowed next to her cot, but Patronas found nothing of value in it, only a few articles of worn-out clothing and a pair of high-top sneakers, no cell phone. Wherever she'd gone, she must have taken it with her.

A group of Syrian women in head scarfs were huddled nearby, watching him with worried eyes. They nodded when he showed them Costas' photo.

Using the language app on his phone, he asked them if they'd seen her, where she might be.

She'd gone to get dinner by herself the previous night, one of the women said, but she never came back.

"Friends, who are her friends?" Patronas asked, typing the question onto his phone and waiting for the app to pick up. He needed to get Liadis, but he was in a hurry and didn't want to wait.

Costas had kept to herself, the woman said. "Watching, always watching."

"Sometimes she played with the children," another volunteered.

Dalia was standing with the women, the doll dangling from her hand. Patronas smiled broadly at her, but she didn't return his smile and secreted herself behind her mother, her face frightened. He wondered if she'd witnessed something, seen the man who'd grabbed Raina Mustafa and maybe Costas. A child would be next to invisible here. If only there was a way he could speak to her.

Patronas walked to the main office and knocked on Liadis' door. He wasn't ready to sound the alarm—if Costas was still in the camp, it would be too dangerous—but he wanted to double check the tents and temporary housing one last time to make sure he hadn't missed something. He was growing more and more convinced something had happened. She always played by the rules; and she should have texted him by now.

Again, Liadis' wife was there, perched on her husband's desk and looking at her phone. She didn't look up when Patronas came in and just kept scrolling down with a manicured hand.

"One of my colleagues is here in Vial," Patronas told Liadis. "I've looked, but I can't seem to locate them." He fought to keep his voice steady.

"You want me to help?" Liadis asked.

Patronas nodded.

"My, my, Chief Inspector," Liadis' wife said, looking up at him. "I am surprised. It's always been my understanding police are supposed to *find* people, not lose them."

"My officer is here undercover."

"Undercover, now that is interesting. And now this person of yours has disappeared." Her tone was mocking. "I'd be worried if I were you. As you know, people have been killed here…Women."

Patronas studied her. "I am aware of that."

"But you sent her into Vial anyway."

Patronas felt sick. He hadn't said anything about Costas being a woman. If Liadis' wife, Chryssoula Papoulis knew, so might others.

• • •

"You must forgive my wife," Liadis told Patronas after his wife left the office. "She thought we'd be living in Athens after we got married, but instead we're marooned on Chios…her words, not mine. It's been a hard adjustment for her."

"She didn't want to come?"

"No. She hates it here. Hates the island. Hates the camp. Hates all of it."

"You could ask to get reassigned."

"I don't want to. I believe in what I'm doing. A person's life must mean something. At one time, my family controlled nearly all the cotton in Egypt, a huge enterprise. But then Nasser arrived; and we lost everything. Still, we lived through it. We managed. What you have isn't important, I keep telling her. Money, where you live, the size of your house, none of it matters."

"What does she say?"

"'They're migrants, those people you work with, ignorant scum'" As if they have no value, as if they're worthless."

"If it's any consolation, my boss says the same thing. He didn't want me to go forward with the case for that reason. 'Migrants don't pay your salary,' he said. 'You need to forget about them.'"

"But you went ahead anyway?"

Patronas nodded. "I didn't think it was right to let it go."

But Liadis was no longer listening. He kept looking around for his wife, waiting pensively for her to return.

"We've only been married a year," he said by way of explanation. "We were both married before; and this was supposed to be a fresh start. She seemed happy at first, but she's not happy now. 'Vlachs,' she calls the islanders. Peasants. I tried to introduce her to some of the shipowners, but they are only here in the summer; and the rest of the year, there's no one she feels comfortable with."

"Must be hard."

"Yes, for both of us. I'm no saint, Chief Inspector—I've done things I'm not proud of—but I'd do anything to make her happy."

• • •

"Costas has disappeared," Patronas told Tembelos when he got back to the station. "I went through Vial and questioned half the people there. No one has seen her."

"When was the last time she sent a text?"

"Two days ago."

There was a long silence as Tembelos processed this.

They both knew two days was the window in a missing person case. After that, the victim was rarely found alive.

"She's resourceful." Patronas said, seeking to convince himself. "She'll make it back alive."

"What do we do in the meantime?"

"We turn over every rock."

They worked the rest of the day and long into the night. Tembelos drove to the hospital, went through their records and got the name and address of the man who'd brought the prostitute in, Petros Akylas. As Patronas had anticipated, he was a local man who lived in Vrondatos, a town on the eastern coast of Chios.

While Patronas waited for Tembelos to return with Akylas, he checked with the harbormaster and the flight controller at the airport. Both said there had been no unusual traffic on Chios in the weeks prior to the murders.

"All was as it should be," the flight controller said. "Regular flights from Athens, nothing else."

He also ran the name of Liadis' wife. Chryssoula Papoulis through the system and was surprised to learn she was the daughter of a man who'd started life as a poor boy in Piraeus and amassed a fortune in the import-export business, which explained her accent. Her brother, Michalis Papoulis, had been arrested twice for rich boy crimes, cocaine in a nightclub, speeding late at night, but had never done time. There was little else about the family.

No wonder she hated Vial.

A woman like that? She'd think poverty was like Ebola, a contagious disease she might catch.

• • •

Akylas was a little bantam rooster of a man, cocky and full of himself. He didn't walk so much as strut as he came into the police station; and the air seemed to crackle around him. He was dressed in tight black pants and a short-sleeved black shirt open to the waist. A snakeskin belt, gold chain and gold-embossed cowboy boots completed his ensemble. Well into his fifties, he was fighting hard to look younger, his ponytail and sad, little goatee, a uniform jet black and obviously dyed. He was heavily tattooed—a snake with fangs winding around his neck, two others doing the same thing on his arms—and he was wearing rings on nearly all his fingers, gaudy chunks of silver.

"Sit down, Mr. Akylas." Patronas nodded to the chair in front of him. "We need to talk to you about your business, such as it is. It is my understanding you are the man in charge of prostitution on the island."

The man bridled. "That's a lie."

"I don't care about what you do for a living," Patronas said. "That's between you and God. I want to know about you and Raina Mustafa."

"The Syrian girl?"

"Yes. The one who was killed and whose body was dumped in Souda."

"Never met her. Arab women are no good in my line of work. They just don't take to it in my experience. That Muslim thing, it cuts deep."

Patronas handed him the autopsy photo. "Take a close look. You're sure you don't recognize her?"

Giving the photo a cursory glance, he handed them back to Patronas. "Yeah, I'm sure."

Picking up a pen, Patronas jotted this down in his notebook. Tembelos was sitting behind Akylas in the far corner of the station and openly recording the conversation. Initially, Akylas had refused to speak on record, but after Patronas had threatened him with a night in jail, he'd relented and given them permission to tape the conversation.

"I want immunity. Nothing I say to be used in court."

"Immunity is off the table. This is a homicide investigation, Mr. Akylas. You confess, you'll be charged."

Patronas would have liked to arrest him for beating up the African woman, but he was afraid Akylas would kill her once he got out. He was that kind of man, the kind who liked to push women around, to hurt them.

Patronas flipped through the murder book. "Where you were from the end of October until November fourteenth?"

"That was over two months ago. How the fuck do know? I spend most of my time at my club, so I was probably there. I know I didn't leave the island."

"What is the name of your club?"

"The Obelisk. It's a gentlemen's club down by the harbor. You need to be a member to get in."

"Anyone see you?"

"Sure. I am like Hugh Hefner, surrounded by beautiful women. The ladies, they like me. Always have."

"You run this operation alone or do you have help?"

"I'm independent. Make more money that way."

"You admit you're a pimp."

"I prefer to think of myself as an 'promoter.'" He smirked. "A promoter of men's fantasies.'"

"How many girls do you have working for you?"

"Seven."

"Seven?" Patronas repeated, counting them off with his fingers.

"That's right." Akylas frowned. "What's this got to do with that girl's murder?"

"We think she was trafficked."

"Wouldn't surprise me. Camp's a rough place. Lots of vermin coming off those boats, riffraff from the Middle East."

"Where do your girls come from? Eastern Europe? Russians bring them in?"

Akylas' face tightened. "I *told* you I work alone."

"Russian mob isn't involved in what you do?"

"I am a bottom feeder, Chief Inspector, a creature of the night. And there are others like me out there, a few a lot worse than I am. I wouldn't bother them if I were you. I'd leave them alone. You mess with those men? You don't survive."

• • •

After cautioning Akylas not to leave Chios, they let him go. He'd made a call before he left; and a woman had arrived at the station a few minutes later to pick him up. Patronas made a note of the license plate. He was sure Akylas wasn't the killer, but he was also sure the pimp hadn't been entirely forthcoming with them. He knew something and had grown increasingly nervous the longer they'd questioned him.

For all his bluster and swagger, it was obvious Akylas was afraid.

"You know what happens when you go against the godfathers of night?" he'd said at one point. "Do you have any idea what they do to you?"

"I thought those men were in Athens?" Patronas said. "You're saying they're here?"

But they were unable to get anything more out of him.

"Let me give you a piece of advice," he told Patronas as he was leaving. "Forget those two women. You have no idea what you're up against. You'll bring destruction down on you and your associates, you keep pushing. You, your friend there. There aren't enough Kevlar vests in the universe to protect you. There aren't enough machine guns. You hear me, Chief Inspector? You go after them? You're going to need tanks."

• • •

Patronas left the station and drove back to the cottage on his moped, Akylas' words ringing in his ears. He went for a walk before dinner, climbing up to the top of a forested hill on the far side of the cove. He stayed there for a long time, taking solace in the birdsong, the rustling of the leaves in the trees.

He'd stopped at a store on his way home and bought toys for Ali. Anything to put distance between himself and Tariro and her lonely vigil in the parking lot, her life as a slave to men's passion, men's greed.

After dinner, he and Ali put together the puzzle of barnyard animals Patronas had purchased. It made a sound every time you put a piece in the right place, the cow mooed, the chicken cackled, the pig squealed. Dreadful sounds, terrible sounds.

Ali imitated the pig, not once, but repeatedly as the night wore on, snuffling and snorting and rooting around. Patronas had always thought parenthood was a relatively quiet affair—it certainly had been in his mother's house—and he was astounded by the amount of noise the boy was making, and he was only four. What would happen when he got older? The racket would be deafening.

"How about a story?" he asked in desperation, holding up the illustrated copy of the Odyssey he'd bought. He flipped through pages before settling on the part about the Cyclops, thinking it would be fun to act it out so the boy would understand.

Unfortunately, Ali understood all too well and began to wail when Patronas reached the part about the Cyclops eating Ulysses' men.

Screaming "*katalhom*" loudly, he went to pieces.

Patronas worked the phone, struggling to figure out the child was saying. It was 'kill people, kill people.'

Lydia was furious. "Next time go with *Cinderella*," she hissed. "Or the *Arabian Nights*. Don't go near Homer again."

"If he's going to grow up here, he needs to have a sense of our heritage."

"He's four, Yiannis. The glories of Greece can wait."

The fire had gone out in the living room; and they'd moved into the kitchen. Lydia had painted the room a kind of persimmon color and decorated the walls with ceramic plates she'd made with flowers of the same color.

It would have been perfect save for the hint of Brussel sprouts that still lingered on the air.

"I filled out the paperwork to adopt Ali today," Patronas said. "I spoke to the lawyer; and he thought this was the best route to take. Not seek asylum for him which we talked about. Just a straight adoption. We can sign everything tonight; and I'll drop it off at his office tomorrow. It's going to take a long time, he told me. We'll need to get character references and testimonials, his mother's death certificate and a bunch of other documents, but with your permission, I wanted to get started on it and set it in motion."

"You're sure, Yiannis?"

He nodded. "I always wanted children."

"Soon we'll be a family." There was a kind of wonder in her voice. "A family, think of that."

Patronas nodded, so moved he couldn't speak.

After they finished signing the papers, they opened a bottle of wine to celebrate.

"He finally started to talk about what happened to him."

Lydia took a sip of wine and set her glass down. "There was a bombing; and the building where he lived collapsed. Rescue workers pulled them out."

"Did he mention his father?"

She shook her head. "Not a word. He'll never get over it, but maybe in time, the memory will fade; and he'll find a measure of peace."

"If I close these two cases, maybe we can take a trip together. Go to Athens and show him the Acropolis. Get his mind off the past."

"What do you mean 'if you close the case?' What happened?"

"Nothing and that's the problem. It's been over two months, but we still have no leads, no clue as to who the killer is or why he did it. Today I interviewed the guy who runs the prostitutes, thinking he might be involved."

Intrigued, Lydia inched closer. "Good God, a pimp. What did he say?"

"He said sometimes he roughs up his women to keep them line, but he would never really hurt them. 'Think of it this way,' he told me. 'I'm a taxi driver and they're the car. Killing them would be real stupid economically.'"

Patronas poured out more wine and drank it down. I sent Melissa Costas into Vial undercover; and I haven't heard from her.

"Oh, Yiannis, no…"

"Stathis wants me to quit the case. 'Those two women weren't even Greek,' he said. 'They're migrants, so why bother with them?'"

"What did you say?"

"I told him to go fuck himself, I'd get justice for them, no matter who they were. Then I hung up on him."

"You hung up on Stathis?"

Patronas nodded. "The way I see it, if there's no justice for them, there's no justice for anybody. That's why when you see those statues of justice, she's always wearing a blindfold. Because justice is *blind*, I told Stathis. It must be. It simply must be."

Lydia's smile lit up her face. "Oh, Yiannis, you're indefatigable.

"What's that mean…that word? Indefatigable?"

"It means made of iron, never to be defeated."

"I've been defeated, Lydia. Defeated in marriage, defeated in life. Before I met you, I didn't know what victory was."

• • •

Patronas drove Dimitra to the hospital early the next morning. He'd turned in the rental car and shown up at her apartment on his moped. She was wearing a dress and complained loudly about showing so much leg, but she climbed onboard, grabbed him tightly around the waist and off they went. He stayed with her at the hospital while she got a special infusion to combat her cancer, wincing at the size of the needle the nurse inserted in her arm.

They talked about a variety of things, anything but what was happening.

"You said you got tested and it wasn't you, it was me," Patronas said at one point. "I was the reason we didn't have kids. If so, why didn't you want to adopt one? How come we never talked about it?"

"Adopt a child? You must be kidding. Who wants to take care of someone else's mistake? People put children up for adoption for a reason, Yiannis. They've got problems, those kids. And no one tells you about them until it's too late."

"I would have liked to have had a child."

"And I would have liked to have been Princess Grace of Monaco. We don't get what you want in life."

She gave him a long, assessing glance. "You're going to do it, aren't you? That's why you brought it up. You and that fool you're married to. You're going to get yourself a child."

"We already did."

That stopped her.

"A Syrian orphan. His name is Ali."

"Jesus, Yiannis. How old are you? Sixty? Seventy?"

"Sixty-two."

"Too old to be a father."

"It's done, Dimitra."

"How old is the kid?"

"Four."

Dimitra did the calculations in her head. "So you're what? Sixty-two now? Not much time left for you and that's not factoring in your being a cop. Chances are you won't live long enough to raise that boy to adulthood; and he'll end up orphaned again. Hardly a kindness, that, Yiannis. Hardly a kindness."

"What do you know about kindness, Dimitra? You of all people?"

"If you're talking about the divorce, that was a long time ago." She made a dismissive gesture. "Water under the bridge."

Her smile was terrible to see. "Now then social services know about this child of yours? I certainly hope so. Best to have your papers in order should they come calling, You can't just pick up children off the street and make them yours, Yiannis. You're a police officer. Surely, you know that."

Patronas exploded. "You fucking bitch!"

Getting up from his chair, Patronas stormed out of the room, got on his moped and roared off. A pathetic gesture, given that it was a moped and had only a single cylinder but it made him feel better.

They were in for it now. He never should have told Dimitra about Ali, never should have given her the keys to the kingdom, the kingdom of his heart.

Chapter 16

Patronas passed an old Turkish water fountain on his way to the police station. Intricately carved, it was dry now, its graceful arabesques out of place in the modern city. The marble basin was full of cigarette butts and candy wrappers; and graffiti covered the base.

There was evidence of the Ottoman occupation all over the capital of Chios, the most notable being the multi-domed bath complex, the so-called hammam, which had recently been restored and now housed a museum.

Six months before, a bulldozer had been digging a hole for a new office building and had inadvertently unearthed the ruins of the ancient capital. Almost immediately, workmen had poured fresh cement over the site in clear violation of the law. Had money done the trick, Patronas had wondered at the time, or was it simply battle fatigue on the part of the officials in charge?

He didn't envy the έφορος, the government employees, who worked for the Greek Archaeological Service. Responsible for the oversight of all archeological excavations and the country's ancient physical heritage, theirs was an impossible task. Chios alone had been occupied since neolithic times; and traces of its storied past were everywhere.

Two women in hijabs walked by; and Patronas greeted them. As expected, they ignored him and strolled on, heading to the cafeteria where aid workers served free meals. There was very little foot traffic, a marked change from the past when the area had teemed with life.

There'd been a demonstration at the harbor when a boat had docked with supplies for Vial. Local people had blocked the streets and refused to let the cargo be unloaded. And things had only gotten worse since then.

Now farmers patrolled the area around the camp nightly to keep migrants from breaking into their homes or stealing their livestock. Alarm systems were selling at a premium, spotlights, guard dogs—things Patronas had never thought he'd live to see on Chios.

Although he didn't want to admit it, Tembelos was right about the migrants destroying the city. Their presence had totally gutted the commercial district. No one shopped there anymore; and many of the stores now stood empty, their owners forced into bankruptcy.

Leonidas, the fabled king of Sparta, had died fighting the invading Persian army, armed to the teeth and hellbent on conquest; and there were those in Greece who wanted to take up arms and physically repel the migrants, these new invaders. In Leonidas' case, it had been war, not what was happening today, desperate people, not soldiers, wading ashore this time..

He hadn't told Tembelos about Ali, afraid he might say something disparaging about the boy's origins; and it would end their friendship. Patronas might have come late to fatherhood, but that child was now his, as much a part of him as the marrow in his bones. He'd walk through fire for him, take on all comers.

"I don't think you're born a parent," Lydia had told him. "I think it's the caring that makes you one, that carves out that space in your heart."

With every hour Patronas spent with Ali, he could feel that space expanding.

• • •

Lydia called the station late that afternoon and asked if she could bring Ali by to see him.

"Not today," Patronas told her. "I'm in the middle of something."

And then Ali got on the phone. "*Baba*," he bellowed. "*Σ' αγαπώ.*" Daddy, I love you.

Patronas was deeply touched. "*Κι εγώ σ' αγαπώ, Αλί.*" I love you, too, Ali.

Lydia got back on the phone. "He's been practicing all morning. He's very proud of himself."

"I can't believe you're teaching him Greek."

"You need to learn Arabic in return. It's only fair."

"I'm no linguist, Lydia, but I'll do my best."

"One more thing and then I'll let you go. Dimitra called and asked me to drive her to the hospital. I told her I needed to check with you first."

"Sure, go ahead, but be careful. And, please, whatever you do, don't let Ali anywhere near her. Dimitra's like that witch in Hansel and Gretel. She feeds on children."

Tembelos had been standing next to Patronas' desk, waiting to talk to him. "Who the hell is Ali?" he asked after Patronas hung up.

"My son, Giorgos. He's my four-year old son."

"That boy from the boat, right? He's living with you now?"

Patronas nodded.

"Does anybody else know?"

"Only Dimitra."

"Shit, Yiannis, you told her, but you didn't tell me."

"What can I say? We were talking about adopting kids; and she figured it out."

"Shit," Tembelos repeated. "A kid, you got yourself an Arab kid."

"I did."

"You going to adopt him?"

"Yes. Lydia and I signed the papers last night."

Tembelos stood there, silently taking this in, then he grabbed his coat and rushed out of the station.

"Where are you going?" Patronas shouted after him.

"On an errand."

A few hours later, Tembelos staggered back into the station with a stuffed donkey the size of a car.

"Something for the kid," he said and plunked it down on Patronas' desk.

"You bought him an ass…"

"What can I say? Living with you? Kid needs to be familiar. Took me a long time to find it. Teddy bears, they got, and unicorns, but asses are hard to come by."

"Ali's not mine yet."

"He will be. I've known you a long time, Yiannis. You're one determined man. You'll move heaven and earth to get what you want."

Patronas shifted the donkey to the chair next to his desk. It had hideous buck teeth and let out a big 'hee haw' when he touched its belly. He didn't know what Ali would make of it, if the boy even knew what a stuffed animal was.

Tembelos grinned. "Welcome to fatherhood, Yiannis."

He smacked him on the back. "Trust me, it's not what you think. Mostly it's good. Not all the time, but mostly."

• • •

"I need to speak to your wife," Patronas told Liadis on the phone. "I have a question for her."

Chryssoula Papoulis came on the line a moment later. "Yes, Chief Inspector, what can I do for you?"

"How did you know my police officer was a woman."

"The one working undercover? That priest was here the other day—the one who's teaching the migrants—and I overheard him talking to her. He wanted to know why she wasn't in uniform. It wasn't that hard to figure out."

"Thank you," Patronas said and ended the call.

He could just imagine the scene: Papa Michalis, deaf as a post, shouting at Melissa Costas, asking her why she was wearing a caftan and hijab.

"Did we tell Papa Michalis that Melissa Costas was going undercover?" he asked Tembelos.

"I don't think so. Why?"

"I am pretty sure he gave her away. He's at Vial. Go get him. We need to find out what happened."

• • •

"Why didn't you tell me?" the priest wailed, wringing his hands. "I saw her in that lengthy garment—all the way to the ground it was—and I chastised her. 'Why on earth are you wearing *that*?' I asked." 'Why aren't you in your police unform?"

"You said, '*police*'?"

The old man nodded.

"Where were you when this happened?"

"Near that building where Liadis works, the administrative center."

"Day and time?"

Papa Michalis ran it through it in his mind. "Monday morning."

"Today is Thursday, so four days ago?"

"Yes. You know me, Yiannis. I'm a vault. I never would have said anything had I known."

Nervously, he smoothed down his robe. "There weren't very many people around when I spoke to her. I don't think anyone heard me."

"Liadis' wife did."

Papa Michalis looked stricken. "I'm sorry," he said again.

"How loud were you? Show me."

"Hey, Melissa."

Maybe not a hundred-fifty decibels, but not exactly a whisper either—anyone within five meters would have heard him.

"I don't like to draw attention to myself in the camp," the priest went on. "It's the migrants' territory, their home as it were; and in their eyes, I am an interloper, an infidel. I am very cautious when I'm up there, Yiannis. Very cautious indeed and not loud at all."

"Has anyone ever threatened you?"

"I've been heckled once or twice, by kids mostly, but that's all. I know as an Orthodox priest, I shouldn't say this, but there is much I admire about their culture. For the most part, their faith in God—Allah, I should say— is intact, unlike ours. And they respect their elders, defer to them even, which is quite refreshing. That used to be true in Greece. People would see a person of advanced years such as myself and they'd get up and give them their seat, but that doesn't happen anymore. It's a different world now and not necessarily a better one."

Papa Michalis' querulousness grated on Patronas. "What did Melissa Costas do when you accosted her?"

"She turned her back on me and walked away which I must say hurt my feelings. We've always been good friends, she and I; and she didn't even look at me."

"Did you go after her?"

"No. It was clear she wanted nothing to do with me."

Raising his head, he gave Patronas a sharp look. "Why all these questions, Yiannis? What happened? What's going on?"

"Costas has disappeared."

"When?"

"Monday. You were probably the last person to see her alive."

"Oh, God, oh, God!" His voice broke. "This is all my fault."

"Father..."

"Don't you see, Yiannis? I gave her away. I gave her away.'"

"We don't know what happened. She might still be out there, pursuing a lead on her own."

"You don't think so, Yiannis. I can see it on your face. You think she's dead, killed just like those other two, those two Syrian women. And I did it. I am the one responsible. Me and my big mouth… I led him to her."

Bowing his head, he began to pray, barely able to mouth the words for his tears.

• • •

"I want you to inspect all abandoned buildings in the rural parts of the island," Patronas instructed the assembled police officers. "Report back to me continually and let me know where you've been, what territory you've covered."

"Where should we start?" a young patrolman asked.

"Concentrate on sheds out in the fields, lean-tos for livestock, that kind of thing. Start with the area closest to the camp and fan out from there. He couldn't have taken her far, not without being seen." Another fucking search and rescue mission.

"Must be my destiny," Patronas told himself sadly. "To run these terrible lost and founds."

"He knows she is a cop," he'd told Tembelos before heading to Vial. "Papa Michalis made sure of that."

"He won't kill her. Kill a cop? No one wants that kind of trouble."

"Which means she might still be alive. Next question, if you were him, what would you do with her?"

"I don't know. Hide her?"

"Yes, but where?"

"Somewhere where no one can see her, where she can't be found."

"That's what I'm thinking. To buy time if nothing else."

They found her scarf in a stone hut about half a kilometer from the camp. There were many buildings like it on Chios, abandoned when the Turks came ashore in 1822. The ruins of an entire village, Anavatos, crowned a hill high on the western side of the island. Dating from the Byzantine age, it was a ghost town now, the bleached stone walls indistinguishable from the stony slope beneath them.

The hut was similar. Judging by its condition, it had long stood empty. The scarf was lying on a pile of rocks near where a wall had collapsed.

The priest rejoiced when they found the scarf, but he grew more and more despondent as the day wore on; and they didn't find her.

"I used to have value. But not anymore. Now all I do is get people killed."

"This is as much my fault as it is yours."

Falling to his knees, Papa Michalis began to sob pitifully, wiping his eyes with a gnarled hand.

"I never thought I'd end up betraying a friend. I'm a rat, A rat, a rat, a rat..."

"Come on, Father. Get up. We've got work to do. Stop this."

But the priest remained inconsolable. "The Mafia kills people who run their mouth. They shoot them dead in the street. It's a grievous sin among criminals. And that's what you should do to me. You should shoot me, Yiannis. Shut me up once and for all."

Not knowing what to do with him, Patronas brought him home with him after the sun went down and it grew too dark to continue the search. Let Lydia tend to him, he told himself. He no longer had the patience.

They rode home on the moped, the priest holding onto Patronas for dear life. His beard kept blowing up and covering his face, thankfully muffling the sounds he was making, the ear-splitting shrieking.

Ali was waiting on the front steps; and he ran down to meet them. Stooping down to the child's level, Papa Michalis introduced himself and shook the boy's hand, said a few words in Arabic. He didn't ask Patronas where Ali had come from or why he was there. For once, he wisely chose silence.

Ali brought out the donkey; and the three of them played with it together, Papa Michalis and the boy shouting 'hee haw,' and laughing uproariously until Lydia called them in to supper.

Papa Michalis praised the food rapturously, laying it on a little thick in Patronas' opinion, given that it was stewed okra and a slimy mess, but then the priest had spent most of his life in monasteries, places not known for their cuisine, where bread and water was considered a meal.

He wasn't a glutton exactly—that implied a sense of taste—he was more of a great white shark. Patronas had read once about a shark that had been found with a license plate in its belly. That would be Papa Michalis. He'd devour anything.

They avoided any discussion of the case for fear of unsettling Ali, then everyone went to bed. Lydia had put a cot in the boy's room for the priest and within minutes, the old man was fast asleep, snoring like a locomotive. Patronas wondered how Ali would cope with the noise. Another nightmare maybe, but of a different sort.

He put on his pajamas and got into bed. He'd wanted to discuss the case with Lydia, but she was in the kitchen, cleaning up; and he lay there in the darkness alone, struggling not to panic when he thought about Costas and what might have befallen her.

Papa Michalis had offered a prayer on her behalf earlier that night; and, for once, Patronas had joined in without protest.

"God return Melissa Costas to us safely and without harm," the old man had intoned.

"Please," he added a moment later. "Please. Let no harm befall her."

Before turning out the light, Patronas repeated the same prayer. "Let no harm befall her," he whispered in the darkness. "Let her be found alive."

• • •

They resumed the search for Costas at dawn the following day. Patronas and the others had already covered five kilometers around the camp; and they expanded the hunt to include the beach of Elida to the west, then worked their way south to the port of Lithi. Two officers were looking for her in the area north of the camp. Patronas had been selective about their targets and ordered them to not to bother exploring Campos, a verdant valley filled with citrus trees, as the area was densely populated; and if the perpetrator had tried to secret her there, he would have been spotted.

"Focus on the places where no one goes," he instructed the men. "The hills above Vrondatos and just beyond."

He was standing outside on the road by the airport. It ran alongside the channel; and, beyond it, he could see the water shimmering in the sunlight. The view had once been a favorite of his-—that vast sweep of the sea overpowering all else before it—but today it did nothing for him; nor did the sight of the gulls riding the thermals high overhead. The sound of their cawing tormented him. It seemed full of anguish to him now, full of pain.

• • •

"Parish priests are keenly aware of everything that goes on in the island, most notably the parishioner's sins." Papa Michalis told Patronas. "We should enlist them in the search."

Chaste in the extreme, he'd used the word, 'peccadillos,' unable to get his mouth around the word, 'sex.'

"People confide in us. They think because we are men of God, we're honor-bound to keep their secrets. And then there's that army of little old ladies, the *yiayias*, who look after us. They're a great source of information, too, gossip mostly, but it's gossip we're after. They have eyes, those women. I swear they can see in the dark. If someone moved Melissa into a building late at night, they would know. I swear they would know."

Reluctantly, Patronas told him to go ahead and put the word out. "You're on probation, Father. No going off on your own. None of that Sherlock Holmes crap of yours. Papa Michalis was an aficionado of the English detective and often cited him as the ultimate authority on homicide.

It was better than the American TV shows, another great favorite of the priest. He was especially fond of the series involving forensics, arterial bloody splatter and the like; and he often relayed what he'd learned from them at meals. Consequently, no one in the station would eat with him; and he was left to dine alone.

Gathering up the folds of his robe, Papa Michalis immediately set off to do whatever one does to alert priests, put the news out on the ecclesiastical grapevine as it were. At the Vatican, they used smoke signals to announce the election of a new pope. Maybe they did the same here, Patronas thought.

Maybe he should go outside and check the sky. Look for puffs of smoke, listen for the sound of tom-toms.

Chapter 17

Costas was naked and unconscious, lying in a pool of her own filth in long abandoned cellar on a remote corner of Chios.

Finding her had been nothing short of miraculous. A dog had been bounding across the rocky headlands high above Vrondatos; and it had started to bark, running around what appeared to be an abandoned building. Troubled, Patronas had walked over to investigate and heard a kind of desperate meowing coming from deep inside.

"Costas!? Costas, is that you?"

Turning on his flashlight, Patronas went in search of the source of the sound.

Costas was in a cage pushed up against the back wall. She was lying face down on her stomach, her ankles and hands tied together behind her back. The rope had also been looped around her neck, so that if she tried to free herself, she'd strangle to death. It was an old Mafia method of execution.

Prying the cage open, Patronas rushed to her side and cut the ropes. Her pulse was very faint, her skin clammy and gray; and she lost consciousness a few minutes later. Someone had put cigarettes out on the palms of her hands and up and down her arms and yanked out tufts of her hair. The insides of her thighs were slick with blood.

Raped. She'd been raped repeatedly.

"Stay with me, Melissa. Stay with me. I'll get you out of here."

Thankfully, there was cell phone coverage; and he was able to summon a medical helicopter. He was vague about her injuries. All he said was they were 'life-threatening.' He didn't want the news of her rape to be bandied about in the department, for her to be the subject of gossip.

"Location?" the dispatcher asked.

"Not sure. Two kilometers northwest of Vrondatos. Maybe a little farther."

"It'll be dark soon. How will we find you?"

"I'll build a fire. Look for it."

Before heading off to build the fire, Patronas covered Costas up with his coat. "I got you, Melissa," he said, stroking her wounded head. "No one is going to hurt you again."

He gathered up some brush and set it ablaze with his cigarette lighter. Scanning the sky, he fed the flames until he heard the helicopter approaching.

It passed directly overhead, the cross on its side clearly visible, then circled around and landed next to the abandoned building. The medics wasted no time. Although the blades of the helicopter were still whirling, two of them came running out with a stretcher.

"Where is she?" one of them yelled.

"In there."

They emerged a few minutes later carrying Costas, an IV attached to her arm, and loaded her up into the waiting helicopter. She was still unconscious, her head lolling from side to side. The engine whined as it picked up speed; and within seconds, she was airborne.

Patronas watched until the helicopter was just a speck in the sky, its red lights blinking as it banked and headed west.

The damage done to her was extensive, the doctor told Patronas on the phone later that night. "Most of her ribs are broken and she was raped repeatedly and not just by one man, by two or three of them. She was also penetrated with objects." Patronas could hear the horror in his voice, the disgust.

"It wasn't just one person?"

"No. I'd say at least three people were involved. A single person couldn't have tied her up that way. At the very least, it would take two to hold her down and a third to work the ropes. I swabbed every inch of her body for DNA. I'll know more when I get the lab results."

* * *

Papa Michalis and Tembelos had heard Patronas' frenzied call for the helicopter, his anguished cry—'officer down! officer down!'—and they anxiously questioned him when he returned to the station.

"She's alive, but just barely," Patronas told them. "You won't believe what they did to her. They took her apart. They literally took her apart."

Everyone else had left for the day; and he spoke freely, relaying word for word what the doctor had said.

"Like the Pharoah's army, erase them from this earth," the priest cried. "The wicked shall perish. They shall vanish. Like smoke, they shall vanish."

"We'll erase them," Tembelos said. "Don't worry, Father. We'll erase them forever."

• • •

As far as Patronas knew, Costas had no family, so early the next day he sent Papa Michalis to Athens to stay with her at the hospital.

"Call me the minute she wakes up. And no last rites or any of that other garbage. She's going to make it, Father. She's going to live."

Patronas took the first plane to Athens the day Costas regained consciousness. She was in KAT, the trauma hospital to the north of the city, in a corner room overlooking the street. Papa Michalis had spent the last three nights sleeping in a chair by her side; and he greeted Patronas wearily.

"She's conscious, but only just. She's not always here. She drifts in and out."

"Can you hear me?" Patronas asked Costas. Her eyes fluttered and she turned her head toward him.

"Where am I?"

"You're in Athens, in the hospital."

"How long have I been out?"

"Three days."

She asked for a glass of water; and he brought it to her. Seeing how weak she was, he held up to her mouth and positioned the straw so she could drink.

After she finished, she fell back on the pillow. "Go away," she gasped. "Let me sleep."

Patronas drove Papa Michalis to the airport and bought him a ticket to Chios. Told him to take the rest of the week off and get some rest.

"Don't go near Vial," he said. "You hear me? From now on, it's off-limits."

The priest started to protest, but seeing the expression on Patronas' face, he stopped. "Very well then, I'll arrange for someone else to teach them. I'll do as you say."

After seeing him off, Patronas returned to the hospital. Costas slept fitfully, thrashing around and crying, 'oxi, oxi,' no,no repeatedly. Sometimes she'd let him hold her hand, but for the most part, all she wanted was to be left alone.

He ended up staying in Athens for over two weeks. By the end of that time, he'd managed to piece the story together. It had been a long, slow process. Overhead, the fluorescent lighting kept flickering; and occasionally it went out, leaving the two of them sitting in semi-darkness.

For the most part, she just lay there in her hospital gown and ignored him. Or else she'd scream and do battle with people only she could see. Witnessing her struggle was one of the hardest things Patronas had ever done in his life.

"I'm sorry," he told her after he'd been there for a week. "Sorry I let this happen to you."

She looked up at the ceiling, her expression hard to read.

Another silent day, he thought, but then she started to speak.

"I knew the risks," she said, her eyes wet. "I volunteered, remember?"

"Do you want to talk about it?"

"No."

"Please, Melissa. Anything you can give me, anything at all."

"A man grabbed me. I was on my way to dinner; and he came up behind me and hit me, hit me hard. The next thing I knew I was tied up in the trunk of a car with a gag in my mouth. We stopped near the harbor—I could smell the sea—and he got out, then another pair of men joined us; and we went on.

"What language did they speak?"

"I don't know. It could have been anything."

"What did they look like? Any scars on their bodies, tattoos?"

She started to weep. "Sir, please. I don't want to remember. I want to forget."

"You must, Melissa."

"Every filthy bit of it?"

Patronas nodded. "Everything."

She lay there for a few minutes with her eyes closed. "When we were near the harbor, I smelled diesel fuel," she said in a low voice. "The old kind that isn't used anymore."

"*Mazout*?"

"Yes."

"A tanker?"

"Maybe. All I know is that's where it started. They pulled over and… and." She hesitated, tears streaming down her face. "That was the first time in an alley there. They laughed, kept laughing at the way I fought them. They thought it was funny."

"How long were you in that alley?"

"I don't know. An hour, maybe two."

Her voice dropped. "There was another man, too."

"Nationality?"

"Greek."

Patronas felt something die inside him. "Greek? Are you sure?"

"Yes. He was in a car; and he pulled up behind us and got out. He yelled at them when he saw what they were doing and told them they were going to ruin everything. I was a cop.

"'You said you'd stop,'" he told them. "'You swore the Syrian would be the last.'" Then he got in the car and drove off. Very fast. I remember. I could hear the tires squealing. I thought he was going to get help, that he wanted to save me."

Her smile was bleak. "My mistake."

"What did he look like?"

"I don't know. The others had me on my stomach then. I couldn't really see."

Patronas looked away, unwilling to meet her eyes. The cement floor under her hospital bed was cracked; and he studied it, seeking a pattern in the damage, a road map that would lead them both away from this, this ghastly place they suddenly found themselves in.

"You're sure he was Greek?"

"Yes. Γαμώ τη μάνα σου" he yelled. I fuck your mother. "Stuff like that."

"I thought because I was a cop, I was invincible, but in the end, it didn't mean a thing. My badge, my standing in the department, none of it mattered. I was just a plaything to them, a piece of meat."

She took a deep shuddery breath. "I was sure they were going to kill me, cut me up the way they did Raina Mustafa."

"The coroner said neither of the Syrian women had been raped."

"You'd think what happened to me was an escalation, but it was just the opposite, a de-escalation. They started out with murder, then turned to rape."

"We don't know what they intended, Melissa. It might have been the same as with the Syrian girl. We just don't know."

Holding up a hand, shouted. "Stop! I don't want to hear."

"Maybe you should talk to someone," he said softly. "It might help."

"You know what would help? Gin, a couple of liters of gin."

"Alcohol is a depressant. It will only make things worse."

"Worse? Are you serious? How could it be any worse?' Something you don't know. I'd never been with a man before. That was my first time. My very first time."

She was screaming now. "I was a virgin."

Against his better judgment, Patronas went out and bought her the gin.

She downed most of the bottle within an hour, drinking it so fast he was afraid she'd poison herself, one little plastic glass after another.

"Here's to me," she said at one point, slamming the bottle down on the tray table. "Here's to me."

"Stop, Melissa…you've had enough."

"Leave me alone. I'm the victim here. If I want to drink myself to death, let me do it."

"Don't relapse, Melissa. You've worked so hard. Don't give them that, don't let them destroy you."

"You don't get it, do you? They already have. I'm gutted, sir. I'm nothing now. A shell of a person, a shell of a woman."

She reached for the bottle again. "You know what else would help?" she said, slurring the words.

"What?"

"If you found those bastards. I'd show them. I'd cut off the part of them they love the most. Cut it off and make them eat it."

Patronas tried to make light of it. "You're a police officer, Melissa Costas. You can't be doing that."

"Just this once, sir. Just this once."

They smiled at one another.

"Okay," he said. "Just this once."

• • •

In the days that followed, Costas made some physical progress, standing up with Patronas' help and walking around the room and then up and down the hall, but emotionally she was gone, lifeless and indifferent to the world around her. The nurses bathed her and combed her hair, but from what Patronas could see, it was like grooming a doll. There was no response from Costas, no acknowledgement.

She had started physical therapy and sometimes practiced her exercises in front of him. It was hard to witness. In addition to the rape, she'd been beaten repeatedly and, as a result, was now unable to bend her knees, unable to stand upright for more than a few minutes without help.

Still Patronas encouraged her and urged her on. "You're doing great, Melissa. Bravo! Bravo! You will be back on the force in no time."

Hoping to cheer her up, Patronas ordered dinner in a taverna and brought it to her—luxury items, a kilo each of *barbounia*, red mullets, and *garides*, shrimp—but she just pushed the plate away. He brought roses, too, huge bouquets of white ones—the florist told him white was the color of hope.

"Get those fucking things away from me." she yelled when see saw them.

The bruises on her face had begun to subside, but the doctor said she'd need surgery to reconstruct her shattered cheekbone. "And a whole new set of teeth."

"You're saying she'll recover…" Patronas said.

"Physically, yes, but psychologically she might not make it back."

• • •

Patronas didn't know what would happen to Costas when she was discharged from the hospital. She wasn't married and had no friends he knew of. He feared for her safety, afraid given her state of mind, she'd take her own life.

They'd gone back over the assault a few more times, Patronas seeking anything that would help identify her assailants.

"You said you stopped by the harbor. Could you hear anything? A ship's horn maybe? Someone dropping anchor?"

He had brought the murder book with him from Athens; and it was open on his lap. He was also taping the conversation.

"Yes," she said. "I did hear a horn. I'd forgotten all about it. Sounded different than the usual ones. Muted somehow."

"Do you think the man who grabbed you boarded a boat when he got out of the car?"

"I don't know. He wasn't gone that long. Like I said, he left and when he came back, he brought the other men with him."

"Crew members maybe?"

She shrugged.

"You must have been getting close if they came after you the way they did."

"I'd spoken to a Syrian woman earlier that day and she told me something important. Raina Mustafa wasn't the only person who disappeared from the camp. There were others. 'Always pretty,' the woman said. "Pretty, pretty."

"How many?"

"Four."

"Either we're dealing with a serial killer or human traffickers."

"Traffickers, sir. Has to be. If it was a serial killer, I'd be dead."

"You said you didn't know what language they spoke. If I play a recording for you, do you think you could identify it?"

"I can try."

He'd found a woman speaking Russian on YouTube and he played it back for her on his phone, He'd chosen a woman on purpose, not wanting Costas to have listen to Russian men and relive the attack.

She listened intently to the tape, her brow furrowed; and then she asked him to play it back again.

"Maybe," she said. "The 's,' the way she says 's.' I remember that. Two of those men spoke the same exact way."

"Russians then."

Costas nodded. "Yes. I think so."

Patronas wrote this down in the murder book and starred it. "But that doesn't explain the man with the car...usually Russian don't get involved with other nationalities."

"Perhaps they needed him to do something they couldn't. A pair of Russian thugs in Chios? They'd stand out. They'd be conspicuous."

Gasping, she shifted in bed, trying to get comfortable.

When Patronas saw how hard she was struggling not to cry, he quickly summoned the nurse. "Give her something. She's in pain, can't you see? She's suffering."

After the shot, Costas started to drift off. "I got nothing else, sir," she whispered. "Go home. Go back to Lydia and that boy of yours. What's his name? 'Ali?' I've told you everything I know,"

"I want to help, Melissa, help you to find your way back to us."

She shook her head. "Some things can't be fixed, sir. What part of 'gutted' do you not understand?"

Chapter 18

Before he left the hospital, Patronas went out into the hall. called the station and spoke to Papa Michalis. "You need to take the next plane to Athens. We can't leave Melissa alone here."

"What is it, Yiannis? Why the sudden urgency?"

"She's lost, Father. I'm afraid she'll kill herself."

"Of course, of course. I've read about this. Women who have been abused often turn the abuse inward and destroy themselves. They do that rather than take on their attackers. Drug and alcohol addiction, suicide, there's a whole litany."

He then went into a lengthy discourse about female depression and hysteria, citing Sigmund Freud.

"Costas isn't hysterical, Father," Patronas snapped. "She's wounded, wounded in body and spirit. The damage is extensive, the worst I've seen in all my years on the force. She was tortured and raped repeatedly. They cracked her ribs and put cigarettes out on her flesh. They fucking urinated on her."

His voice rose. "So don't go quoting Sigmund Freud to me or giving me any of your other bullshit."

There was a lengthy silence.

"I'm sorry, Yiannis. I was only trying to help."

"Well, don't."

He lowered his voice. "There's a plane this afternoon and I want you on it. We will stay with her at the hospital, working in shifts, one week at a time. I'll leave when you come and vice versus, one of us always at her side. You got that, Father? Morning, noon and night, one of us will always be by her side."

"I'll look after her, I promise."

"One last thing, she's to hear nothing about 'forgiving those who trespass against us,' understand? It will only add to her misery; and I won't have it."

"What should I do instead?"

"For once in your life, just shut up and listen."

• • •

Costas frowned when she saw Papa Michalis standing in the doorway of her hospital room. He'd made some effort with his appearance, both his robe and his person freshly laundered. He'd even gotten a haircut and trimmed his beard.

"Well, look who's here," she said. "The man of God."

"Good to see you, Melissa."

He pulled the chair closer to the hospital bed and sat down. They chatted amicably the rest of the afternoon, gossip mostly about other members of the force, but then when dinner arrived and Papa Michalis suggested they say grace and thank God for the food, it all went to hell.

"Don't you see me?" she shouted. "He can go fuck Himself for all I care. I begged Him to save me, but He didn't. He didn't."

She started to weep. "You don't know what it was like…that cage, the smell of them. Where was God? Answer me that, Father. Where was God?"

"Are you familiar with the *Brothers Karamazov*? In it, Dostoyevsky asked the same question you're asking. He describes how a landlord locked a serf child in an outhouse one night; then the next morning set his dogs on him; and the dogs ripped the boy to shreds. If God is just, why do children suffer, Dostoyevsky asked. They haven't sinned. They're innocent."

She wiped her eyes on her sleeve. "Why are you telling me this? What the fuck does Dostoyevsky have to do with me?"

"You're the child in that outhouse, Melissa. You're the one who's been ripped to shreds."

Something collapsed in her face then; and she began to sob. A nurse rushed in and wanted to sedate her, but Costas waved her away.

"Just give me a minute."

Eventually, she calmed down. "You're an odd one, Father. An odd kind of priest."

"I'm an old man, Melissa. I wouldn't say I'm wise, but I've learned a few things. First, that religious dogma doesn't go far in human life. Hindus won't eat a cow, for example, and yet they slaughter their Muslim neighbors. And Christians, don't get me started on Christians. The esteemed fathers of the church."

Her smile was faint, but it was there. "Don't let the bishop hear you say that."

"Oh, he knows. That's why I'm working for Patronas. The bishop won't have me. According to his Eminence, I am a blasphemous, lazy and gluttonous old fool and nothing can be done with me. 'A lost cause,' he said, 'Irredeemable.'"

He reached for her hand. "I like Jesus. Don't get me wrong. But sometimes I think he expected too much of us. He was only thirty-two when he died. He didn't really know life, what happens to people over the years, the pain every one of us experiences on this earth. All those parables about forgiveness and so forth and so on. I'm not sure it's possible. A man once threw me off a balcony and would have killed me if he could. I've wrestled with it for years, seeking to forgive him, but the truth is, I still haven't. And I'm a priest, a professional turn-the-other cheek kind of fellow."

"What happened to him, the man who did that to you?"

"An old woman took revenge on him for the murder of her grandson."

"That's what I want to do."

"Take revenge?" She nodded.

"Jesus never spoke of rape, how one reconciles such an act with God's grace or mercy."

"What does Jesus say about revenge?"

"I'm not sure he would endorse it. Nor would your colleagues on the force. Let justice take its course, Melissa. It will. Trust me, inevitably it will."

The next morning, they spoke again about the attack. Outside the room, Papa Michalis could hear the rattling of dishes, the sound of breakfast being delivered; and he got up and closed the door.

"Something occurred to me last night while you were sleeping," he said, settling back down on the chair. "How did that man—the one you said was a Greek—know you were a cop?"

She thought this over, her face furrowed in concentration. "I have no idea," she eventually said. "There were no Greeks living in the camp. The only Greeks in Vial work for the relief agencies."

"So how did this man know you were a cop?" the priest repeated.

"Maybe he saw me at the station. Patronas assigned me to the front desk. Anyone who came in then would have seen me."

"Anyone special you remember?"

She shook her head. "You know what it's like. There are always people milling around the lobby."

"Did those men who attacked you come into the station during that time?"

"No. I would have remembered. There was nobody with an accent, only local people."

"This might be the break we're looking for. I'll call Patronas and tell him to look at the logbook and see who signed in on those days."

"Good idea, Father."

He studied her. She had always been such a strong woman in his mind, strident and mighty, but no longer. There she lay in her hospital bed, her hair shaved off in places, a row of stitches showing on her scalp. Worse still was how her attackers had damaged her face. Most her teeth were gone; and her gums were bloody. She had two black eyes and anger-looking bruises along her neck.

"I know we spoke of forgiveness yesterday," he said gently. "I wish to seek yours."

She looked up at him. "Why? What did you do?"

"I gave you away that day in the camp. It was an accident, true, but I cannot sleep at night thinking about it. You'll never know how sorry I am."

They stared at each other for a few minutes.

"Will you bless me if I kill them?" she asked.

He stroked his beard, his face thoughtful. "Old habits die hard, Melissa. But I will do my best."

• • •

Patronas staggered up the steps to his house and opened the front door. He hadn't slept much during the two weeks he'd been in the hospital; and he was very tired. Lydia wrapped her arms around him and led him into the living room. A fire was dying in the fireplace, Ali half-asleep in front of it.

"I'm going to take a shower," he said. "Why don't you put Ali to bed?"

It took Ali a long time to get settled. He kept calling for Lydia in a frightened voice.

Patronas had seen a photo of a child Ali's age. Pulled from the wreckage of his home in Damascus, he had been covered with blood. Worse had been his eyes, the suffering in his eyes.

They'd taken Ali to a pediatrician a few weeks before. "He's got scars on his back," the doctor told them. "Shrapnel probably. Do you know his history?"

Patronas demurred, saying he knew nothing about the child. The boy's mother had wanted the boy examined; and the camp administrator had asked him to see to it. Language, culture, it would have been impossible for her.

Lydia had given him a long look after they left the doctor's office. "You lie exceedingly well."

"Only in service to others, my love. Only in service of others."

Lydia threw a log on the fire and stood there watching it burn. "You seem to have set him off tonight."

"I know. It's like he can sense the violence I'm dealing with, smell it on me."

"It's not just him. It's having a corrosive effect on you, too, Yiannis. The migrants…the murders in that camp. You should hear yourself; you scream in your sleep sometimes the same way Ali does. It upsets me. It upsets him. It's no good."

"What do you want me to do? Quit my job?"

"I don't know. Maybe."

Not wanting to discuss it, he left the house in his pajamas and wandered down to the cove. He ended up chucking rocks in the sea again until his body ached all over. But unlike previous times, it brought him no relief. Nothing did anymore, save for the hours he spent with Ali…their silly games, the trill of his laughter.

Lydia would have lots to say when he told her about Melissa. He was sure of it.

She had set out some cheese and crackers, a rare concession, and lit some candles. He always mocked her when she did that—saying the candles reminded him of funerals—but tonight it seemed appropriate.

"She was a virgin," he blurted out. "They raped her repeatedly, kept her in a cage in the ruins of a building. A cage…Lydia, a cage."

Overcome, he got up, walked over to the liquor cabinet and got out the scotch, poured himself a shot and tossed it down.

"What's going to happen to her?"

"I don't know," he said. "Maybe she can be salvaged...but then again, maybe not."

"Salvaged!"

"Cured. She can be cured."

She stared at him. "She was raped, Yiannis! There's no 'cure' for rape."

"All I'm saying is with time and proper medical care, she might be all right. People are resilient."

"Up to a point, Yiannis. Up to a point. For some victims—women especially—all that's left, after all is said and done, are the scars."

Patronas continued to drink. In solidarity with Costas, he told himself.

Picking up a poker, Lydia stirred the embers in the grate. Her auburn hair caught the light, her face shiny from the heat.

"I hate what this is doing to us." She gave the fire a fierce jab. "You go away for two weeks and when you come home, you stink of hospitals and talk of rape."

"It's my job, Lydia. You knew it was my job when you married me."

"Ali needs you here."

"What about you? Do you need me here?"

"Of course, I do."

He drew her to him, pressing her hard against him, the warmth of her body easing something deep within, something he couldn't name.

"You're my salvation, Lydia. Of course, I need you."

• • •

The next morning Patronas left the house early to drive Dimitra to the hospital. She was standing outside her apartment building, waiting for him in a flowered pink dress.

"Thank God it's you! I was afraid I was going to have to deal with that wife of yours again."

"Lydia told me you did all right."

"Sure. It was fine. I insulted her. She insulted me back. Like tennis. Being an American...she was a little slow, so I won most of the time. I could always tell when I got to her. She'd go all quiet."

His ex-wife had bought a new blonde wig. It was slightly askew; and there was far too much of it. Maybe that American woman, Dolly Parton, could pull off it off, but Dimitra was no Dolly Parton.

Settling herself in the car, she fastened her seatbelt. "Go slow," she commanded.

The *laiki,* open air market, was open today; and the surrounding streets were blocked off. Men were selling watermelons out of the backs of pickup trucks, the sound of their loudspeakers following them as they turned toward to the hospital.

"Gypsies." Dimitra waved a hand dismissively.

Dimitra liked to air her prejudices, so he knew what was coming and turned on the radio to drown her out. She had three major ones: first, she believed that green-eyed people cast the evil eye and should be avoided at all costs. Second, that Americans were gullible children and, consequently, easy to take advantage of. And third, that gypsies were thieving rascals and stole anything that wasn't nailed down.

"Turn the radio off," she commanded. "I have something to tell you."

Reluctantly, he complied.

"The doctor says my new therapy is working and I'm in remission. He's very optimistic about my prospects. So no more rides to the hospital."

"That's wonderful, Dimitra," he said.

"I am grateful to you, Yiannis. That wife of yours also. I want you to come to dinner. Both of you. My way of thanking you. And, of course, you must bring that fine, fine boy of yours."

There was an edge to her voice as she said this, a little flicker of spite. "I've been wondering where he came from, this child you spoke of. Did the stork bring him, Yiannis? If not, then where did you get him?"

• • •

Patronas called Lydia from the parking lot of the hospital. "Dimitra wanted to know where I got Ali."

"What did you tell her?"

"Nothing. But knowing her, she won't let it go. She'll contact the authorities here or worse, my boss in Athens and tell him I've got an undocumented Syrian child living in my house."

"You really think she'd do that?"

"I don't know. All I know is if she talks to Stathis, I'm done for. I could lose my job."

Lydia was silent for a few minutes. "Stathis calls, you tell him she doesn't know what she's talking about. We were only housing Ali temporarily until we could find a place for him in one of those children's shelters; and he's gone now."

"What about the adoption?"

"Say that you are planning to adopt him, but there's a big backlog of cases and you are waiting for the paperwork to clear."

"What about the local authorities? She alerts them, they could take Ali away."

More silence. "We'll fly to Athens and hide out there. That way no one on Chios can get to us. We'll have a good time, Ali and me. We'll go to museums and walk around the city. It will be his heritage one day; and he needs to know it."

Patronas reached for his cigarettes. "I'll book your tickets and talk to the lawyer. I don't know how long it will take. You might have to stay away a couple of months."

"No problem."

"What about the cat? Who's going to take care of it?"

Lydia chuckled. "You are. It'll be good, give the two of you a chance to bond."

Lydia was big on bonding. Along with 'mindful' and 'awareness,' it was one of her favorite words. Being Greek, he hadn't known what it meant at first; and she'd explained it to him. It had taken some time, but he'd eventually gotten it. Bonding was a kind of gluing process that took place between people.

That said, he seriously doubted it applied to cats, that a person could glue oneself to a cat or vice versa. No, cats were cats and people were people; and most probably, it would be business as usual with Jinn while Lydia and Ali were away, the scratching and clawing and hissing, and, ultimately, the beast would bestow upon him the gift of mange; and all his hair would fall out.

"How can I take care of it? I don't know anything about cats."

"All you need to do is feed it and water it and, when the time comes, scoop the poop out of its kitty litter box."

Poop. He knew it. Along with the mange, Jinn would be the gift that kept on giving.

"I'll call the airlines," Lydia said. "See if we can't leave tomorrow."

"That would be great, Lydia. The sooner the better."

Maybe he was overreacting, but in his experience, people didn't change. Once a troublemaker, always a troublemaker—it was one of the basic tenets of police work—and Dimitra was a first class one. The ancient furies had nothing on her, those terrible goddesses who were consumed by anger and sought only revenge.

She wouldn't kill you—he was sure of that— but she'd ruin your life if she could. She'd certainly done her best with his. And he wasn't about to let her do that to Ali.

"*Ελα εδώ μπαμπά*," the boy shouted into the phone. Come here, daddy. Oh, Ali, my son, my son.

"*Μόλις μπορώ μικρέ.*" Patronas answered. As soon as I can, little one.

Chapter 19

Patronas called the lawyer from his desk at the police station and instructed him to expedite the adoption. "Money is no object. Bribe whoever you need to bribe, falsify documents. Whatever it takes, I don't care. Just get it done."

"You're in luck," the lawyer said. "It used to take up to six years to adopt a child, but a new law was passed in 2018; and it changed all that. Now it takes between six and eight months. That said, there are certain requirements that must be met before an adoption can go through. I'll go over them with you. First, you and your wife have been married three years, is that correct?"

Not quite, but Patronas said 'yes' anyway.

"Good, good. Next, a certified social worker will need to write a report on the child's background. They will also need to interview the child."

"He's a migrant from Syria."

"Hmmm, so you don't know his background?"

"Correct."

"As this will be a transnational adoption, the governing authority will be the Center for Social Welfare of the Region, as well as the Central Authority for Transnational Adoptions at the Ministry of Labor. Given the circumstance, I'll check with them and see if I can get the background check waived."

"How's the social worker going to talk to him? He doesn't speak Greek."

"You'll need to get an interpreter then, someone certified in Arabic."

Another hoop to jump through.

Agitated, Patronas drummed his fingers on his desk.

"Now then, are you under sixty?" the lawyer continued.

"No. I'm sixty-two."

"I'll see about getting that requirement set aside also. How old would you say the child is?"

"Four."

"Excellent. There must be an eighteen-year difference between the two of you."

Then he delivered the bad news. "By law, adoption of a minor requires the consent of the child's natural parents. Only in exceptional cases can this be surmounted by a court order, for example, if said parent is mentally ill or the child is in danger. Neither of which is the case here."

"His mother drowned," Patronas fought to keep his voice down. "I saw her die."

"Are you sure the woman who drowned was the child's mother? Would you be willing to swear to this under oath to it in court?"

"Yes.," Patronas said.

For him, Ali's grief was sufficient proof.

• • •

After he had worked out the final details with the lawyer and set a timetable for the adoption, Patronas hung up the phone. 'Four months if you're lucky,' the lawyer had said. "I'll do my best, but it might take as long as six."

Hopefully, Lydia and the boy would leave Chios without incident and ride out the time in Athens until Ali was officially theirs, safely out of harm's way. The people dealing with transnational adoptions were there, so Lydia's presence might even expedite the process.

Papa Michalis had called repeatedly while Patronas was on the phone with the lawyer. "Check the logbook at the station," he squalled when they finally connected. "See who signed in at the station on the days Costas was working the front desk."

"Did Costas suggest this?"

"Actually, it was my idea." He sounded a little smug. "I reviewed the evidence and came up with it all on my own. And make sure to make note of the Greeks, when you check, Yiannis. It's imperative. I'm convinced if we find the man Costas said witnessed the attack, he'll provide the key to cracking the case."

'Cracking the case....' Patronas shook his head.

What had it been this time? NYPD? CSI Miami? No doubt about it, Father had been watching one of them.

Nevertheless, he did as the priest suggested. He retrieved the logbook from the front desk and began going through it. He could look on the computer—it would probably be faster—but he distrusted modern technology. In his mind, policework was best done the old-fashioned way. Inevitably, it came down to pen and paper and hope for the best.

He printed out Costas' schedule and matched against the dates in the logbook, checking and cross checking the names against the days and times she'd worked, paying particular attention to the Greeks. Some of the names he recognized—people, who were feuding with their neighbors—but a few were strangers to him.

It took him nearly two hours, but he came up with five names:

- Achilles Kourelas
- Costas Milonas
- Thanassi Alexandropoulos
- Georgos Travayakis
- Lefteris Papadopoulos

The administrator of the camp, Dimitri Liadis, had also signed in a couple of times, but Patronas assumed it was when he'd come there to translate and drew a line through his name.

He handed the list to Tembelos. "Run these names through the computer. Get everything you can on them."

By the end of the day, the list had been reduced to three. Papadopoulos had been born in 1922 which made him 97 years old. Travayakis suffered from Alzheimer's; and his daughter had come to the station with him to inquire about becoming his legal guardian. Costas had made a note of the case, stating she referred the daughter to social services and given her the numbers to call.

"Milonas is interesting," Tembelos said. "Golden Dawn and then some. A patrolman caught him spray painting a wall in old migrant camp."

"Was he charged?"

"Doesn't look like it."

"What about the other two?"

"Nothing."

Standing up, Patronas gathered up his gear and headed toward the door. "Let's go find them. See what we've got."

• • •

Kourelas lived on the side of shallow ravine west of Vrondatos. An unpaved road led down to the house; and the smell hit them long before it came into view.

In addition to the stench, there was a strange undercurrent of noise, a far-off rumbling.

"Pigs," Tembelos declared

Chocolate-colored and enormous, there were six of them, rooting around in a make-shift corral in front of the house. Their snouts were buried deep in the watery muck; and they were defecating on a regular basis, hence the stench. When Patronas was a boy, he'd been standing outside a butcher shop when a man drove up with a pig in the back of his truck. The pig had begun to squeal—an unearthly sound that had tormented him for years after—and kept on squealing as it was dragged inside. A few minutes later, the butcher hung its head on a hook outside. That pig had known what was coming, Patronas had told his mother later that day. It had known it was about to be destroyed.

A farmwoman, she'd had no sympathy for the pig. 'Χοιρινές μπριζόλες' was all she said—pork chops— which, of course, Patronas refused to eat forever after.

Over the years, he'd seen much worse as a policeman, but somehow the image of that struggling pig had stayed with him, its palpable and noisy despair; and he eyed the ones at the front of Kourelas' house with sympathy.

Patronas knocked on the front door. "Police! Open up!"

A woman was hanging up laundry on a clothesline at the side of the house. She set her basket down when she saw them, a wary look on her face.

Patronas quickly introduced himself. "Chief Inspector Yiannis Patronas, of the Chios Police. And this is my colleague, Giorgos Tembelos. Are you Mrs. Kourelas?"

Ducking her head, she gave a stiff nod. "My husband is not here." She had a harelip that had only partly been repaired and had trouble forming the words

"Where is he?"

"Working."

Dressed in a sleeveless dress and stained cotton tennis shoes, she had a strange, agitated manner, continually dipping her head as she spoke.

"When will he be back?"

"I don't know. He comes when he comes."

Returning to her work, she hung up a sheet, shielding herself deep in the folds of the fabric.

In addition to the pig pen, there was a vast vegetable garden. Tomato bushes were planted in orderly rows along with eggplants, cucumbers and peppers, green beans tied to lengths of string. All of it well tended.

Patronas gestured to the yard. "You own this land or are you squatting?"

"What's it to you? You're not the owner. He's in Australia."

"As I told you, I am the Chief Inspector of the Chiot Police Force; and what you're doing here is illegal. If your husband calls me or, better yet, if he comes to the station, I might be willing to overlook it. Otherwise, I'll have to charge both of you with criminal trespass."

"I'll make sure he comes to the station," she said, keeping her head averted.

"Good. See that you do."

• • •

"Jesus, how can people live like that?" Tembelos asked. "The smell alone is enough to kill you."

"Poor people don't have a lot of choices," Patronas said. "And she was poor."

"Eleni's is going to burn my uniform when I get home and me along with it."

"Send it out to the dry cleaners."

The woman had depressed him; and he longed to get away.

Three years before, there'd been a tremendous fire in the area; and underfoot the ground was blanketed with pine saplings. A bird was calling from the stump of a burnt tree, its mate answering deep in the thorny brush.

Kourelas and his wife had probably set up shop after the fire, Patronas concluded, surveying the landscape, built their house on the ashes when no one was looking.

"I don't think Kourelas is our man."

Tembelos looked over at him. "I don't know, Yiannis. His wife was hiding something. You notice how she kept ducking her head? Couldn't look us in the eye?"

"It was her face she was hiding, Giorgos, that harelip. Nothing more than that. Kids probably teased her when she was a child. Ducking was how she survived. I got picked on when I was a kid; and, believe me, it does something to you."

"Why'd they pick on you?"

"Because my mother knitted shorts for me out of wool. They were hideous and itched like crazy; and the other boys would yell, 'keep away, keep away, he's got lice.' Later when I was older, I asked my mother why she'd done it. 'That was all I had,' she told me. 'There was nothing else.'"

"Jesus, Yiannis."

"You know the worst thing about being poor, Giorgos? The shame. You never really get over it. And I think that's what's going on with her. Not shame because she's poor, shame because of the way she looks, because her face doesn't fit together."

Patronas started the car; and they drove through the town of Vrondatos. Beyond Vrondatos was the Plateau of Aepos, an immense rockbound wasteland once inhabited by ancient man. A hiking trail, called the 'path of Homer,' wound through the region. Patronas had only been there once; and it was like walking on the surface of the moon. Nothing but outcroppings of gray rock as far as the eye could see. Ruins were scattered throughout, ash-colored tumulus and '*grismata*,' a local term for the stone encircled fields. Few people ever ventured there; and he'd thought it was as bleak a stretch of earth as he'd ever seen.

They'd found Costas on the periphery of that same plateau.

• • •

Kourelas' hair was greasy; and he reeked of pigs and sweat. He was dressed in thin black cotton pants and a threadbare white shirt, cheap plastic flipflops on his feet. His fingernails were rimmed with dirt; and he had a crude tattoo of a cross on his right forearm.

Patronas motioned for him to sit down. "This isn't your first visit here, is it? You signed into the station a couple of weeks ago."

He nodded. "I lost my ID; and I came here to see about getting it replaced."

"You spoke to my colleague, Officer Melissa Costas."

"That's right. A woman. I don't remember her name."

"I don't know if you know this, but she was attacked not long after you came in. Beaten half to death." He didn't mention the rape.

Kourelas frowned. "What's that got to do with me?"

Patronas was watching him intently.

There were many myths about 'tells' during police interrogations. Supposedly suspects blinked when they told a lie or shifted around in their seat, did something physical that gave them away. As a student at the police academy, he'd been instructed to watch for them.

"Fidgeting, sweating, digging their nails in their palms, there are many signs that indicate a suspect is lying," the teacher had said.

Papa Michalis was a firm believer in 'tells,' but then he was a priest; and priests had always been seekers of signs, of the Almighty's presence mostly and His benevolence and boundless love of mankind. Patronas on the other hand had never had much faith in 'tells.' As for God's benevolence and love of mankind, the jury was still out on that one.

Kourelas didn't seem surprised when Patronas described the attack on Melissa Costas.

Who had told him about it? Patronas wondered. Only members of the police force were aware of what had happened that night; and he was sure none of them were responsible. Which left the perpetrators. Kourelas must know the perpetrators.

"She's with a police artist now. They are working on a composite sketch."

"She saw the three of them?"

Patronas and Tembelos exchanged glances. Neither of them had said anything about three people being involved.

"Yes," Patronas said. "We get them in a police line-up, she'll be able to pick them out."

"Your wife said you were working," Tembelos said. "What's your job?"

"I load cargo onto boats down by the harbor. Hard work for very little money. That's why I went into pigs. They bring in a whole lot more."

Patronas entered this in his notebook and drew a circle around it. The harbor was the site of the initial attack on Costas. It also wasn't that far from where Raina Mustafa's body had been dumped. If Kourelas worked in the area, there was a good chance he'd encountered the men who'd assaulted Costas. They had been very familiar with the harbor, those men. They'd known about the alley where they'd taken Costas, known they wouldn't be seen there.

Kourelas narrowed his eyes. "This isn't about the squatting, is it?"

"No. It's about your visit to the police station that day. Who you saw, what they looked like…that kind of thing. These are dangerous men we're after. We believe they also killed those two Syrian women. As I told you, we're putting together a composite sketch."

Patronas continued to stir the pot. "It's only a matter of time until we catch them."

Kourelas mulled this over for a few minutes. The smell he gave off was even stronger in the confines of the office, the stench nearly overwhelming. But there was something unsavory about him that went far beyond the pigs, a false note Patronas kept hearing in everything he said.

He kept glancing slyly at Patronas, obviously weighing the possibilities, how best to turn the situation to his advantage.

"You want information, right?"

"Yes."

"I saw a poster of that dead girl. Said there was a reward."

"That's right."

"Just a phone call. I wouldn't have to point a finger or anything?"

"That is correct. All we want at this point is information."

He rubbed a hand over his grizzled cheek. "Like I said, I work down at the harbor; and it is a rough place. No one checks your papers. You just show up and do what needs to be done. Some of the men I work with, they're quick with a knife. Fellows you wouldn't want to meet up with late at night. Could be they're the ones you're looking for."

Patronas nodded. "Go on."

"I'd be willing to keep an eye on them and report back to you. You wouldn't have to pay much. I'm not going to bleed you dry. Let's say fifty euros a week. And if I end up identifying the killer of that girl, I get another one hundred euros"

"Fine. I'll pay you week-to-week. See how it goes."

Patronas handed him the fifty euros and they exchanged phone numbers. "Don't come back here," he warned. "I'll drop the money off at your house. I don't want anyone to know you're working for us."

"Got a spy, you think?"

"I don't know, maybe."

Kourelas gave him an assessing glance. "These men really as bad as you say?"

"They killed two people so far and came close to killing a third. What do you think?"

"Okay, okay. I hear you. I'll be careful." He stood up to go.

"One last thing," Patronas said. "We'll need a DNA sample from you. It's just a formality, a way to eliminate you as a possible suspect. We're asking everyone who was in the station that day to give us one."

Although Kourelas was clearly reluctant, he opened his mouth and let Patronas swab his cheek. He also allowed himself to be fingerprinted, complaining bitterly about how the ink would stain his clothes.

Patronas smiled to himself. Kourelas had been fingerprinted before.

He doubted he'd hear much from him in the future. Kourelas would string him along for a couple of weeks, then disappear.

But maybe, just maybe, he would pass along the information about the composite sketch; and the perpetrators would show themselves.

Kourelas paused at the door on his way out. "You ask me, it was the brother killed that migrant girl. They do that, you know, migrants. They're poor, same as me—you saw where I live—but it's a different kind of poor. It's poor like Jesus said, poor of spirit. They're broken, those people, broken like twigs."

Chapter 20

"What do you think?" Tembelos asked Patronas after Kourelas left. "I couldn't get a read on him."

"He's a strange fellow. One minute, he's selling out his friends, the next he's quoting the Sermon on the Mount."

"You think he's involved?"

"No. He's shady, no question about it. But he didn't know a thing about Raina Mustafa. She didn't have a brother. She came to Chios alone."

"Sell you bait and swear it's caviar," Tembelos said. But you're right. I think that's as far as he goes. He's no killer."

"Run his prints anyway and see what comes back."

"Will do."

Tembelos hesitated. "You're putting him in harm's way, you know, asking him to spy."

"I didn't ask him, Giorgos. You heard him. He volunteered."

"So did Costas."

It was a low blow.

"It's not the same."

"No, it's worse. She was a cop and he's a civilian."

"All he wants is the money, his miserable fifty euros a week. He'll call me a couple of times and that will be that. He's not going to risk anything for us. Nothing's going to happen to him."

"I still don't like it. I spoke to Costas yesterday; and she told me what happened to her. These aren't normal people we're dealing with, Yiannis. You need to remember that. There was an element of sadism in everything they did to her. Everything."

• • •

It turned out Kourelas was not originally from Chios. He'd moved there from a small village in central Crete, where he was well known to the local authorities. "In trouble since he was a kid," the officer in charge told Patronas on the phone.

"What did he do?"

"Stole a bike, hotwired a car. Kid stuff. If wasn't nailed down, he took it."

"Any crimes against women? Rape? Assault?"

"No. He's a thief, sure. But nothing more than that. He's not the kind of man who hurts people."

"If he told you something, would you believe him?"

"Depends on what it was. He's a greedy bastard. He'd string you along if he could, milk you for money."

"He offered to be an informant."

"Could be useful. Based on what I know of him, he's doesn't hang around with saints."

• • •

After Lydia and Ali departed for Athens, it was very quiet in the cottage. Desperate for the sound of a human voice, Patronas turned on the radio and left it on. Most of the broadcasts were from Turkey, but he preferred them to the silence; the silence was killing him.

Dimitra continued to call and ask for favors: a brand of ice cream only available in Chora, disposable diapers she needed for her mother. This last had brought great shame down upon Patronas. The store owner had assumed the diapers were for him and inquired if Patronas needed anything else. 'Rubber underpants and sheets for the bed?' he'd asked in a voice that carried. 'A portable urinal?' 'Viagra?' Patronas had blushed to the roots of his hair.

Still, not wanting to antagonize her, he continued to do as she asked. She had not spoken about Ali again; and he wanted to keep it that way. If that meant a run to the store for ice cream or diapers., so be it. It was a small price to pay.

Beyond the radio, the only other sounds in the house came from Jinn, who started meowing at first light and continued throughout the day. Nothing appeased it. Maybe the cat had bonded with Lydia, but it was obvious it would never bond with him.

Hoping to win it over, Patronas purchased imported treats at great expense and a kilo of fresh sardines. He coaxed and cajoled, even let the animal sleep in the same bed with him. As a result, he now had a persistent itch which was growing worse by the day. Mange, he was pretty sure. It had finally happened. Jinn, the cat, had given him mange.

Earlier that day, he'd stood stark naked in front of the mirror and inspected himself. Sure enough, there were blotches of red everywhere.

If he were a crying man, he would have cried then. He was like Job in the bible. All that was missing were the boils; and he was pretty sure they were on their way. It was only a matter of time.

• • •

The second man on their list, Costas Milonas lived in Kardhmayla, a town in the northeastern corner Chios.

"An attack like the one on Costas?" Patronas told Tembelos as they got in the police car. "Whoever did that was no stranger to violence. We'll know right away if Milonas is involved."

Lighting a cigarette, he inhaled deeply. "I can't believe we're looking at a Greek for this."

"Twenty five years on the force and you still think we're all saints. I don't know, Yiannis. You and reality need to get better acquainted."

The streets were empty: a pair of famous sculptures stood nearby, one of sailor, the other of the sailor's wife, each looking out at the ocean with a kind of yearning. The bronze statues had been erected to honor the generations of seamen from Chios, who'd lived and, far too often, died on that water, and the women, who'd waited at home, praying for their safe return.

Milona was standing outside, watering his garden with a hose when Patronas and Tembelos drove up to his house. There were ceramic decorations scattered throughout his yard—kittens, rabbits, frogs—and a shell-shaped fountain gushing water. The latter seemed out of place in the yard. With a trio of carved dolphins, it seemed a little showy to Patronas, pompous.

Flashing his badge, he introduced himself. "Is there someplace we can talk?"

Milonas led them into the front parlor of his house and motioned for them to take a seat. Well into middle age, he was rotund man with a fleshy, open face and more chins than he needed.

The room itself was full of heavy Victorian furniture, the seats of the chairs upholstered in peach-colored brocade. There was crochetwork on the backs and arms of all of them. Looking around the room, Patronas felt like he'd gone back in time. Those kind of doilies—starched to look like bowls—he hadn't seen them in years. There were also silver trinkets and souvenirs from weddings and baptisms, at least a lifetime's worth. Every surface was covered.

Opening his notebook, Patronas explained why they were there. "We are interviewing everyone who signed the registry at the police station on the days Officer Costas was on duty."

"Yes, yes, I was there," Milonas volunteered. "There was an issue with a wall my neighbor had built encroaching my land; and I went there to file a complaint."

"You spoke with Officer Costas?"

"Briefly. It was very busy; and she suggested I come back later when she'd have more time."

"Did you see anyone suspicious while you were there?"

"Now that you mention it, there was someone. Greek, I think he was. He didn't go near her, just stood out in the hall, looking at her through the glass and talking to another man. It seemed odd to me at the time. Why come to the police station if you're just going to stand around?"

"What did he look like?"

"Prosperous. Hair just so, sweater draped over his shoulders. You know the type. A ship owner's son maybe."

"Young, old? Tall, short?"

"Medium on both. Forty or thereabouts and about the same size of your colleague there." He pointed to Tembelos.

"Handsome, ugly? Tattoos?"

"Okay looking, but nothing special. As for tattoos, I was too far away to see. I remember looking for him when I got out—curious, you know—but he'd already left."

"What about the man he was talking to? What did he look like?"

"He might have been from the Middle East. Dark hair, dark eyes. A little sinister in my opinion. Tough."

"Did you happen to see the kind of car the Greek was driving?"

"As a matter of fact, I did. It was a black BMW."

Patronas dutifully wrote all this down in his notebook. "Besides the Greek and his companion, did you see anyone else?"

"Only a bunch of men, Afghans maybe. They were standing around on the front steps, staring at women the way they do, taking their clothes off with their eyes. Made me mad.

He spat. "Μαλάκες." Assholes.

After thanking him for his help, Patronas and Tembelos drove back along the coast. They passed Panagia Myrtidhiotissa, a monastery built out over the sea and sped on, passing a series of forested hills before the land leveled off near Vrondatos. In the distance, Patronas could see the island of Oinoussos, legendary home of some of the richest ship-owners in the world and beyond it, Lesbos, another island in the Northern Aegean.

The migrant crisis on Lesbos was far worse than the one on Chios. At one time, the Moria camp there had been the largest in Europe. Built to house three thousand people, at its peak, more than twenty thousand people had been living there; and it had been roundly condemned by human rights organizations as an 'open-air prison' and 'concentration camp.' It had been burned to the ground in 2020, allegedly by four Afghans protesting the lock-down during Covid. The fire had been catastrophic for the residents, destroying everything they had and forcing them to sleep out in the streets.

The situation in Vial was tame by comparison. Patronas knew his counterpart on Lesbos, Gregoris Maistralis well—they had been at the police academy together— and he called him when he got back to the station.

"I've got a killer loose in Vial," He quickly brought him up to speed.

"I don't know what to tell you," Maistralis said. "It's terra incognita in those camps. The Afghans won't help no matter what, so forget them. As for the Syrians, they've been through hell at the hands of Assad and his security forces; and they think we're the same. If I were you, I'd go back and re-interview those women, the ones the first victim was living with. See if there isn't something new that they remember."

"Hard without a translator."

"I've got a man, who can help you. I'll send him to Chios tomorrow. Name's Papadopoulos. He grew up in Syria. Knows the people and the culture well."

Patronas thanked him, relieved he'd no longer have to rely on Liadis.

"I'm a very busy man, Chief Inspector," the camp administrator had said the last time Patronas had summoned him to translate. "Isn't there someone else you can call?"

Since then, Patronas had relied on the translator app on his phone which was no good, not in police work, not with potential suspects. Translating Greek into Arabic took far too long, gave the truth time to scurry away.

He and Maistralis continued to talk a few more minutes, weighing the pros and cons of a search and seizure effort at the camp.

"If you could find the weapon it would be a start," Maistralis said. "DNA would go a long way toward solving a case like this. I'd come to Chios myself and lend you a hand, but there's no way I can get away. Lesbos is under siege. Migrants moved into an olive grove near the camp and cut down 5000 trees, some of them centuries old, to use as firewood. And now the villagers are all up in arms. They've had enough. Their houses have been broken into; their property defaced. It never ends."

"No murders?"

"None that I know of, but then again, who knows. There are just too many dead people, Yiannis, especially now after the fire. The coroner has his hands full. He can't perform autopsies on all of them.

Patronas kept pushing. "Nothing like I described?"

"No, but like I said a lot goes on in those camps that I don't know about, that I don't *want* to know about."

"I spoke to a policeman in Turkey; and he said the same thing. A 'jungle' was how he described it.

"There's a certain order in the jungle. A kind of natural law. There's nothing like that in the camps that I've seen. It's not even dog-eat-dog, it's worse. A hundred times worse. You know 10,000 children have gone missing since the crisis began. 10,000 kids. Can you believe it? Where are they? What the hell happened to them?"

Patronas nodded. He knew about the missing children; every law enforcement official in Europe did. It was one of the reasons he'd taken Ali home with him. He hadn't wanted the boy to join their numbers.

Just thinking about it made him want to vomit.

Chapter 21

The last person on their list, Thanassis Alexandropoulos lived in a decaying apartment building outside Chora, the capital of Chios. Although it was late in the afternoon, he was still in a bathrobe when he opened the door.

"What?" he stammered.

"Police." Patronas flashed his badge.

Alexandropoulos stood off to one side so that they could enter. Unlike Milonas' home, there was very little in the way of furniture here. Only some sickly-looking plants on the windowsill and a pair of mismatched kitchen chairs. It reminded Patronas of the place he'd lived in after Dimitra kicked him out, everything broken and taped together, painted over to look like new.

Staggering in after them, Alexandropoulos shut the door, leaning on it like a boat taking on water. He reeked of alcohol.

Patronas changed his mind. Not hungover. The man was drunk.

"We wanted to ask you about your visit to the police station."

Milonas raised his hands in a gesture of surrender. "What can I say? My ex-wife came by and we got into it; and I punched a hole in the wall."

He enunciated the words carefully. "She gets all worked up and before I know it the cops come and drag me off to the police station."

"What happened once you got there?"

"I spoke to some woman. Real crime and punishment, she was, not sympathetic at all."

"Officer Costas was nearly killed shortly after your visit."

He backed away. "I swear I didn't touch her. Couldn't even if I'd wanted to. Had a desk between us. The cops who brought me in told her what I'd done; and I stated my case, real careful-like, but I got nowhere with her. My court date is in a couple of weeks. I can show you the papers."

He kept looking first at Patronas, then at Tembelos. Wanting sympathy, the way drunks do. Self-pity, the extent of their emotional range.

Patronas had an uncle, who used to do the same when he came home drunk. He'd talk and talk, looking first at his wife and then at his kids, seeking a safe place to land. He'd knocked over the Christmas tree one year; and it had caught on fire. The kids had saved their presents before rescuing him, which said about all there was to say. No doubt, the situation with Alexandropoulos was much the same, hence the divorce.

"Did you see anyone suspicious hanging around while you were there? Anyone watching Officer Costas?"

"No, no one."

"Thank you, Mr. Alexandropoulos. We appreciate you taking the time to talk to us."

Alexandropoulos tried to see them out, but it proved to be too much for him; and he sank back down on the chair.

"*Adio*," he called faintly, good-bye.

• • •

Costas called that afternoon and said she was being discharged from the hospital and would be flying back to Chios the following day.

"I think you should stay in Athens," Patronas told her. "You'll be safer there."

"I won't be alone. Papa Michalis has volunteered to stay with me until I'm on my feet again."

"Those men are still out there, Melissa. You'll be in grave danger if you return to Chios."

"I've got no place else to go, sir. Chios is the only home I've got."

Patronas could hear the tears in her voice. "Come and stay with me then. My house is very secluded; and you can hide out there."

"That's very kind of you, sir, but I'd prefer to be back in my own apartment, for everything to go back to normal."

Poor Melissa. There would be no going back to normal for her, not tomorrow or the day after, not ever. She just didn't know it yet. Patronas had been nearly killed himself and he knew. Even now, years later, he still flinched when people approached him in a certain way, his body instinctively recoiling. Worse were the re-occurring dreams, haunted always by gunfire and splattered with blood.

"Lydia and Ali are in Athens. And it's very lonely in the house. It would help to have you and Father there, Melissa. To have some company. It would only be for a short time. It wouldn't be forever."

He continued to plead with her. "The loneliness is really getting to me."

"All right," she finally said. "I'll stay with you."

"Good. I'll pick you up at the airport tomorrow."

She gave him the time of her flight and what she needed—the list of medications she was taking was a long one—and they sorted out the details. "I need a lot of care," she whispered. "Personal care."

"Don't worry. We'll get a nurse."

"You'll also need to buy a lot of food. Papa Michalis never stops eating. I've never seen anything like it. He consumed an entire jar of spoon sweets in one sitting and wiped the syrup off his face with his beard. The staff at the hospital calls him το ηλεκτρικό πιρούνι. The electric fork."

Smiling, Patronas wrote 'food' on his list and drew a star next to it. "Anything else?"

"Bring my computer from the station so that I can work."

"But you're on sick leave."

Her voice rose. "I need to work, sir. It's important. Speaking of which, did you follow-up about those people I told you about? Those four people who went missing?"

"No, not yet."

"Do it, sir. Do it today. I was calling to tell you about them right before I was abducted."

Patronas' interest quickened. "You think someone overheard you?"

"I've been thinking about it and I'm pretty sure that's what happened. You didn't pick up and I remember I was leaving you a message. There was a lot of noise in the camp then; and I was fighting to make myself heard. Ten minutes later, that man was all over me."

"A coincidence?"

"Not a chance, sir. The timing. It had to be related. I'm not saying the men who attacked me were migrants, but they were in the camp in some capacity. I'm convinced of it. They are doing something in Vial, something they don't want the police to know about. I think that's why they killed Raina Mustafa. They wanted to silence her."

Patronas nodded. It fit. The camp was the key. He was sure of it. The men he wanted were in the camp. And he was pretty sure he knew where to start looking for them.

· · ·

"Melissa is being discharged from the hospital," Patronas told Tembelos. "She's coming back to Chios tomorrow."

"That's crazy, Yiannis. If those men catch her, they'll kill her."

"I convinced her to stay with me. It'll be all right. I'll station a patrolman in the driveway and speak to the Coast Guard. We'll be all right."

He patted his holster. "I've got a gun."

"You can't do this alone, Yiannis. It's too dangerous. I'll stay at the house with you. We can protect her together."

"Papa Michalis is coming with her. He can help, too."

"What's he going to do? Hit them over the head with a bible?"

"We could give him a gun."

"But will he use it? Will he kill someone? Me, I've got no trouble killing people. Shoot a bad guy? There's a certain symmetry to it. It balances things out. But he's a priest and priests operate with a whole different set of rules."

They stopped off at the station and gathered up all the guns they could lay their hands and four bulletproof vests. Patronas drew the line at the bazooka in the evidence room, fearful he'd blow a hole in the house. Ditto with the pile of ancient grenades, gunpowder being inherently unstable.

He called a friend in the Coast Guard and asked him to anchor a patrol boat at the entrance to the cove.

"Keep a searchlight on the water. If you spot any kind of boat near my house, arrest everyone onboard; and if they resist, sink it."

"Most of the inflatables, the Zodiacs and the like, are made of black rubber which makes them difficult to see, but I'll do my best."

He paused. "What's going on, Yiannis? What's happening? Who are you after?"

"A couple of murderers."

"I'll be there, be there as long as you need me."

· · ·

As soon as the sun went down, Patronas and Tembelos carried the weaponry along with the murder book and all the computers out of the station and put them in the trunk of the cruiser. They drove around for a few minutes; and when they were sure no one was following them, they turned north and headed to Patronas' house.

Sneaking around in the dark, Patronas felt like he was reliving the scene from *The Godfather* when the mafia men 'went to the mattresses,' during a war with another crime family. They'd camped out in an apartment in their undershirts, he remembered, cooked and eaten copious amounts of pasta. Fortunately, they hadn't had someone like Papa Michalis among them whose gluttony probably would have cost him his life, mobsters not liking it when someone took more than their share, be it money, drugs or spaghetti.

On the way to the house Patronas called Dimitra, told her what was going on and that because of the danger, he'd be out of commission for the time being. "Call the station if you need anything. There are men there who can help you."

"Be careful, Yiannis," she said and sounded like she meant it. "It would break my heart if something happened to you, my mother's, too."

• • •

"Not Alexandropoulos," Tembelos said, adding their notes on him to the pile of papers on the table.

Although it was close to three a.m., he and Patronas were still hard at work, the lamp in the living room, an island of light in the darkened house. Patronas had the nagging sense he'd missed something; and they were going through everything they had, trying to find it.

They wanted to get as much done as they could before Costas arrived. After that, they'd have to put the case aside and focus on protecting her.

Patronas had brewed a pot of coffee and drank most of it. Still, he didn't know how much longer he could keep going. They'd been working for hours—reviewing the entries in the murder book and playing back the tapes of the interviews—but so far, they had come up with nothing.

"Alexandropoulos is capable of violence," he said. "That was a very big hole he punched in the wall—but rape, murder? No. He's too far gone as an alcoholic."

"He's the last Greek man on the list. What do we do now?"

"I don't know. Kourelas might be involved, but, if so, only in a peripheral way. It's got to be someone else."

They looked at one another.

"How much do you know about Liadis?" Tembelos asked quietly.

"Not much. I took him at his word for the most part. He was the camp administrator; and I just assumed he was what he said he was."

Tembelos pointed to the police registry. "Look here. 'Liadis' is written on every single one of the dates in question, the days Melissa was on duty."

"There's something else. Right after we found the body of Raina Mustafa, I went to see him; and I asked him point blank if anyone else in the camp had gone missing and he told me 'no, no one else had disappeared.'"

"Nothing about those four women?"

"Not a word. Shit, it's him. He's been there the whole time; and I missed it. He's the prosperous man, Milonas said he saw at the station, the one who looks like a ship owner."

"You want me to bring him in?"

"Not yet. Let's turn him inside out first. See what we can find out. He's married to a woman who values money. Could be he borrowed from the wrong people; and they roped him in."

"The godfathers of night."

"That's what I'm thinking."

• • •

Grey with fatigue, Tembelos spent the rest of the night searching the internet for information on Dimitri Liadis. As Patronas had suspected, the camp administrator was heavily in debt. He didn't own the house in Campos where he lived, he rented it; and, according to court documents, the landlord was after him for back payment. As was his first wife, who currently lived in Athens and was after him for child support. All his credit cards were maxed out; and he had no savings accounts, certificates of deposit or other investments that Tembelos could find.

"Could be his money is in Cyprus," Patronas said. "His father-in-law is in the import-export business; and those people are maestros when it comes to hiding money."

"I don't think so, Yiannis. From the look of things, he can barely make ends meet. He's broke."

"You never know. His wife might be paying their bills."

"That woman? She wouldn't give you water if you were dying of thirst."

They'd also pulled up everything they could find on Liadis' brother-in-law, Michalis Papoulis. Patronas made a note to call Athens and see what his colleagues had to say about him. Could be the brother-in-law wasn't just using drugs, he was dealing them, strengthening the possibility the godfathers of night were involved.

Perhaps they'd expanded their sphere of influence, those men, moving on from cigarettes to far more lethal endeavors; and Liadis and his brother-in-law were assisting them.

"Trafficking," Patronas said to himself. "They're trafficking people out of the camp. But where does Liadis fit in? Is he in charge or just their pawn?"

Near dawn, Patronas called a halt. "Get some sleep, Giorgos. We have a long day ahead of us. I'll call Stathis and get a wiretap put on Liadis' phone."

Stathis had been appalled when he learned of the attack on Costas; and he was more than willing to do what Patronas asked if it meant catching the men responsible.

"This is a brotherhood. An attack on a single police officer is an attack on all of all of us,"

"Brotherhood?" Patronas rolled his eyes. The fact that Costas was a woman seemed to have eluded Stathis, but then many things did. It was like his boss heard every third word.

"Sir, I need your help. I have serious concerns about the camp administrator…"

"That man, Liadis? You think he's involved?"

"He withheld critical information which makes me suspicious. He was also at the station on the days in question. I want to put a wiretap on the phone in his office and another on his cell. Find out who he's talking to."

"Very well. I'll get the necessary paperwork together and see that the judge signs it." Stathis lowered his voice. "I want them caught, Patronas. I want them caught and sent to hell."

He paused. "Legally, of course, if you can manage it. But, as you know, unfortunate things occasionally happen in police work. A gun goes off or a suspect accidentally trips and hits his head. You know how it is. Can't be helped. I would not hold you responsible if that happened here, not in a case like this. Not at all."

Patronas almost dropped the phone.

Stathis had just given him a license to kill.

Chapter 22

The charade was an elaborate one.

First, they cut the power at the camp, albeit briefly—no reason to panic the residents unnecessarily—and then a man in a DEH uniform, the major supplier of electricity in Greece, barged into Liadis' office and told him to clear out.

"There's a problem with the power grid, and we need to check the wiring."

Patronas had recruited a young traffic cop from Athens to pose as the repairman, afraid if the camp administrator would recognize anyone local. A tap was already in place on Liadis' cell phone, placed there by a wizard in the police department in Athens. Stathis had tried to explain how a tap could be placed remotely, but Patronas had been unable to grasp the concept—Chios was here, Athens was there.

Liadis quickly gathered up his things and headed to his car, a black BMW, another strike against him. His hair was shiny with gel and recently dyed, a shade darker than the last time Patronas had seen him. He was dressed in khaki pants, a polo shirt with the collar turned up and loafers with little brass buckles across the instep. Gucci or its first cousin.

His briefcase matched the shoes which ruined the effect. Shipowners didn't carry briefcases; only their employees did. Liadis should have known better.

Stepping forward, Patronas intercepted him. "Good morning, Dimitri. I have a questions for you."

"I'm afraid it will have to wait. I'm very busy now." Turning, he moved to open the door of the car, but Patronas blocked his path.

"We're closing the case," he said. "That's why I'm here. I wanted you to be the first to know."

Liadis froze. "You identified the men who killed Raina Mustafa?"

"Yes. A witness has come forward, a man who was in the vicinity when they dumped the body. He took a picture of them with his cell phone."

"A photo?" Patronas could hear the panic in his voice.

"Yes. He did a good job. You can see their faces clear as day." Enjoying watching Liadis squirm, Patronas went on—making it up as he went along and laying it on thick. He praised the steely nerves of the photographer, his steadfastness and courage, and exclaimed again and again how rare it was to meet a man like that these days.

"We're afraid the killers will come after him, so we placed him protective custody."

"Where?"

"At the station. We're short staffed these days what with Officer Costas being out on sick leave, but he should be all right there. We outfitted the room in the back for him."

This was all part of Patronas' plan. He was setting the trap. Stathis had sent him reinforcements from Athens—ten men well trained in combat—to keep watch on the station while Patronas and Tembelos guarded the house. Liadis' associates made a move in either direction, he'd have them.

"I sent the photo on to Athens, also to Interpol and all the other international agencies," Patronas added, still toying with Liadis. "Once we have their names, we'll put out an all-points bulletin. With any luck, we'll have them in custody by tonight, tomorrow at the latest."

"Well done, Chief Inspector. Congratulations."

"Thank you."

"Now if you'll excuse me…" Liadis got into the BMW, started it and roared out of the camp, scattering gravel in all directions. Visibly agitated, he was shouting at someone on his cell phone.

Not checkmate, but close.

Patronas watched him go with a sense of satisfaction.

"Gotcha you, you fucking asshole, you fucking son of a bitch."

• • •

Patronas saw the Syrian woman Raina Mustafa had been living with on the road outside the camp. She was carrying a bag of groceries; and he stopped and offered her a ride.

Recognizing him, she gave a sad smile. "Mr. Police," she said. "Good afternoon."

He'd taken a picture of Liadis with his cell phone; and he showed it to her. "Is this the man that Raina Mustafa was afraid of?"

"No. That man, he was big, no office person like him." She tapped Liadis' image on the phone. "A soldier maybe, fighter."

Raising her arms, she flexed her muscles.

"Was he Greek?"

"I don't know. I only know my people."

"Could he have been Russian?"

"Too dark. Dark in face, dark in heart. Like Raina, I am also scared of this man.."

• • •

Melissa Costas was exhausted when she arrived in Chios. Patronas had given strict instructions that she should be the last one off the plane and not pass through the airport, but instead be brought over in her wheelchair to where he was waiting in an unmarked van.

An elderly vehicle, the van belonged to a bakery; and the inside smelled faintly of freshly baked bread. The windows had been painted over; and with the help of Tembelos, he had rigged up a portable ramp so that she could get on and off in her wheelchair. The logo of the bakery—a parrot holding a plate of cakes—was a familiar sight on Chios; and hopefully, they would be able to drive through town undetected.

The owner, another old friend of Patronas, had loaned him the van for the duration. "Just bring it back without bullet holes," he'd said with a laugh. "Hard to explain bullet holes to people buying donuts."

Before Papa Michalis had boarded the plane with her, he had texted Patronas what he wanted for dinner. How he'd learned to text was anybody's guess, but he'd obviously mastered it and was very specific. To start with he said he was sick of hospital food and yearned for grilled octopus, followed by a 'kilo or two of *barbounia*,' little red mullets that cost seventy euros a kilo, and for dessert, pasta flora.

"And don't forget the wine," he'd texted a moment later, this followed by ten exclamation points.

Patronas hadn't shot him yet, but he felt like that day was fast approaching.

Given the number of people now residing in the house, he'd have to take out a loan from the bank to feed them all. Maybe he should follow the gangsters' example and buy a couple of kilos of pasta, call it a day.

Tembelos was already at the cottage; and he'd called Patronas and told him all was well. The Coast Guard boat was anchored at the entrance to the cove and the police cruiser was in the driveway.

The sun was setting by the time they reached the village of Nagos where Patronas lived; and he waited until it was fully dark before turning onto the road that led down to his house. He parked the van, slid open the side door and lowered the ramp. Costas was sitting in a wheelchair, held in place by a couple of wooden blocks. After removing them, he turned the chair around and started to wheel her out.

"Stop," Costas said. "I'm not crippled. I can walk."

"Chair might be better. It's a long way to the house."

"I'll get there, sir. It will just take me some time."

He turned the light on his cell phone and used it to light her way, praying no one would see them. He'd planned to give her his bedroom, but she wouldn't have it and settled herself in Ali's room instead.

Jinn was sleeping on top of the bed; and he looked up when she came in and began to purr, a sound Patronas had never heard before. It even licked her hand.

At Costas' request, Patronas got out her computer and set it up on a table next to her bed.

"I need to work," she told him. "It makes me feel good, like my old self again."

He quickly brought her up to speed about the case. "We think now Liadis, the camp administrator is involved. Right after we found Raina Mustafa's body, I asked him if any other people had gone missing from the camp; and he said 'no.' He had to have known about those four women; and yet he denied all knowledge."

"He knew about them, all right. That Syrian woman told me she went to him first when they disappeared."

"Find out everything you can about him. Tembelos did some preliminary work, but we need more. Also check out Liadis' wife, Chryssoula Papoulis, and his brother-in-law, Michalis Papoulis. We need to know where they get their money, who their associates are."

"I thought her papa was rich."

"Check that, too. I'm suspicious of everything Liadis told me."

Costas grimaced as she leaned over the computer, but immediately started typing away.

"On it, sir. If it's out there, I'll find it."

• • •

Tembelos had brought an enormous air mattress for himself and Papa Michalis and laid it out on the floor.

"Trust me, Giorgos, you don't want to sleep with him. You know how other people snore when they sleep, well Father eats. He chews and smacks his lips all night long, burps, sometimes even farts. It's disgusting."

And so Papa Michalis ended up in Patronas' room. Thankfully, the room had a door and they could shut out the sound of him.

Patronas intended to bed down on the porch. It would be easier to spot an intruder from there, hear his footsteps on the stone steps. For the first time in years, he was wearing a gun. He'd put it away after the massacre of the goats, afraid he'd shoot it off again by mistake, but now he'd taken to wearing it again. The machine guns, the *Kalashnikovs* and AK-47s he and Tembelos had taken out of the police department were on the floor next to him.He and Tembelos had debated how best to set up a perimeter around the cottage. If one of them saw someone, they needed to be able to communicate with the other and with patrolman outside in the cruiser without alerting their target they were on to him.

"No way to do it that I can see," Tembelos said. "Fumbling around with the phone in the dark? He'll hear us."

"What do you suggest?"

"Open fire."

"Maybe not that far."

"Okay, okay. A warning shot."

And that's what they agreed to do.

As a precautionary measure, they'd closed all the shutters; and it grew hotter and hotter inside the house as the night wore on

• • •

Stathis called around eleven o'clock to report Liadis had spoken to a man with an accent.

"Man told Liadis he'd take care of 'it.' We are trying to trace the call, but for God's sakes be careful. Be on your guard."

Patronas took a deep breath. No time like the present. "Sir, I need to speak to you on another matter."

The case had taken a dangerous turn; and he didn't know what the outcome would be, if he would even survive. He didn't want Lydia to have face Stathis on her own, to have to plead with him to keep Ali. He needed to see to it now. The Social Services people wouldn't care, but his boss was a stickler for rules; and, when it came to the boy, Patronas had broken many.

"What is it, Patronas?" Stathis barked. "For God's sakes, it's late. Spit it out."

"I've been meaning to ask you, sir," he said, "what are your feelings about transnational adoption?"

"I'm old-fashioned," Stathis said. "I don't believe in co-mingling of the races."

Another miss by Stathis. Syrians were not a different race. They were white people.

His boss paused. "What's this about, Patronas? Why are you asking?"

"There's a humanitarian effort underway on Chios now that I thought you should be aware of. People are taking refugee children into their homes, the little ones who have lost their parents."

It wasn't a complete lie. There *was* a humanitarian effort underway, but only on his part.

"They aren't doing anything illegal, Patronas," Stathis said. "I'm sure child services has screened them. I'd say this is out of our jurisdiction."

"Sir, the reason I'm telling you this is I have one of those children living with me now. His mother drowned the night that boat capsized."

"How long do you intend to keep him?"

"Forever."

Patronas held his breath.

"I am assuming given what happened, he has no papers, no birth certificate and so on and so forth."

"That is correct, sir. All Ali came with were the clothes on his back."

"Ali, huh? He's Muslim then."

"As far as I know."

"Highly unorthodox from the sounds of it, especially given that you are a police officer."

"I had no choice, sir. I couldn't send him to Vial alone. He's only four-years old."

There was a lengthy silence. "I always said you were a fool, Patronas, but so be it. You have my blessing."

"Thank you, sir."

Stathis chuckled. "It's working with that priest that's done it. Softened you up so much it's a wonder you can do your job. Before you know it, you'll be saying prayers when you arrest someone, praying for their immortal soul."

"Not this time, sir. These men? I'll shoot them on sight."

"See that you, Patronas. See that you do."

• • •

Hanging up the phone, Patronas turned to Tembelos. "They're coming."

"I'll see to the house. You take the cove."

Grabbing the AK-47, Patronas slipped out of the cottage and hurried down to the beach, taking care not to make any noise. A new moon was rising; and he touched his gold wedding ring for luck. An ancient custom, it was one of the few he adhered to. There was a lot of folklore about the moon in Greece, always had been.

There'd even been a goddess, Selene, associated with it. Supposedly, she rode across the heavens in a silver chariot, pulling the moon behind her with a crown shaped like a crescent moon on her head. He still remembered the words he'd been forced to memorize about her in school.

'From her immortal head a radiance is shown from heaven and embraces earth; and great is the beauty that arises from her shining light.'

Looking up at the moon now, Patronas understood his forefathers' fascination.

The sea was silver in the moonlight, waves slipping over and pooling around the whitened rocks. On the hills which surrounded the cove, the trees were majestic, their dark forms silhouetted against the starlit sky.

He sat down on a rock, raised his binoculars and scanned the water.

The cruiser's spotlight played across the surface now and then, the circling beam like that of small lighthouse. The coverage it provided was spotty; and as the Coast Guard officer had warned, a man could easily slip ashore without being seen.

No one came the first night or the second; and slowly Patronas began to relax his guard.

"Maybe it was a false alarm," he told Tembelos at breakfast on the third day.

Tembelos shook his head. "Not these people, Yiannis. They're smart. They're biding their time. "

Although it was very cramped in the cottage, the four of them had quickly settled into a routine. Costas stayed in her room, occasionally working on the computer when she had the energy while Tembelos and Patronas kept watch on the cove from inside the house with binoculars. As to be expected, Papa Michalis spent most of his time lurking in the kitchen, opening and closing the refrigerator door, looking for food.

The nurse came in the afternoon; and she had been enlisted to bring them dinner from a local restaurant. This had caused an uproar the first day when the priest had ordered luxury items for himself—the lobster spaghetti had been an especially galling purchase—and refused to share. As punishment, he was now subsisting on lentils and would be for the foreseeable future.

• • •

"I'm heading down to the cove," Patronas told Tembelos.

Binoculars in hand, he hurried to his usual place. The cruiser was lying at anchor out by the entrance to the cove. Although the spotlight was on, tonight there were no sounds coming from the boat.

Strange as they were a noisy crew. Maybe they'd bedded down early. A creature rustled in the underbrush, but then all was still. The only sound, the soft whispering of the wind.

He laid down on the rock and looked up at the sky, picking out the constellations one by one. No wonder people believe in angels, he thought. No wonder heaven seems like a possibility. The glories of the night sky would convince anybody.

The creature continued to scurry through the underbrush, an owl closing in on it now. But the creature was too fast for it: and the bird rose again, its talons empty.

He dipped his hand in the sea and let the water trickle through his fingers. He'd have to teach Ali to swim one day. To convince the child the sea was a source of joy, not pain. Perhaps he'd even go paragliding with him like the kids he'd seen off the coast of Turkey.

The sound of a splash jolted him out of his reverie.

A few seconds later, there was another splash, louder this time. He could make out a dark shape swimming in his direction from the north side of the cove. It kept coming, a fin breaking through the surface now and then marking its passage through the water.

Not a fin, a flipper, he realized. The dark shape coming toward him was a man in a wet suit.

No way this was innocent, not a man in the water at this hour.

He reached for his gun. It was the killer. Had to be.

Chapter 23

The man emerged from the water a few minutes later. Pulling off his flippers, he looked around, then started walking toward the house. He had a knife in his hand, the metal gleaming dully in the moonlight. He took his time and proceeded cautiously, taking a step or two and then stopping. Patronas followed close behind, ducking behind the trees, taking care to stay hidden.

It was hard to make out the man's features in the dark, but Patronas could tell he was a brute, broad-shouldered and muscular. If he tried to wrestle a man that size to the ground, he wouldn't stand a chance. David against Goliath, only this time Goliath would win. As quietly as he could, he unholstered his gun and raised it. Guns were good that way. They evened the score.

Stepping out from behind a tree, he fired off a warning shot. "Police! Freeze!"

The man spun around. Seeing Patronas standing there, he rushed him and knocked him back into the water. The gun went flying as they grappled, grunting and clawing at each other. Patronas' hands kept slipping off the rubber wet suit and he couldn't get traction.

Raising his fist, the man smashed him hard in the gut. Patronas felt something give way. Cartilage, bone, he wasn't sure. The pain was tremendous. It was like his insides were collapsing.

Then grabbing him around the neck, the man dragged him further out into the water, pushed his head down and held him there. Clawing and writhing, Patronas fought to breathe, bubbles of escaping air engulfing his face.

Suddenly, the man let go and stumbled backward, thrashing around like a fish on a line, Blood was pulsing from a wound in his arm; and it darkened the sea around them. A moment later, he took off. Splashing out of the water, he disappeared up into the woods on the far side of the cove and was gone.

Patronas staggered out of the water and collapsed on the sand. He tried to wipe the blood off his face, but he lacked the strength, could barely move.

The last thing he remembered before he blacked out was the sound of Tembelos screaming.

• • •

Patronas woke up on the air mattress in the porch, a blanket over him. He had no memory of walking to the cottage. Tembelos must have carried him.

Papa Michalis was sitting in a chair next to him.

"You gave us quite a scare, Yiannis," he said softly. "There was a moment there when we thought we'd lost you."

His eyes filled with tears. "Gone, the only friend I ever had."

"What happened?"

"Giorgos brought you in and laid you down. You weren't breathing, so he went to work on you and begam performing CPR. Even unconscious, you kept fighting, pushing him off like you wanted him to stop. That's when we saw the wound on your side. We tore up the sheeting and wound it around you, did everything we could to staunch the flow of blood."

"Where's the man who attacked me?"

"In the wind. You were in bad shape; and we figured we'd save you first, then go after him."

"For what it's worth, he had a tattoo on his hand. Cyrillic."

"Russian?"

"Maybe. It was hard to tell with the wetsuit."

"The doctor is on his way. After he looks you over, we'll deal with it."

Tembelos poked his head in. "Brought you a shot of whisky." He set the glass down on the table next to the bed. "Drink up. It'll make you feel better."

Patronas couldn't hold his hand steady; and Tembelos had to raise the cup to his lips. He was surprisingly gentle and wiped Patronas mouth with a napkin after he'd finished. The warmth of the whiskey helped ease the pain in his throat, but not the wrenching in his gut

"Jesus, that hurts. He must have cracked a rib."

"Nope," Tembelos said. "He stabbed you. That blood in the water? Most of it was yours."

Patronas slid his hand carefully down his side. Bandages, great wads of them. "Father said the two of you taped me up."

"Had to. You were bleeding out. Worse was I had to resuscitate you. You weren't breathing, so there I was. Smooch. Smooch." Pursing his lips, he made a kissing noise.

"You get the knife?"

Tembelos nodded. It's a 'Storm.' I looked it up. It's a tactical combat weapon, used by underwater warfare units in Russia."

"Man came prepared."

"Indeed, he did."

"Could it be the murder weapon? Coroner thought the killer used a hatchet or an axe. Something with a thick blade."

"Knife's plenty big. It's a real nasty piece of metal."

"Nothing about this makes sense. Why would a Russian kill a Syrian refugee?"

"Maybe they met in a bar; and she didn't want to sleep with him."

Patronas fell silent, reviewing the details of the case. "Maybe we're wrong and he wasn't Russian. Could be he was something else."

"The tattoo, the knife… what else could he be? And not an ordinary one. The way he conducted himself. Ex-army probably. Special forces or whatever they call themselves in Russia."

"I don't get it. What is he doing on Chios?"

"My guess is he is a mercenary. Someone hired him."

"A foreign national. Stathis is going to go berserk."

"To hell with Stathis. It was a righteous shooting by any standard. That man was trying to kill you, Yiannis; and I shot him. Anyone would have done the same. My only regret is I didn't kill him. It was too dark. Even with my scope, I couldn't see well enough to take him down."

Patronas shifted on the air mattress. He could taste blood in his mouth; and it scared him.

"How bad am I hurt?"

"Pretty bad. On a scale of one to ten, I'd say you're a ten. Why the hell did you go after him alone? A man twice your size? What were you thinking?"

"I was worried about Costas. I couldn't let him get her."

"So, idiot that you are, you let him get you instead."

Patronas shrugged. "I didn't think about it. I just rushed in."

"You cut it close this time, Yiannis. Way too close."

He nodded to Papa Michalis, now asleep in the chair. "He lost his mind when I brought you in. Wanted to give you the last rites. I did, too, truth be told. You weren't breathing and you'd gone all pasty and cold. 'That jackass has finally gone and gotten himself killed,' I told myself. But then like the true friend you are, after I breathed into you a couple of times, you opened your eyes and vomited all over me."

The front of Tembelos' shirt was caked with blood. Worse was the expression on his friend's face, the fear.

"You saved my life," Patronas said. "If it hadn't been for you, I would have died. I don't know if you know this, but in China that means you're responsible for me now."

"First off, we're Greek, not Chinese; and I, for one, intend to stay that way. And second, I don't want to be responsible for you. Not today, not tomorrow, not ever. Keeping you alive? It's a full-time job. You have no sense of self-preservation, Yiannis. None whatsoever. It's amazing you've lasted as long as you have."

"Lay off, Giorgos. I'm a wounded man." Patronas looked around the room.

"Where's Costas?"

"I sent her off to stay at the police station. I didn't know who else was out there; and I didn't want to take any chances."

"Good thinking."

"I'm glad it's over."

"It's not over, Giorgos. Trust me, we're not even close."

"Speak for yourself. I'm done. Remember when I told you I had no problem shooting people? Well, turns out that I do. I keep feeling the kick of that gun in my hand."

"It'll go away. Just give it time."

"Not sure I want it to. Get too casual about shooting people…you end up like Dirty Harry. Making your day by making people dead."

• • •

The doctor, a dour young man with a soul patch, gave Patronas a shot of novocaine and stitched up the wound in his side. Then he painted him with a yellowish solution that stung like hell and ordered him to keep his movements to a minimum.

"How long do I have to stay still?

"I don't know. You lost a lot of blood."

Reaching for his stack of gauze, he began to pack up his bag. "You're a lucky man," he said. "An inch to the left and I wouldn't be sewing you up, I'd be signing your death certificate."

Patronas didn't feel lucky. He could still feel that sudden jolt of pain and feel the blood coursing down his side. He couldn't seem to get past it. It was always there.

Stathis called later that morning and congratulated Patronas for shooting the Russian and closing the case. "Well done," he said. "A masterful plan, using Costas to lure your quarry out into the open."

Although Patronas vehemently disagreed, he kept silent. The case was for from over in his mind no matter what his boss said. Too many loose ends. Who had sent that man to the cottage and why? He hadn't come on his own. Someone had sent him: and what role had Liadis played in all of it. There was something going on in the camp, a malignancy of some sort. Patronas was sure of it.

"Doctor wants me to take it easy," he told Stathis, "so I won't be able to do much with the case for the time being."

As always there was some truth in what Patronas said. He never lied to Stathis directly, fearful his boss would catch him. Stathis had an ear for bullshit; and it rarely failed him.

He planned to continue investigating the case, although he didn't tell Stathis this. Maybe not in person—the doctor had told him if he re-opened the wound, he would hemorrhage to death—but that didn't mean he couldn't use Tembelos and Papa Michalis in his stead. Between them, they'd get it done, they'd catch the killer.

Patronas had a complicated relationship with the truth. He considered it legitimate to withhold information—a tactic he often employed at work and in his marriage to Lydia—but to tell a lie, no, that was different. That crossed the line. In his opinion, the road to hell wasn't paved with good intentions, it was paved with falsehood.

"Don't worry about Tembelos," Stathis said expansively. "I'll make sure he sails through this. No need for internal affairs to get involved. It was impressive what he did. He should be commended, not punished."

"I agree, sir," Patronas said. "The way he came running and fired off that shot, hit the perpetrator. I still don't know how he did it."

"I'll tell you how, Patronas. He was *trained*. That's how he did it. He was trained to respond. That's what we all do as officers of the law. You, me, Tembelos. Twenty-four hours a day, we *respond*."

Stathis was getting ready to speak to the press, Patronas could tell. 'A gunfight on the beach...' He could almost see the headline.

It was impressive the way his boss had woven himself into the narrative, almost as if he'd been there when Tembelos shot the man in the wetsuit.

After he hung up, Patronas lay there on the air mattress and mentally went over what had happened. He remembered looking up at stars before the man emerged from the water, his wetsuit gleaming in the moonlight like the skin of a malevolent serpent. How peaceful the cove had been.

Probably the knife the man had stabbed him with was the same one used on Raina Mustafa. There'd be no way to prove it, of course. The salt water had seen to that. And there was a good chance, he'd murdered Almira Al-Bashir, too, and attacked Melissa Costas.

Hard to believe such a person walked the earth. Disguised as a human, but something else entirely. The devil's own.

"Don't they have mothers?" Patronas' mother used to say of criminals. "Don't they have mothers?"

In other words, weren't they raised like the rest of us? And yet they'd gone one way and everyone else had gone another. What caused the deviation? Surely, the man, who attacked him, had been given a choice; and yet he'd chosen to kill an innocent sixteen-year-old girl. Again, what caused the deviation? Was it hatred? Love of money? Why had he done what he'd done? Why?

Maybe it was the lateness of the hour, but the evil on Chios suddenly seemed manifest.

Chapter 24

Papa Michalis resumed his teaching at Vial, spending most of his days there and returning to Patronas' house at night to sleep. Patronas had given him strict instructions not to meddle.

"Don't play detective, you hear me? It's too dangerous. And, for God's sakes, keep your mouth shut. Conjugate Greek verbs and nothing more, you hear me."

The old man now had help. A local woman named Kupia Toula had volunteered to assist him in his make-shift school.

"I can teach the women how to shop," she said. "Wash clothes the way we do here, tasks you are unfamiliar with. My grandparents came from Smyrna, so I well understand what these women are up again. She was a good person, my grandmother. 'Throw good deeds to the wind,' she always said. 'Don't expect them to come back to you or for people to thank you. See them as confetti.'"

Papa Michalis smiled at her. "Confetti?"

She nodded. "Confetti."

She had been there ever since, appearing in Vial early in the morning and working with the priest until he left at night. She was especially fond of Dalia and had made a bed for the girl's doll and sewn a little coverlet to go on the top of it. She'd also stitched a bunch of caftans with lace trim and velvet edging for the toy, exactly like Dalia's mother wore. The girl's Greek continued to improve; and Papa Michalis often saw the two of them conversing together.

Full of energy, Kyria Toula was a robust little woman with a gold front tooth; and Patronas had liked her immediately when Papa Michalis introduced her.

"I'm going to organize a clothing drive," she told him. "And I want the police to help me."

And to his great surprise, Patronas agreed. His officers would collect clothes from all over Chios and bring them to her. She would then sort through them, mend what needed to be mended and distribute them within the camp.

"After that, we're going to put in a garden. Grow our own food."

She was that kind of person. It was like she had a force field around her, one that drew you in

'Turn Greece over to the women,' Lydia often said. 'And you'll own the world."

Watching Kyria Toula in action, Patronas thought Lydia might have a point.

She was an amazon, that little Greek woman. Not in size, but in spirit.

• • •

In the days that followed, Patronas continued to listen to the wiretap of Liadis, although he learned little. The administrator spoke frequently to his wife; and those conversations were painful to listen to. Liadis was always polite and conciliatory while his wife was abusive and nasty. . "Love is blind". Theocritus, the poet, said. Apparently, it was deaf as well.

The administrator also spoke to his wife's brother, Michalis Papoulis, who inevitably asked him for money.

"After what I did, you owe me," he said at one point.

Patronas wished Liadis' brother-in-law had been more specific. Outlined exactly what he'd done for Liadis, if it had involved criminal activity.

It was obvious something had happened since the shooting. Liadis no longer called men with foreign accents and every word he spoke was innocuous. "He's using a burner phone now," Patronas told Tembelos. "Got to be."

"Maybe he doesn't need a phone. Maybe the men we want are in that camp; and Liadis speaks to them there."

The next morning Patronas visited Kyria Toula, described the situation and asked her to spy on Liadis.

"I need you to spy on Liadis."

"The camp administrator?"

"Yes. I want you to keep track of where he goes and who he meets with."

"I'll do it," she said without hesitating. "I have a daughter the same age as that Syrian girl, the one they killed and dumped in Souda. I cried when I heard what had happened to her."

"You can't let him catch you."

"I won't."

"And never call me from Vial. Wait until you get home to report in. And never —and I do mean never—discuss him or what you're doing with anyone connected to the camp."

"I'll pretend to hang laundry up along that fence. I can see right into his office from there."

"Don't pretend— actually do it—that will be safer."

She nodded. "How soon should I start?"

"Now."

"You can't be doing this," the priest told Patronas later that day after the Greek woman departed. "You saw what happened to Melissa. I'm not long for this earth, let me do it instead."

"Father, people have seen us together. They know you're with the police."

"Surely, they wouldn't attack a man of the cloth."

"You must be kidding. These people? They'd kill their own mothers."

• • •

After the doctor took his stitches out, Patronas returned to the place where he'd found Costas. Waving his flashlight around, he inspected the room where she'd been held. He hadn't gathered much in the way of evidence that day—he'd been too focused on getting her to safety—and he was worried he might have missed something.

The cage was gone. He didn't remember ordering it removed and wondered if Tembelos had seen to it. He'd have to check. He feared her captors had returned and taken it, the forensic evidence it contained irretrievably lost.

Underfoot, the ground was littered with greasy gyro wrappers and pizza boxes, empty beer bottles. Someone had been hiding out here.

He gathered up the garbage and stowed it in evidence bags, labeling everything as to date, time and location. He'd ask the forensic people to check the glass bottles for fingerprints and DNA. Hopefully, they would get a hit. He'd also send Tembelos here to keep watch, in case the squatter returned.

Patronas took one last look around. Why risk coming back here? he asked himself. To remove the cage and any other incriminating evidence?

Or because no one would ever think to look for you here?

He called Tembelos as he walked back to the moped. "What happened to the cage they put Costas in? Did you send it off to forensics?"

"Nope. It was still there when I left that night. Why? What happened to it?"

"It's gone."

"Those bastards are still in business."

"Someone has been camping out in the building. There were food wrappers everywhere. I want you to assign someone to keep watch out here for a couple of nights. See if anyone turns up."

"Will do. Anything else?"

"Check and see if Liadis served in any other camps. What his work history is."

• • •

Patronas called Lydia and told her to stay in Athens for the time being. "I'll let you know when it was safe to come home."

He didn't tell her about the man wading ashore and stabbing him. Didn't tell her he was hosting a nightly slumber party at the house or share the fact that Tembelos, Papa Michalis and Melissa Costas were bedding down with him. He and his wife spoke about Jinn mostly. How to make the cat happier in her absence.

The beast had gone silent since Patronas was injured, skulking around at night. It still scratched him on occasion, but now it only raked his ankles with its claws; it never ventured near the wound on his side.

A bond of sorts.

He continued to stand guard at night, sitting outside on the front steps with the AK-47 across his lap until Tembelos took over for him at midnight. The patrol car was still parked in the driveway, the young policeman fast asleep in the front seat; and the Coast Guard cruiser remained anchored at the entrance to the cove, its searchlight playing across the black water. Patronas was taking no chances.

He felt like a soldier on the eve of battle. These men weren't finished with them, he was sure of it. There'd be another round of violence, he just didn't know when or how.

• • •

Three nights later, Patronas was fast asleep on the porch when there was huge crash; and the front windows exploded in a hail of broken glass and flames.

The lights went out a few seconds later.

Jumping to his feet, Patronas ran into the bedroom where Costas was sleeping. "Melissa, wake up!" he yelled. "They're here. They're here. Take cover!"

He then did the same with Papa Michalis.

Within minutes, the entire front of the house was on fire. Patronas couldn't see for the smoke, couldn't see his way clear. Stumbling around, he tripped and fell headfirst into the flames. Within seconds, his pants were burning, tendrils of fire consuming the flesh of his legs.

"Help! Oh, God, help!"

Writhing in pain, he tried to crawl away.

Costas heard him screaming and came running. "Roll yourself up in the blanket!"

She and Papa Michalis then dragged him to safety. The fire department arrived a short time later and within minutes brought the fire under control.

"It wasn't a Molotov cocktail," one of the firemen told Patronas. "It was dynamite, a couple of sticks of dynamite."

They were standing outside, assessing the damage.

"When that young cop—the one you got stationed in the driveway— saw the man throw the dynamite, he opened fire on him and the man retaliated. He had a big gun, the cop said, a Kalashnikov maybe. Lit up the night. Mowed the trees down like a chainsaw."

Looking around, Patronas felt sick. Every living thing in the front yard was destroyed, the trees and bushes, the flowers Lydia had so painstakingly planted, all of it, gone. The house itself was badly damaged. All the windows in the front had been shot out and what remained of the porch was pockmarked with holes, huge gaping bullet holes in the wooden siding. Lydia would be heartbroken.

"Just one man?"

"As far as we know."

"Got balls, whoever he is."

"That he does. Fuse was lit. A moment's hesitation and he would have gone up, too, boom, just like the house."

"What happened to the electricity?"

"He cut the wires. DEH is coming to fix it, but it's going to take some time. You'll need to get some kerosene lanterns. We'll rig a tarp up over the front. You should be all right for the time being."

Patronas made a mental inventory. The windows and siding could be replaced; and new rose bushes planted. As for himself, he wasn't so sure. He was in shock and fast losing heart in his ability to do much of anything.

Maybe Stathis was right; and he should abandon the case.

"Boss wants us to quit," he told Tembelos after the firemen left.

"No way. Got to be Churchill not Chamberlain at a time like this Yiannis, and fight no matter what. We'll get them, we'll get the men who did this. And when we do, we will feast on their entrails."

Patronas ached all over and he let himself down on the step. He'd been patched up by the doctor, who'd dressed the burns on his legs and advised him to air them out. They would heal faster that way and there'd be less chance of infection. Patronas had readily complied and had hacked off the bottom half of his pants with a knife.

He didn't have much in the way in the way clothes anyway; and what he did have was now covered with ash at the bottom of the closet. Not that he cared. Usually, he bought shirts and pants in bulk and wore them until they were rags; and he was already long overdue for a restock. Lydia would have chided him about his state of undress; but she was not here, thank God. She and Ali were tucked safely away in Athens.

He still felt like he was on fire. Post-traumatic stress, the doctor had called it. Patronas had suffered from it before; and he recognized the symptoms, the agitation and bouts of terror. The previous episode had occurred after he was shot during another murder investigation. He'd spent the next three years dodging imaginary bullets and crying in his sleep. There were cops he knew who never got over it and suffered the rest of their lives.

It seemed unfair to him. Something terrible happens, it should only happen once. But it didn't work that way, not in his experience. Instead, it stayed with you, and you couldn't forget it, no matter how hard you tried. Trauma lived on forever. It had an afterlife like nuclear waste.

• • •

A reporter had been listening to the police scanner; and he arrived at the cottage and took a picture of Patronas in front of his bombed-out house.

It was a few hours after the explosion and Patronas' face was still covered with soot—the whites of his eyes gleaming like a madman's. Part of his scalp had been burned away and both of his legs were bandaged, the strips of white gauze visible below his abbreviated pants. He looked like he'd gone to war and lost.

The following day the photograph appeared on the front page of the national papers and on the television news. It was picked up by the international media and traveled around the world at the speed of light. "Mafia in Greece," was the headline.

Stathis was beside himself. "I'm organizing a task force," he told Patronas. "Same as they did in Sicily after the mafia blew up that magistrate, Giovanni Falcone, on the highway. We cannot have this, not in Chios, not in Greece. It simply will not be tolerated. The Ministry of Justice is monitoring the situation and I just got off the phone with them."

"When is the task force coming?"

"Tomorrow. We'll bring in the army if necessary. We need to shut this done."

"What about my house?"

"First, catch the perpetrator. After that we'll see."

"A whole wall is missing and the windows..."

"All in good time, Yiannis. All in good time."

Stathis continued to talk, recalling other bombings in Greece and their aftermath. They'd been politically motivated for the most part and had all happened a long time ago; and Patronas quickly tuned him out.

"A cautionary word, Patronas," Stathis said before he hung up. "In the future when you have your picture taken, you might want to put on some pants."

• • •

Leaving Ali in the cab, Lydia ran across the yard, fell into Patronas' arms and wept all over him.

"Yiannis, oh, dear God, Yiannis!!"

After establishing his injuries were not life-threatening, she then proceeded to berate him. This time the lecture was a lengthy one and focused on the need for trust in relationships and taking responsibility for one's actions which, according to her, he very rarely did. There'd been too many times when he'd held out on her. The stake-out at the house, being only the latest one.

"Tembelos said you got stabbed. Stabbed, Yiannis, stabbed! And you never said a word."

"I didn't want to upset you."

"And then you brought Costas here, knowing full well they'd come after her. But did you say anything about that? No."

"I was honor-bound to protect her."

"Honor-bound? Who are you? Sir Galahad? Nobody talks about honor anymore."

"I do. I believe in it."

"What about family? You believe in that, too?"

"Of course."

"Well, you need to start acting like it. You need to *share*."

The way she said 'share,' it was like she was holding up the Holy Grail.

"Can we talk about this another time?" Patronas said. "I've been injured and I'm a little tired now."

But like a dog with a bone, she kept gnawing. "They stabbed you and blew up our house. You put us all in danger and for what? To catch a phantom. I won't have it, Yiannis. I won't have you bringing criminals into our lives anymore."

"I'm a cop, Lydia," he said wearily. "Criminals come with the job."

"Fuck your job."

Patronas was stunned. Lydia was not one for salty language. She must be seriously upset.

"I'm tired, too." she continued, her voice thick. "Tired of coming in second, of being an afterthought with you. I wait at home night after night while off you go playing cops and robbers, and I never say a word. But this...this is too much."

She pointed at the house, the fire-blasted garden.

"I didn't do this, Lydia."

"Yes, you did. You set it in motion; and this is the result. At the very least, you should have told me."

"I needed to protect Costas. I have a responsibility. To her and those two dead women and all the other victims of these men. It's what I do, Lydia. It's who I am."

"What about your responsibility to Ali and me? Did you ever think of that? Suppose we'd been in the house when that man threw the dynamite? Suppose we'd been killed?"

Reaching down, she touched one of the rose bushes she'd planted. It had been sawed in half by gunfire and was obviously dying.

"Gone. Everything's gone."

"It'll be okay, Lydia. We can rebuild."

"It's no good, Yiannis. You and me. It's no good."

Patronas winced. The tongue has no bones and yet it can crush you.

"I am a cop," he said again. "And I have been for a long time. It's all I know. All I am. You knew that when you married me."

"Yes, but I never thought it would come to this." She was sobbing now, tears streaming down her face.

"I can retire."

"You must be kidding! Being a cop is your life. It always was and it always will be."

"No, it isn't. You are my life, Lydia., you and Ali. You're my life."

Usually this did the trick, but not this time.

"If only that were true," she said. "But we both know it isn't."

Patronas began to panic. "What do you want? What do you want from me?"

She was silent for a long time. "I don't know. All I know is you can't keep doing this. Ali has had enough trauma in his life. We can't subject him to more."

"Let me close the case. After that, we can talk."

"You don't get it, do you? You just don't get it. Sure, go ahead and close your damned case. I've had enough. I'm out of here and I'm taking Ali with me."

Turning on her heel, she walked back to the cab, said something to the driver; and he started the car. Ali had his face pressed against the window. He was saying something, but Patronas was too far away to hear it. *'Baba,'* it might have been. *'Baba.'* Daddy.

A moment later, they were gone.

Waving his arms in the air, Patronas hobbled after them on his wounded legs, "Lydia! Don't go! Stop! Stop!"

Tembelos had been standing in the doorway, listening. He helped Patronas back into the house. "You gonna go after her?"

"Not now. Later. After I solve the case."

"Might want to do it now. From the sound of things, that guy didn't just burn down your house, he burned down your marriage."

Chapter 25

Two days later, Kourelas called and told Patronas he had some information for him.

"Don't want to be seen talking to you," he said. "Get my throat cut same as that girl. There's a café called Zefyros In Vrondatos. Meet me there."

Given the burns on his legs, Patronas couldn't drive; and he asked Tembelos to take him. Vrondatos was very quiet; and the café was empty. Kourelas was sitting in the back, wearing sunglasses and a wool seaman's cap pulled low over his face. He was very nervous and kept looking around.

"Need my money," he said as soon as Patronas sat down.

"I need to hear what you've got."

"There's been talk of a boat. Men saying they got to work late a couple of nights from now, well after 2 a.m. A boat's coming in and they have been ordered to be on hand to load it."

"What's suspicious about a boat arriving?"

"Give me the money and I'll explain it to you."

Pulling out his wallet, Patronas counted out the fifty euros and slid them over to him.

Kourelas quickly stuffed the money in his pocket, then after taking one last look around, he leaned forward across the table. "No one loads a boat that late," he said in a low voice. "Maybe in a big port like Piraeus they do, but never here on Chios. And I do mean *never*. There's only one reason you would load a boat that late and that's because you don't want to be seen, that your cargo is illegal. Could be drugs, weapons, a whole lot of things. But illegal, for sure. One more thing. Those men, the ones I heard were talking, they're afraid of the owner of that boat. Real scared of him."

Pushing back his chair, Kourelas stood up. "I'm done here. If it's who I think it is, I don't want to be involved."

Patronas grabbed his arm. "I need a name."

"You think I'm stupid? No way."

• • •

"She's a sly one, Kyria Toula," Papa Michalis told Patronas when he returned from Vrondatos. "She organizes games with the children and tells them stories, all the while listening, listening. The little girl with the doll is a great favorite of hers; and they spend hours together. I wish I'd thought of it. It's a great cover."

"Father, children and priests?! For God's sakes! Don't you read the papers?"

Papa Michalis bristled. "Not all priests sin against the young, Yiannis. Only a few. And, I most assuredly, am not one of them."

"I never said you were."

"I would never hurt a child."

"Of course, you wouldn't."

This continued for some time. The priest proclaiming his innocence and Patronas trying to get him back on track.

"You were talking about Kyria Toula."

"Ah, yes, that's right. She said Liadis had a phone call yesterday—not on his office phone, a different one she'd never seen him use before—which caused him great distress. I can attest to that as I heard him, too. He was shouting something about a boat. 'No! No!' 'I won't do it.' And so forth and so on."

"A boat? Are you sure?"

"Absolutely. He was very loud, Liadis. Everyone in the camp could hear him."

"Thank you, Father. That's very helpful."

"Don't thank me, thank Kyria Toula. She's a maestro, that one. Took to espionage like a duck to water. Women do, I suppose. Subterfuge and deceit, it comes natural to them. One might say they are 'shape shifters.' First, they are one thing and then, presto, like magic, they turn into another."

"Shape shifters?"

The old man stroked his beard. "An interesting concept, don't you think? I got it from a science fiction show I saw."

Patronas sighed. No longer would it be be Sherlock Holmes, now it would be extraterrestrials and man-eating plants.

He was too tired to argue with Papa Michalis about the wisdom of gaining knowledge from television shows. As for women, he was as out to sea as the priest on that topic. He'd survived being blown up, but had that made Lydia happy? No, it had done just the opposite. As for Dimitra, his first wife, he'd never understood her either. Malice greased her wheels—that much he knew —but that was about it.

He knew he'd failed her as a husband. In love with another woman, he'd never been there for her, not even at the beginning. He hadn't withheld information as was the case with Lydia. No, with Dimitra, it had been much worse. It had been his heart.

Patronas' mother had assumed Dimitra had money—she certainly presented herself that way—and she'd forced him to go forward with the marriage for financial reasons. A terrible mistake as Dimitra turned out to be nearly as poor as they were, her dowry a wretched house next to a gas station.

Like Dimitra, the house itself had delusions of grandeur with a fancy portico and marble columns. Inside was a different story. A stage set in other words, in spirit identical to the phony villages Potemkin had built along the Volga River to fool the tsar.

Lydia had moved on from Dante and had him reading Russian history now which was how he knew about Potemkin.

He had liked the story—the idea of a fake front with nothing behind it. That had been him and Dimitra, the long hard years of their marriage.

It was different with Lydia. He'd been happy with her and now she'd up and left him.

No doubt about it, when it came to females, he'd given himself the *moutza*. Usually, you gave it to others—the open-handed gesture being the equivalent of 'shovel shit up your nose'—but time and time again he'd given it to himself. Shit and more shit. He was drowning in shit.

He and Papa Michalis were sitting together in the kitchen. The task force had duly arrived from Athens, but it hadn't amounted to much—two rookies from Kifissia, a wealthy suburb of Athens, who'd never investigated a murder before—and they'd all eaten souvlakis and drunk beer while Patronas brought them up to speed. The rookies were now fast asleep in the back of the cruiser, there being no room in the inn. Costas had also retired and just turned off the light in her room. Tembelos was outside, patrolling the beach with a gun. He'd refused to let Patronas accompany him.

"As the ancients said, 'making the same mistake, does not indicate an intelligent person."

"But I'm your superior officer."

"In what way are you my superior, Yiannis? Fire prevention? I'm standing guard and standing guard alone and that's all there is to it."

It was drafty in the house, the tarp being inadequate against the wind blowing in from the sea. Wrapping himself up in a blanket, Patronas struggled to get comfortable. The burns hurt worse at night, so bad there was no point in trying to sleep. He kept telling himself soon it would all be over. The killer would be in jail and the case solved; Lydia and Ali would return to him; and life would be good again. He wasn't comfortable praying—he'd forsaken God his entire adult life—but tonight he prayed for that. For his life to be as it once was. Nothing more. Just that.

• • •

Kourelas turned up dead the following morning. His body was found by a fisherman, floating near the entrance to the harbor. His tongue had been cut out; and he had been strangled.

A small crowd of onlookers were gathered around the body; and Patronas ordered Tembelos to hold them back.

The coroner, his face intent, was bending over the body. "You see the hyoid," he told Patronas, pointing to the bruising on Kourelas' neck. "That U-shaped bone? It's fractured. He was strangled, no question about it."

"Bare hands?"

"As I see no evidence of rope, no fibers of any kind, I'd say yes, most probably whoever did this, used their hands. But I can't say for sure until I get him back to the morgue and examine him more thoroughly."

"Let me know."

"Of course."

Patronas walked over to where Tembelos was standing. "Nothing more for us to do here, Giorgos. Let's go back to the station."

"What do you think happened? They catch him spying?"

"No. I think he was blackmailing them. Probably been doing it all along, playing me, playing them, trying to get as much money as he could out of both of us. I spoke to his wife earlier; and she said he was talking about being flush, buying himself a big flat screen television."

He looked back at the crime scene. "Poor fool. Taking a chance like that. He didn't know who he was dealing with."

Tembelos started the car. "He does now."

Chapter 26

"Dalia?" Kyria Toula called.

The Greek woman was standing outside the girl's tent in Vial, shielding her eyes from the sun. She'd bought the child a toy—a pink plastic convertible for her doll—and she wanted to give it to her.

"Dalia," she called again. "Come here, child. I have something for you."

The doll in the red dress was still there, upside down on the ground beside the bed Kyria Toula made for it, but the girl was nowhere to be seen.

The doll's position on the ground alarmed the Kyria Toula. Dalia always took great care of that doll. This was something she would never do.

She questioned a woman standing nearby, who told her Dalia's mother had gone shopping and perhaps the little girl had gone with her.

When the child's mother returned, though, she was alone. Liadis had come by earlier, Dalia's mother said and offered to take the child for ice cream. As he was the camp administrator, Dalia's mother assumed it was all right and had given her permission to go.

As they were communicating through the language app on the phone, it took some time before Kyria Soula fully understood what she was saying, Liadis' name not coming through clearly.

When she finally realized, she immediately called Patronas on her cell phone.

"A child's gone missing," she said. "Dalia, little Dalia, the one with the doll. The girl's mother said that Liadis took her for ice cream."

"How long ago?"

"Not long. Less than an hour."

• • •

Shouting to his staff, Patronas issued an all-points bulletin. "Arrest Liadis on sight. He might have a child with him, so proceed cautiously. No gunfire. No high-speed car chases. Once you have him, bring him here, the child, too, unless she needs medical attention. If she does, summon an ambulance and have her taken to the hospital."

He then ordered the manager of the airport to stop Liadis from boarding a plane. "Public or private, it makes no difference. If he shows up, hold him until I get there. "

He did the same with the Coast Guard, requesting they seal off the harbor until further notice.

"Just the ferries?" asked the Coast Guard officer.

"No. Yachts, tankers, everything."

He feared the worst. If the child had witnessed something incriminating in the camp, these men wouldn't hesitate. They'd kill her.

Kourelas had said the boat was coming in late that night; and Patronas was certain the girl's disappearance was connected to its arrival.

• • •

Liadis was sitting in the front seat of his BMW on the far side of the harbor. It was near where the trucks disembarked from the ferries which was why Patronas and Tembelos hadn't spotted him sooner; the trucks had obscured their view.

They'd been parked there for over an hour, watching him through binoculars. Patronas had alerted the other members of the force; and they were all in position, ready to move in and make an arrest.

"Can you believe that asshole?" Tembelos said. "He's wearing a fucking polo shirt. You'd think he was on his way to play golf."

"Just like John Gotti."

"Who the hell is John Gotti?"

"An American mafioso. They call him the 'dapper don.'"

"You do know your gangsters, Yiannis. I'll say that for you. I've always wondered why the mafia never took hold here. We're pretty much the same as the Sicilians."

"Couldn't get a group of Greeks to agree on anything, let alone how to run a criminal enterprise. You know the saying, 'two Greeks, three opinions.' It's true."

"What about the godfathers of night?"

"According to Stathis, they're a loose outfit, nothing like the mob in Sicily or the states."

Sitting in the cruiser, they continued to monitor the camp administrator. Patronas had held off arresting him, wanting to see if anyone approached the BMW, but with each passing minute, he grew more and more anxious about the girl. He needed to know where she was, what Liadis had done with her.

"I'm going to go get him," he said.

Drawing his gun, he walked over to the parked BMW and rapped on the window. He could hear music playing inside. Liadis was listening to *ksenitia*, a genre of Greek folk songs about emigration and homesickness, being a stranger in a strange land.

Liadis didn't know it yet, but he was about to become one of the men in those songs, not because he'd be leaving Greece, but because he'd be leaving civilized society and going to jail, a far more hostile and unforgiving place.

"Get out of the car!" Patronas shouted.

Smiling uncertainly, Liadis did as he was told. "What's going on, Chief Inspector?"

Patronas pushed him up against the BMW. "Where's the girl? What have you done with her?"

"What girl?" Liadis asked.

Patronas hit him in the face with the barrel of his gun. "Dalia. The one you took from the camp."

"I don't know what you're talking about."

"Stop fucking around." Raising his gun, Patronas pressed it to Liadis' forehead. "Where is she?"

Closing his eyes, Liadis sank down against the car. "She's in the trunk."

• • •

The child was lying on her side in the back of the BMW. She had a filthy gag stuffed in her mouth and her hands were tied behind her back with a length of wire. Her eyes widened when she saw Patronas and she struggled to free herself, her cries muffled.

Patronas lifted her out of the car and quickly undid the wire. It had torn her skin in places; and she was bleeding. But other than that, she seemed to be all right.

"You're safe now, Ralia. "We're going to take you to your *Omm*." He used the Arabic word deliberately, wanting her to understand it was over.

"*Omm!*" she wailed. "*Omm!*"

Dalia panicked when she saw Liadis standing next to the car. Backing away, she pointed at him and screamed and screamed.

Patronas showed her that Liadis was handcuffed, then looked up 'safe' in Arabic on his phone and repeated it over and over, but the child remained inconsolable.

Summoning a female officer from the station, he ordered her to drive the child back to Vial. "I'll take her statement later. Right now, she needs her mother."

"It's not what you think," Liadis told him. "I didn't hurt her. I'd never hurt a child."

Chapter 27

"I couldn't do it. I couldn't turn her over to them," Liadis said. "I was supposed to meet them and make the transfer, but I drove down to the harbor instead. I like to be by the sea. I find the water soothing. It calms me."

He'd made the same claim repeatedly since Patronas arrested him and read him his rights. According to him, he'd regretted seizing the child and was planning to return her to her mother unharmed. Not innocent, but not guilty either. A man caught up in another man's web.

As soon as they'd gotten to the station, Patronas had led him down the hall to the interrogation room and bolted him to the floor with a chain. Although the two of them had been in there for more than two hours, Liadis had yet to reveal the names of his co-conspirators. He denied all knowledge and kept saying that business at harbor had all been a great misunderstanding.

He'd asked repeatedly to speak to his lawyer

Ignoring the request, Patronas explained it would go better for him if he assisted the police in their investigation. A judge would take it into account and go easier on him.

Tembelos was standing outside the interrogation room, watching them through the one-way window. Patronas had refused to let him participate, afraid Tembelos wouldn't be able to control himself and would attack Liadis again.

When they'd opened the trunk and found the girl, Tembelos had yelled Liadis' wasn't fit to live and fired off a couple of rounds in the man's direction—a scene out of the wild west—and then proceeded to beat him half to death, cursing and spitting on him. Within minutes, the camp administrator had been covered with blood.

"*Τέρας!*" Tembelos kept shouting. "*Τέρας!*" Monster.

Patronas had taken his time pulling Tembelos off Liadis.

"Easy, Giorgos," he'd finally said. "Don't kill him. We need him."

Initially, Papa Michalis had sat in on the interrogation. Patronas had wanted him there as the priest was brilliant at eliciting confessions, but the old man had quickly withdrawn, after seeing Liadis' injuries, mumbling a prayer as if to protect himself from what was happening.

"I can't, Yiannis," he whispered. "Such venality not just on that man's par, but on ours."

"He was trafficking children, Father. Children."

"I know, I know. But still…"

"'Judge not' does not apply here,"

"It should, Yiannis. We should hold fast to decency even when faced with the devil. Hold fast to honor."

• • •

Patronas banged his fist on the table. "You keep talking about 'them.'" he shouted at Liadis. "Who are they? Who are these mysterious people you keep referring to?"

"They're from all over," the camp administrator replied. "Chechnya, Turkey, Greece…I don't know where I fit in. Greece, I suppose. I've lived here longer than I have lived anywhere else."

He said all this in a conversational manner, as if they were standing on the corner passing the time of day. He'd been behaving like this since they brought him in, never answering Patronas' questions or acknowledging in any way the trouble he found himself in.

It was an interesting performance—that studied obliviousness—given that he'd been charged with kidnapping and attempted murder and was handcuffed and chained to the floor. But, nevertheless, there he sat, his clothes stiff with blood, chatting amiably as if nothing was wrong.

Lydia had a name for this kind of behavior, 'compartmentalizing,' she called it. Patronas knew because she'd often accused him of it—boxing up whatever troubled him and refusing to acknowledge it. But Liadis took it to a whole new level.

Still to profess your innocence after a child has been found in the trunk of your car…That took some doing.

Patronas kept after him. "Who's the ringleader?"

"As I told you before, I am unfamiliar with him, nor do I know much about the hierarchy of his organization. I was nothing really, Chief Inspector, a low-level factotum at best. I never dealt with him, this so-called mastermind of yours. I only dealt with his employees, the foot soldiers in his army as it were."

Another lie. Liadis had to have been at least halfway up the criminal ladder. They wouldn't have paid him all that money otherwise. It had been one fairy tale after another; and Patronas was fed up with it.

"Do you know where their headquarters is? Where they're based?"

"It varies. One week here, one week there. These men have no allegiance to any country or any one person. They're nomads, both physically and emotionally. And, as you've seen, they do not hesitate to do what they're paid to do, including murder. They're mercenaries in every sense of the word."

Another non-answer.

"How did you get involved?"

"The usual way. Money. I borrowed from the wrong people and one day they came calling. It started small—'just point out the pretty women in the camp,' one of them told me—and then it escalated." For the first time, there was a hint of emotion in his voice, grievance. Those money lenders hadn't played fair.

Patronas had the feeling there was someone else lurking behind the man's carefully constructed façade, but who that person was, was anybody's guess.

He didn't buy Liadis' story about backing out of the transfer. If that were the case, why had he been at the harbor? There were far better places to look at the sea on the island. The man hadn't had a change of heart, no matter what he said. He'd been there to hand over the girl.

"Who put you in touch with them?"

"My brother-in-law, Michalis Papoulis. He knew who to go to."

"What's his relationship with them?"

"Drugs. They are his supplier."

"What was the process? First, you identify a woman, then what happens?"

Liadis wouldn't meet his eyes. "They take them, put them in cages and load them on a boat."

"Cages?"

Liadis nodded. "Like the one they put that officer of yours in. They only have a couple of them; and they re-use them."

"Raina Mustafa?"

"What can I say? She got in their way. After they murdered her, I wanted out, but they refused to release me. I had a dog, a little Yorkshire Terrier named Rambo, and the man they sent snapped his neck with his bare hands. He told me if I didn't cooperate, he would do the same to me."

Laidis' hands shook as he told the story. "After that, they had me. I would have done anything they asked."

"Can you describe him? This man they supposedly sent?"

"He was big, very big with jet black hair. His eyes, I remember his eyes especially. They were empty, totally devoid of light. He was from Chechnya, I learned later, and his name was Khasan."

"Anything else about him you remember?"

"Yes. He had a tattoo on his left hand."

"What kind of a tattoo?"

"Writing. Some kind of writing in a ring of stars."

"Was he the one who knifed me? The guy in the wetsuit?"

Liadis nodded. "Yes. That was Khasan. A true psychopath. The others wouldn't let him near the merchandise. They were afraid he'd damage it."

"Merchandise?" Patronas fought to control himself.

"That's what they call the people they're trafficking. 'The merchandise.'"

"Did he dynamite my house, too?"

"No. That was a Greek named Manos. No need to search for him. One of your men shot him that night and his wound got infected. He died of sepsis. As for your Officer Costas, that was different. They sent three recent hires after her. I don't know their names. They were only supposed to rough her up, but they got carried away."

"I repeat: who is this 'they' you keep referring to?"

"I don't know. As I told you before, there is no structure to any of it as far as I could see. One day Khasan is in charge. Another day, someone else. It depends on what needs to be done."

"If you wanted someone killed, who would you send?"

"Khasan. Khasan for sure. Like I said, he's from Chechnya. I don't know who trained him, but whoever it was , they did a good job. He's like a machine. Dead to life. No feelings whatsoever."

"How many of these men are there on Chios?"

"Usually two or three, but sometimes as many as five."

He began to weep. "Chief Inspector, I beg you, please don't judge me. I truly regret what I've done."

Patronas pushed back his chair and stood up. "All you regret is getting caught."

"Say what you will. I shall never forgive myself."

"Neither will we, Liadis. Rest assured, neither will we."

"I never intended to harm anyone."

"You were going to give that little girl to them!" Patronas shouted. "The one who was in the trunk of your car. That's one victim. How many others have there been?"

"You know already. Those four you questioned me about. The ones who went missing."

"I thought they were women."

"No, they were kids, Chief Inspector. All four of them were kids."

"You said it was pretty women they were interested in."

"I lied. It was always kids. From the very beginning, it was kids. I just couldn't admit it. Not to you, not to myself."

"What do they want kids for? What the hell do they do with them?"

"I never asked." Liadis looked down. "I didn't want to know."

"What happened to them?"

"I repeat I don't know and that's the truth. My role ended at the camp, what came after... It was out of my hands."

Liadis asked to call his wife before he was locked up, but Patronas refused.

"We are going to arrest your brother-in-law, Michalis Papoulis; and we don't want you to warn him. The two of you are going to jail for a very long time, Liadis. Chances are neither of you will last very long in prison. Different rules there. Men inside don't much care for people like you, people who hurt children."

• • •

After locking Liadis in a cell, Patronas returned to his desk, called Stathis and relayed what he'd learned.

"Kids," Stathis said. "Mother of God, Mother of God."

"Liadis' brother-in-law, Michalis Papoulis, put him in touch with the traffickers. He's in Athens. You need to arrest him."

"I'll see to it. Anyone else?"

"A man named Khasan. He's from Chechnya."

"He in Athens, too?"

"No. I have reason to believe he's still on Chios."

"First name?"

"Unknown. He might well be the ringleader."

"You want help tracking him down?"

"No. I want to do this myself."

"Very well, Patronas. I'll see what I can find out about him and get back to you. A man like that, he's got to have a record."

"Thank you, sir."

"From what you've said, Chios is just a way station; and the real trafficking is going on elsewhere, so he might well be employed by someone else. We'll need to pool our resources if we are going to be effective, locate the leadership of this organization and root it out."

"I know a policeman in Turkey; and I'll call him and see what he knows. Raina Mustafa was living in a camp along the Syrian border; and that's where it all started."

"This Liadis, he's from Egypt, isn't he?"

"That's what he told me."

"Good, good. That will make it easier when I speak to the press. No one wants a Greek to be involved in something like this. It's always better if it's a foreigner."

Patronas swore under his breath. As if Liadis' nationality mattered. Fighting to keep his voice level, he said. "A trawler is arriving late tonight and I'm heading down to the harbor to see if I can intercept it.

"A trawler, huh? That means they are clever. You could put a nuclear bomb in one of those boats; and no one would be the wiser."

They talked for a few more minutes; "Be on your guard, Patronas. These aren't ordinary criminals you're dealing with. These men are σατανικός." Satanic.

Chapter 28

"Starting at nine o'clock tonight, we will monitor all traffic in and out of the harbor," Patronas announced. "You will examine every truck that arrives, every car and every boat."

"What are you looking for?" a young patrolman asked.

Ten people were assembled in the conference room at the police station; and Patronas was explaining the logistics of the operation he had planned. Based on what Kourelas had said, nothing would happen before two a.m. when the boat arrived, but he wanted them in place at the harbor well before then.

"We are after all merchandise arriving by any means and the people responsible for that merchandise. Ideally, we will intercept it before it gets loaded onboard the boat and arrest whoever might be connected to it. I repeat, we are after all merchandise—no matter how innocuous it appears. We'll sort it out later. We want whoever brings it, the longshoremen who handle it and the crew of the boat it is bound for. But, most importantly, we want the man or men in charge. The one who owns it."

Patronas then handed out walkie-talkies and went over how to use them.

"Station yourselves twenty meters apart in places where you won't be readily seen and check in with me every fifteen minutes. Alert me of any movement. You see something? I want to hear about it."

• • •

It had started to rain again; and the bars along the waterfront were empty. The aging trawler was tied up near the custom house on the eastern side of the quay, rust showing beneath its white paint. Judging by the name painted on the stern, *Okhotnik,* it was Russian.

Patronas hadn't seen the trawler in the harbor before. It must have arrived when he'd been preoccupied with Liadis. One of his officers had spotted it earlier that evening and phoned it in.

"Something strange about it," the man told the dispatcher at the station. "No one's onboard as far as I can see. The crew must have left before we got here, before we started the stake-out."

Cautiously, Patronas drove closer and parked. The boat was registered in Panama which he found suspicious. In Greece, luxury yachts, oil tankers and container ships frequently had Panamanian registration, their owners seeking to avoid taxes, but trawlers and other fishing boats rarely did. Russia? Panama? It didn't compute.

The metal door to the pilothouse was hanging open, clanging in the wind, but as far as he could tell, there was no one inside.

He was wearing a Kevlar vest as was Tembelos. Both were heavily armed, his friend with an AK-47, himself with a Glock and an Uzi. The rest of the force was spread out along the quay, waiting to move in when Patronas gave the signal.

Before boarding the trawler, Patronas took a picture of the stern with his phone and sent it off to the Coast Guard. The captain of the boat would have needed permission from the Coast Guard to enter the harbor which meant there'd be a paper trail.

If the trawler had indeed started in Odessa, its journey would have been a long one, traversing the entire Black Sea, the Sea of Marmara and the Dardanelles Straits before docking in Chios. Much too far to catch fish. The cost of fuel alone would be prohibitive. In addition, it had no nets that he could see, no visible haul lines or winch drums. If anything, it looked abandoned.

Perhaps Chios wasn't such a backwater, after all.

Keeping his head down, Patronas sprinted up the ramp and stepped out onto the deck of the trawler. He stood there for a few minutes and listened for voices, but he heard nothing. All was quiet.

He began slowly inching toward the pilothouse, his footsteps loud against the metal. It was after eleven o'clock at night; and he was counting on the darkness to hide him.

The trawler didn't smell of fish, nor did he see any of the paraphernalia he associated with fishing, no nets or towing blocks, no grappling hooks. It had been swept clean.

The pilothouse stank of cigarettes and diesel fuel. A map was lying open on the console, a line drawn on it from Odessa to Chios. Apparently, it had stopped off on the Greek island of Lesbos, then made its way on to Izmir in Turkey before arriving at the harbor in Chios.

Leaving everything as he'd found it, he exited the pilothouse and explored the rest of the deck and the quarters below, doing as much as he could in the dark and only switching on the flashlight when necessary. He saw nothing personal, nothing that might have belonged to a crew member. The boat was strangely anonymous.

Although Patronas was convinced the crew had fled, he turned on the walkie-talkie and ordered the men on the quay to continue their watch.

"Warn me if you see anyone coming."

Most trawlers had a hatch near the prow where the crew emptied out the nets and dumped the fish; and Patronas quickly located the one on the *Okhotnik*. Moving as quietly as possible, he slid the cover back and let himself down into the hold.

The darkness was total, the only sound the occasional creaking of the boat. Again, there was no smell of fish, only a faint hint of human feces. Switching on the flashlight, Patronas got down on his hands and knees and examined the metal floor, marking out a grid in his mind and going over it as carefully as he could.

He found the broken fingernail first. Painted pink, it was lying in one of the grooves. It was so small it could only have come from a child. Also small was the bracelet he discovered a few minutes later, the chain so thin it was almost invisible. It had a single charm on it, a disc with an Arabic letter engraved on it.

As he'd feared, the cargo of the trawler had not been fish. It had been young children. But what had become of them? They weren't on Chios. He would have known. Turkey maybe. He remembered what the policeman in Izmir had told him— the area was fast becoming one of the centers of sexual trafficking. Maybe even the heart of it, women arriving daily from Russia and Eastern Europe.

"They think they're going to be models, movie stars," Hazmas Arsian had said. "And you see where they end up. Selling themselves in a field like the one by the airport."

But kids, Hazmas had not mentioned any kids.

Patronas placed the bracelet in one evidence bag, the fingernail in another. He'd have to remember to label them as to the time and place of their discovery, maintain the chain of evidence.

Playing the flashlight over the surface, he studied the Islamic charm. He hadn't wanted to believe what Liadis had told him, but here was proof, irrefutable proof.

He looked around in despair. Not women, not adults...kids.

Still on his hands and knees, he made his way forward until he reached the far end of the hold. The smell of feces was stronger here as was the stench of fear. He could almost hear the kids crying as he crawled, weeping for their mothers.

Perhaps the man, who owned the boat, had intended for a certain child to make this journey—a child Raina Mustafa knew and cared for—and she'd resisted; and he'd had her killed. As a motive for murder, it worked.

A knife across the throat would have been merciful compared to this.

Patronas had no idea of what had transpired within the dank walls of the hold, how many children had been trapped in here or what had happened to them. Like Liadis, he didn't want to know.

He hoisted himself back out onto the deck and stayed there for a few minutes, breathing in the night air and weeping.

Tembelos walked toward him. "You okay, Yiannis?"

Patronas waved him off. "Go away, Giorgos."

Turning his face away, he continued to cry.

• • •

Although it was very late, the Turkish police officer, Hazmas Arsian, was still working. He was surprised to hear from Patronas. "Chief Inspector, have you found the man you were after?"

Stammering in English, the only language they had in common, Patronas quickly shared what he had discovered.

"Young children?" Hazmas Arsian said after Patronas finished. "No, no. This cannot be."

"I have a signed confession from one of the participants. There's a criminal syndicate operating in the migrant camps, kidnapping children and selling them. I'm not sure of the last, but it is the only thing that makes sense."

"Why? What do they want them for?" Hazmas Arsian asked, his voice shrill. "These children? Are they harvesting their organs? Using them for sex? What? What?"

"I don't know. They were transporting them on a Russian trawler, the *Okhotnik*, which they have since abandoned. The crew has left Chios and most probably is headed your way which is why I'm calling. They can't fly out of Greece. All the airports have been alerted. And crossing the border into Albania or Bulgaria is no longer possible. Turkey is their only hope."

Hazmas Arsian's voice took on a new urgency. "These men, how will they come?"

"In a small motorboat, I believe, or perhaps in an inflatable, a Zodiac or something similar. Nothing flashy. They don't want to draw attention to themselves. They're mixed in terms of nationality and will probably be traveling with fake passports."

"How will I identify them?"

"Five to six foreign men on a Zodiac? It shouldn't be too hard."

"I must abide by the law. On what grounds should I arrest them?"

"Kidnapping. Murder. Whatever it takes. Thousands of migrant children have gone missing since the crisis began. These men are responsible for at least some of them."

"I will find them; and they will name names. This is a vile thing; and it must be stopped. The search will take some time—there are many coves and inlets, places where a little boat might drop anchor—but I assure you, they will be found and dealt with. You have my word."

• • •

Before leaving the harbor, Patronas and Tembelos cordoned off the Russian trawler. Patronas had spoken to Stathis; and he was sending a team of forensic technicians to go over it. The Coast Guard was also at work, tracing the boat back to its point of origin, seeking to find out the name of its owner.

The sun had risen; and the water of the harbor was awash with light. There was Turkish word in Turkish for sunlight on the Bosporus, the legendary channel of Istanbul, but Patronas couldn't remember it. He'd always found solace in the play of light across the sea, but today it brought him no comfort.

"You know, Giorgos," he said. "If it hadn't been for me, Ali might well have been one of those kids on that boat. It makes me sick just thinking about it. Is it luck? Is that all it is? One kid makes it; and the others don't?"

"You're asking the wrong question. What you should be asking is why people do such things. We figure that one out, we could save the world."

"I'd be happy just to save a corner of it."

"You did, Yiannis. Trust me, you did."

• • •

Liadis' brother-in-law, Michalis Papoulis, was arrested; and Stathis assigned a forensic accountant to go through both his and Liadis' finances, seeking to trace the illicit money the men had received back to its source.

The prosecutor had already presented the case to the investigating judge, a necessary step given Greek law which stipulated it must be done within twenty-four hours after a person was arrested.

The judge had quickly agreed to pre-trial detention, stating Liadis should be remanded into custody, based on 'the reasonable suspicion he was guilty of the crime under investigation.' As evidence, the photo of the girl tied up in the trunk of the administrator's car had been irrefutable.

Patronas still wasn't sure what role Liadis had played in the trafficking. Whether or not, he was the mastermind.

"He's not man enough," Tembelos insisted when they discussed it. "You ever catch a whiff of him. He must bathe in aftershave."

"You can smell good and still be a killer."

"Come on, Yiannis. You know what I'm saying."

In other words, Liadis was too much of a sissy. He also appeared to have genuine remorse about the killing of Raina Mustafa, the remnants of a conscience. Not much of one, it was true, but it was not completely absent either. He knew what he'd done was wrong, not just in the legal sense, but in the moral one.

Still, Patronas had his doubts. Even in jail, the man had held back, unwilling to reveal his true nature. In addition, he had served in three different camps which meant he could easily have set up the trafficking operation—and then there was his love of money.

Papa Michalis had quoted the bible when he and Patronas had spoken of Liadis.

"His gold and silver are corroded. Their corrosion will testify against him and eat his flesh like fire."

"But what role did he play? Was he in charge?"

"I don't think so. His greed makes him weak. Even if he'd set it up originally, he wouldn't have lasted as godfather. Others—far more ruthless than he is—would have quickly pushed him aside."

Khasan, Patronas thought.

From Liadis' description, the Chechen fit the bill. A man who thrived on violence, welcomed it even.

Interestingly, Liadis' wife, Chryssoula had yet to visit her husband in prison and so he spent his days alone, his crimes rendering it too dangerous for him to mingle with the other inmates. The warden had insisted on this.

"He won't survive if we release him into the general population. The men here, they hate people like him. They'll kill him."

• • •

The Turk called back three days later. "We have four men in custody," he said. "There were six, but two of them drowned when we rammed their boat."

"You rammed their boat?"

"Yes. Perhaps we were overzealous, but they gave us no choice. When we approached their vessel—as you anticipated it was an inflatable—they tried to outrun us. An unwise decision on their part, very unwise."

"Where are they from?"

"It was a very mixed group. Two Russians, a Greek and a Turk. A kind of United Nation of criminals."

"Any Chechens?"

"No. I spoke to them at length. One of them—the Turk—was very familiar with the trafficking. It wasn't easy to get him to talk, but in the end, I prevailed."

"What did he tell you?"

"That your murder victim, the girl Raina, was very brave. She witnessed the kidnapping of a child in a camp on the Syrian border and tried to stop the same thing from happening in your camp there, the one on Chios. They ordered her to stop, but she wouldn't; and they killed her."

"Who gave the order?"

"He wouldn't say. He's like a canary now and singing his head off, but only up to a point. He's no fool. He doesn't want to incriminate himself. As for the others, they are not so talkative. But they will be. Trust me, they will."

"What happened to the children?"

"Some of them were sold to men and women who cannot have children of their own. People who are too impatient to go through the proper channels and wait their turn. These adoptions generate a lot of money, he said, and they were very popular for this reason. Other children were sent off to be trained as pickpockets. There's a kind of factory, apparently, where they teach them to be fast with their fingers and fast on their feet. It's in Greece. I will send you the address."

"And the rest?"

"Their fate is a sad one. The pretty ones, they became the playthings of men."

• • •

Hazmas Arsian emailed Patronas the transcript of the interview; and Patronas took the names of those arrested, ran through the international database and quickly traced them. They were low-level criminals for the most part and didn't appear to share the same appetite as their customers— not a single charge of child abuse or pedophilia had ever been filed against them. In the end, it had been about money, only money.

The Turk had also sent him mugshots of the men; and Patronas laid them out on his desk and studied them, searching for some sign of the evil which had possessed them. But there was nothing.

"What do you expect?" Tembelos said when Patronas showed him the photos. "Horns and a tail? Can't you see, they're just like us. A little vacant maybe, but that's how people look in a mugshot. Like someone hit them over the head with a hammer."

Remembering Eichmann, Patronas kept shifting the photos around on his desk. The German had been called 'colorless' and 'ordinary' by the reporters at his trial, exactly like the men in these photographs. Somehow, that made it all worse.

"I will leap into my grave laughing because I have five million human beings on my conscience," Eichmann had said.

Patronas shook his head. Maybe Tembelos was right; and psychopaths didn't have 'evil' stamped on their foreheads, but it was there. The evil was always there.

Later that day, he forwarded the material Hazmas Arsian had sent him Stathis in Athens, who in turn alerted Interpol and other international law enforcement organizations. Within twenty-four hours, plans were in place to roll up the entire network both in Greece and abroad.

Working with local police forces, Interpol raided the sites where the children were held; and by the end of the operation, more than a hundred children had been found. Many of them were orphans—children no one would miss—which was why they had been targeted by the traffickers. The rest would be returned to their parents as soon as their parents could be located.

Over fifteen people were arrested; and, like Hazmas Arsian had said, it was a United Nations of criminals. Patronas wanted to believe the leader had been captured in the raid—the person who had set it all in motion— but there was no way of knowing as those arrested refused to speak. Khasan was not among them. Patronas didn't know how, but the Chechen had managed to slip through the net and escape.

They had no photograph of him to post in airports, no way Interpol could alert law enforcement officials across the world. He was in the wind.

• • •

The trafficked orphans would all end up in state-run facilities. "I wish it were different, but that's the way it is," Stathis told Patronas.

In preparation for the upcoming trial, Patronas interviewed a few of the children in one of the facilities. The staff members seemed to care deeply for them; and they were being taught everything—art, music, mathematics, science and, most importantly, Greek. Far more important, there was a sense of warmth and security in the place. He felt it as he walked down the halls, the walls bright with pictures the children had painted. Still, no child should have to grow up in an institution and he would have gladly adopted the lot of them if he could, taken them home with him and been a father to them.

Interpol had not found all the children missing from the camps in Greece. Patronas had trouble accepting this. The fate of the lost children haunted him; and he often found himself unexpectedly in tears.

He and Hazmas Arsian spoke on the phone after it was all over.

"We've done what we could, but it is like an octopus, this thing," the Turk said mournfully. "An ugly creature with tentacles. You cut off one of them and another grows in its place."

"What are you saying?" Patronas asked.

"As long as there are men with these hungers, there will be men who feed them.".

Chapter 29

The day after the raid, Stathis called a press conference. Standing in front of television cameras and a huge group of reporters, he discussed the operation and paid tribute to those under his command and, of course, to himself. "These officers have saved the lives of innumerable children This cancer has been removed from Greek soil."

Liadis was never mentioned. It had been a group of foreigners—'evil men from abroad' was how Stathis characterized them—who'd been responsible.

Stathis also announced he was establishing a protocol to protect the children residing in the camps. "In the future," he intoned, "staff members will be required to know the names of all the children in these camps, also the identity of those responsible for them and the nature of their relationship. In addition, camp administrators are to institute a daily roll call and make sure all children are accounted for. Personnel have been instructed to remain vigilant during their shifts and report any suspicious activity to the appropriate authorities. Strangers will have to sign in before entering the camp and present valid IDs."

On and on it went.

Clutching the podium, Stathis ended with a great crescendo. 'I promise you the children of Greece will be safe, whether they are recent arrivals or native-born. I shall protect them. My men shall protect them. It is our scared duty as officers of the law."

Remembering what Hazmas Arsian said about the migrants pouring into Turkey, how in the end the numbers had defeated him, Patronas doubted Stathis' mandate would make much difference. He himself would do his best as would Tembelos and the other members of the force on

Chios, but even if they succeeded in getting rid of the traffickers forever, the camps would remain. Hell on earth, places where no human being should ever be forced to live.

The press played up the fact that the children had been housed in cages. Tembelos had found the cages under a tarp when he and Patronas had returned to the trawler with the forensic team. They were the same kind farmers used to house animals bound for slaughter, which in a sense, the trafficking had been.

Tembelos had gone berserk when he saw them and kicked one of them into the sea.

"Don't be doing that," Patronas cautioned." We need to go over them and check them for fingerprints. They will be crucial evidence when the case comes to trial."

• • •

Liadis didn't survive. He was found lying on the floor of his cell without a mark on him. He'd been in solitary confinement; and no one had gone near him since he was locked up. Only a single guard, who passed his meals through a slot in the door on a tray. Consequently, the coroner, Dimitri Constantinou, ruled that he died of natural causes.

"You have to do an autopsy," Patronas insisted. "Someone killed him. I'm sure of it."

"How?" the coroner asked. "There's not a mark on him."

"Poison?"

"Unlikely. He ate exactly what the other inmates did; and they are all still with us."

Patronas and the coroner were in the morgue, standing next to the steel gurney. Patronas motioned to the administrator's body. "What do I have to do to convince you?"

"Chief Inspector, what do you want from me? He was alone in a locked cell. Not every dead person is murdered."

"Somebody got to him. As you know, he was the key witness in a major child trafficking case."

Constantinou shrugged. "I repeat, he was by myself. The other prisoners didn't have access to him."

"Maybe a guard. I don't know."

In the end, the coroner gave in and performed the autopsy with Patronas in attendance. He recorded himself as he worked, chattering into a mike as he pulled out lengths of intestines and weighed Liadis' heart and lungs.

Patronas held it together until Constantinou started in on the skull, at which point he fled the room. He only wished he could block out the sound, the terrible whine of the saw that the coroner was using.

Constantinou called him back a few minutes later. "All done."

"Find anything?"

"He died of a myocardial infraction. In layman's terms, heart failure."

"No evidence of poison?"

"None whatsoever. I'll run a toxicology screen just to be sure, but it will take some time. The coroner looked down at the body. "I remember when I was in medical school, there was a very religious student who thought he'd see the human soul when he opened someone up. After a time, he gave up the search. 'We're nothing,' he told me. 'Just liquids and flesh.' And so we are...sad, isn't it?"

• • •

Liadis was to be buried in Athens and Patronas flew there to attend the funeral. He planned to photograph those in attendance and run their pictures through the police database. It wouldn't hurt; and there was a chance he'd learn something.

It was a very small gathering. Liadis' brother-in-law was in jail, but the warden released him to attend the funeral. He entered the church in handcuffs with a policeman on either side of him. He stood next to the open coffin for a long time, weeping quietly, then took a seat in the back. Patronas watched him, wondering if it was his dead brother-in-law he was crying about or himself.

He searched the pews for Liadis' wife, Chryssoula, but she was nowhere to be seen which surprised him. In Greece, you are required to attend the funerals of people you know. It was an iron-clad rule, especially if you are a close relative, let alone a spouse. Yet the grieving widow hadn't seen fit to show herself.

Poor Liadis. He'd been enraptured by Chryssoula. Patronas had seen the way he'd looked at her, the longing in his eyes. She would have been an expensive toy, especially given the twenty-year difference in their ages. Liadis had desperately wanted to please her—that petulant brat of a woman—and he had ended up selling his soul to do it.

Outside a doll, inside plague.

And, so, it had been.

As for the other attendees at the funeral, they were mostly reporters, who left before the service was over. A single wreath marked Liadis' passing. It was from his assistant in the camp—Patronas recognized the name—and it was very modest, a single ring of faded, yellow carnations.

In a few years, they would gather up Liadis' bones and put them in a metal box as was the custom in Greece. Most probably no one would come forward to claim them; and he would join the legions of the nameless dead. Not mourned on this earth and in hell forever after.

With the police escort standing by, Patronas questioned Liadis' brother-in-law, Michalis Papoulis, after the service. Even in handcuffs, he was a compelling figure.

'He has the milk of birds,' Patronas' mother had always said of such people. In other words, he'd been blessed with good looks, blessed beyond measure.

Other than admitting he'd given his brother-in-law the name of the money lender, he denied all knowledge of the affair. Like Liadis, he, too, claimed he was innocent, unwillingly caught up in a criminal conspiracy he'd wanted no part of.

"Dimitri would still be alive if I hadn't given him that name. It was an alias as it turned out; and his phone number has been disconnected."

They talked for nearly an hour; and in the end, Patronas believed him. 'A person without bones,' again his mother's words. Dissolute and indolent. He lacked the energy to be a criminal, a godfather of night.

• • •

The coroner called Patronas and told him he was releasing the bodies of Raina Mustafa and Amira Al-Bashir; and they were buried two days later. The delay was not in keeping with Muslim custom, but there was nothing Patronas could do about it. The Syrian woman in the camp had seen to the ritual bathing of the bodies and the placing of them in white cotton shrouds. They'd then overseen the burials, making sure the dead women faced Mecca, in keeping with Islamic tradition.

Patronas had insisted that the funeral announcement with the women's names be plastered all over Chios; and he was gratified at the number of people who came. Many were from the camp, but there were Greeks there as well.

He remembered what Hazmas Arsian had said about Raina's courage, how she'd tried to protect children both Turkey and Greece; and he grieved for her.

The Syrian women, who had known Raina, spoke to him with tears in their eyes after the service was over. He had no idea what they were saying—it wasn't the time to consult his phone—but, judging by their expressions, they were mourning her, too.

Amira Al-Basjar's family was distraught and withdrew immediately after the funeral. Patronas could hear the children crying inside the tent, the voice of an older woman comforting them.

Her death was his fault. He should have realized the danger she was in and put her in some sort of witness protection program away from the camp, saved her somehow.

Patronas stood outside the tent for a long time, staring at the language app on his phone, trying to find the right words to say to Amira Al-Bashir's family. Kyria Toula finally pulled him away.

"Leave them."

"I want to tell them how sorry I am."

"Words are cheap. Do something for them instead. Buy coats for the children or books so they can learn. Tell them you're doing it in memory of her."

Chapter 30

Every morning before he drove to the station on his moped, Patronas would call Lydia. The phone would ring and ring, but she would never pick up. Still, he kept at it. It was a kind of ritual for him. First, he'd take a shower and get dressed, then he'd drink a cup of coffee and make the call, letting the phone ring exactly ten times before hanging up.

It couldn't be over, the two of them, he kept telling himself. One day she'd answer and all would be as it once was between them. They might have lost the house, but surely not each other.

The week after Stathis' press conference, she finally answered the phone.

"Oh, Yiannis," she said. "Those children. I saw it on the news. Cages. They put them in cages."

They talked for a long time. "I'm sorry," she said. "I had no idea what you were doing, what was at stake here. But no matter, I should have stood by you. I shouldn't have run away."

"It's okay, Lydia. It's not easy being married to a cop."

"You saved those children. If it hadn't been for you, they would have perished." Her voice faltered.

"I had help. Tembelos was with me all the way. Costas and Papa Michalis. I wasn't alone in this, Lydia. Even Stathis lent a hand."

"Ali and I are coming back to Chios tomorrow night. I already bought the tickets."

• • •

The next morning Patronas got a haircut and, knowing it would please Lydia, had his moustache trimmed. The barber waxed it a little and twirled up the ends, Poirot-style. Put some pomade on his hair.

Next he bought himself a jaunty new tangerine-colored shirt and pair of khaki pants and purchased a train set for Ali, a fancy one with lights and a steam engine that smoked. He also bought groceries, mopped the kitchen floor and changed the sheets on the air mattresses. The house was still a wreck, but at least it was clean. He even shined his shoes.

A crew of workmen were hard at work outside, installing new windows; and he'd hired a local man to replace the dead bushes in the garden. A row of new rosebushes now graced the path leading up to the front door. He hadn't known what color Lydia preferred and had bought one in every shade, a sort of a rainbow effect.

He got to the airport early, a bouquet of roses in hand. Passengers were already milling around outside, saying their good-byes and gathering up their suitcases. Many were tourists, sunburned and exhausted, but there were Greeks in the crowd as well.

They never traveled light, his people, Patronas thought, eyeing the boxes of food piled up in the parking lot. Tins of olive oil and spoon sweets—fruit preserved in sugar—bunches of oregano, bottles of mastic liquor and ouzo. You name it, his fellow islanders were transporting it. Did they not know there was food in Athens?

He'd seen the same phenomenon once in a local supermarket. There'd been an incident with Turkey; and old women had been filling their grocery cars with bags of sugar in preparation for war. Famine had followed the German invasion in World War II and more than a million Greeks had died. Those old women with the sugar hadn't forgotten and were taking the necessary steps to protect themselves and their families.

Like many things, going hungry leaves an indelible mark, not just on you, but on subsequent generations. Trauma, he concluded, trauma yet again.

Suddenly, a blonde man wearing sunglasses and a Greek fisherman's hat rushed by him. Although the plane to Athens wasn't due to leave for over two hours, he was running. Strange, Patronas thought. Also strange was the man's blonde hair, even a little jarring given his Middle Eastern coloring and those ferocious black eyes. A wolf in sheep's clothing. There was something familiar about the way he moved, the way he held himself.

Pushing open the glass door, the man entered the terminal. He had a tattoo on his hand. Cyrillic letters enclosed in a circle of stars. Patronas recognized it instantly.

Khasan.

Patronas pulled out his cell phones and called Tembelos.

"He's here. Khasan is here. He's about to board the plane to Athens. Call the head of the airport and tell him to delay departure, then round up as many people as you can and get here as fast as you can."

"You armed?"

"No. I left my gun at home. Lydia is flying in with the boy; and I didn't want to scare him."

"Wait for us. We're on our way."

Patronas followed Khasan into the terminal. It wasn't large—one room basically with a single exit—and he easily tracked the Chechen's progress as he checked in at the ticket counter and made his way through security.

The man behind the Hertz counter was watching Patronas. "This about those kids?" he asked in a low voice, pointing to Patronas' badge. "You after one of those fuckers?"

"Yes," Patronas said. "The man in charge."

• • •

Both Tembelos and Melissa Costas were in Kevlar vests and heavily armed, rifles, handguns, the works. Seeing the weapons, the people in the terminal began backing away; and the atmosphere shifted and became alive with fear.

Within minutes, the entire airport was surrounded. The two police officers were in position by the door leading out onto the tarmac, two more standing by the entrance in front, effectively sealing off the building.

The plan was to encircle Khasan, handcuff him and drag him out to the police cruiser in the parking lot, read him his rights in the car.

"Go!" Patronas shouted.

Tembelos and Costas ran toward the Chechen with their guns raised, shouting for him to freeze.

But Khasan was too fast for them. Grabbing an elderly man, he whipped out a knife and held it up to his throat.

"One more step and he dies!" He shouted in English.

He dug the knife into the man's neck, not deeply, but enough to draw blood.

The elderly man cried out, writhing in agony, his face contorted with pain.

Seeing the blood, the crowd inside the building immediately panicked, people shoving and pushing, desperate to get away. An old woman got knocked out of her wheelchair and the noise was deafening.

Taking advantage of the chaos, Patronas snuck up behind Khasan and jumped up on his back.

Grabbing the Chechen around the neck, he held on for dear life. Startled, Khasan released the elderly man, who dropped to the floor and lay there, whimpering and holding his bleeding neck.

Khasan struggled to shake Patronas loose. Raising the knife, he tried to slash him with it, but Patronas kept shifting his weight and darting out of the way.

The two of them continued their savage dance through the terminal, the Chechen, an immense bear of man, stumbling around with Patronas, who was half his size, clinging to his back. When the knife failed to dislodge him, Khasan smashed him hard against a cement wall and then into one of the glass doors, shattering it into a thousand pieces. Still, Patronas held on.

"Drop the knife or I'll shoot!" Tembelos yelled to Khasan.

Then, raising his gun, he shot and killed him.

• • •

It was not exactly the homecoming Patronas had anticipated. The floor of the terminal was slick with blood, and there was the body of Khasan, splayed against the Hertz ticket counter. Patronas had no idea what had become of the roses he'd intended to give Lydia or the balloons he'd bought Ali. They'd fallen by the wayside along with his peace of mind.

He was a mess. He kept hearing the pained animal noises Khasan made when the bullet entered his body, felt the man jerking beneath him as he died.

The Chechen had bled to death all over him. There wasn't enough time to go back to the house and change, so Patronas did what he could in the washroom of the airport, wetting paper towels and, when they ran out, toilet paper and wiping himself off. His new clothes were ruined; and he knew he looked like hell.

Lydia's smile faded when she saw him.

"Don't worry, it's nothing," Patronas said, seeking to reassure her. "There was an incident here before you arrived."

Her voice rose an octave. "What do you mean, 'there was an incident'?"

Patronas gestured toward Khasan, lying dead beneath the yellow Hertz sign.

"Was he one of the traffickers?"

"Yes. He was the man in charge."

"Well done," she said and kissed him.

• • •

Ali panicked when he saw the blood and began to scream. Patronas tried to explain that he was all right; he hadn't been hurt; but the boy refused to understand. He screamed when he saw Khasan, too, and kept on screaming during the entire taxi ride to the house—for a solid hour. The driver wanted to charge Patronas double. Again, not the homecoming Patronas had hoped for.

The boy was shy with Patronas when they first arrived at the house. He refused to look at him and stayed in his room the rest of the day, playing with the cat.

"He thinks I abandoned him," Patronas thought sadly.

The next morning Patronas took Ali fishing, paddling the kayak he'd bought for the two of them out into the channel. He demonstrated how to bait the hook and cast off, then had Ali do it. Within minutes, the boy caught a little red fish the size of a finger which he proudly carried home and put in a bowl of water, seeking to restore it to life. Patronas let him fuss, planning to swap it out for a live fish as soon as he got the chance.

The boy followed him around for the rest of the day. Every time Patronas turned around, Ali was there. He even kept Patronas company in the bathroom, happily flushing the toilet after he'd finished.

"What's he doing?" Patronas asked Lydia. "What's with the plumbing?"

"He's trying to help. To show you how useful he can be."

"But why?"

"He's afraid you'll go away again, that he'll lose you the way he did his parents."

"What should I do?"

"Nothing. Just give it some time."

Lydia wept when they first got the house; and Patronas showed her the new rosebushes.

"It's just the start," he said. "I'll fix everything, Lydia. Better than ever. I'll be the husband you always wanted."

"You already are, Yiannis. I realized that in Athens. Where we live doesn't matter. All that matters is you and me and what we are to each other."

Patronas very much doubted this, but he thought it best to keep silent. Lydia was a rich American and as such, she had certain expectations when it came to living quarters, a functional roof being one of them, followed by windows that opened and close; and furniture that didn't smell like smoke.

Patronas had purchased new beds in anticipation of their arrival, but they hadn't arrived yet; and the three of them ended up sleeping on air mattresses that night. The kitchen was still in shambles, so she couldn't cook. Not exactly a tragedy, this last, but Lydia carried on like it was the end of the world.

"How will we live?"

"We'll eat gyros and pizza."

They replanted the front yard together two days later, Lydia demonstrating how to handle the seedlings while Ali ran around with mud on his face.

"They're delicate, Yiannis," she kept saying. "Don't shove them in the ground like that. You must be gentle. Gentle."

Patronas did his best, setting the roots of the trees down into the holes and covering them with dirt.

They say in Greece, a man plants trees for his grandsons. Maybe that would be the case here. The trees would grow into maturity as would Ali. And Patronas' life would be complete.

• • •

Ali's adoption came through at the end of the month. The necessary paperwork had all been filed; and the adopted minor—in this case, Ali— duly registered at the Special Civil Registry in Athens by Patronas' lawyer.

Patronas didn't understand everything the lawyer told him on the phone. The process, as the man described it, had been extremely tedious, requiring an adoption order to be issued by a Greek court, but it had now been completed; and Ali was legally his.

After thanking the lawyer, Patronas ended the call.

He'd been standing outside, tending to the trees with Ali, when the call came in and he'd started to cry. The boy hugged him around the knees. *"Baba?!"*

Patronas typed 'happy, not sad,' on the language app; and had the phone read it back to the boy in Arabic. The child was confused by the device and kept thumping it with his hand, trying to make the woman who was talking appear.

"*Omm?*" he said, holding his head to the phone. "Mama?"

• • •

When Patronas told Lydia the news about the adoption, she swooped Ali up and danced around the room with him, singing the song about the child from Babylon Patronas had taught her.

"We'll have a feast," she said, setting the boy down. "I'll cook us something special to celebrate."

Here we go, Patronas thought. "But we don't have a stove."

"I'll figure something out."

She came back a few hours later, carrying a huge bag of groceries and a cardboard box. "I brought a crockpot," she said gaily, unpacking the box. "You plug it in; and it cooks all day."

Patronas inspected the device. "You can't use it here. It's American and American appliances run on 110 volts while in Greece it's 220 volts."

"No worries. I bought an adaptor."

Patronas' face fell. Vegetables didn't have much to begin with and cooking them all day would not enhance their appeal. Baby food, they'd end up eating baby food.

"I have a better idea, Lydia. Why don't we go to that taverna you like in Vrondatos, the one by the sea."

Lydia took her time getting ready and emerged wearing a green satin dress Patronas had never seen before and sparkly high heels. She smelled of gardenias.

They dined on lobster pasta and an assortment of appetizers, drank a bottle of wine each and watched the moon rise over the sea. Ali fell asleep not long after they arrived; and they laid him down on two chairs they pushed together and covered him with Lydia's shawl.

Reaching over, Lydia took Patronas' hand. "I love you, Yiannis. You're the finest man I know."

Remembering what she'd said about sharing, how important it was, he decided to give it a try. "You're pretty good yourself."

She looked down at Ali, asleep on the chairs. "We're a family now."

"Yes."

"It feels good. It feels right."

Feelings. It was always feelings with her.

"Yes, it does, Lydia. It feels right."

• • •

That night Patronas dreamed he was back in the water again, only it was Ali this time, Ali who was being borne away by the waves, Ali, he couldn't reach. There were children everywhere in his dream, splashing around in desperation, drowning right before his eyes. He couldn't reach them either and woke up screaming.

Lydia shook him. "Yiannis! Yiannis! Wake up!"

They ended up going for a walk on the beach. There was no wind; and the sea was still. Nothing like it had been in his dream, it was like a sheet of hammered silver in the waning light of the moon. In the distance, a boat was heading north in the channel. A Coast Guard cruiser maybe, on the prowl for migrants.

Picking up a rock, Patronas heaved it into the water. Lydia selected a smaller flat one and sent it skipping across the surface. They ended competing, sending stone after stone dancing across the channel, counting each skip they made and laughing.

"Four," Lydia sang out. "I win."

Throwing the rock like a frisbee, Patronas made it to five and declared himself the winner.

"Time to go back," she said.

"Not just yet."

Pulling her close, Patronas buried his face in her neck. She still smelled of gardenias. "Not just yet."

Ali was standing on the steps in his pajamas when they eventually returned to the house. He ran to Lydia's side, then seemed the think twice about it, and embraced Patronas.

"*Baba*," he cried. "*Baba*."

Chapter 31

Patronas still struggled with the case, going over it again and again in his mind. He regretted not taking Liadis down sooner and sparing little Dalia. However, the child appeared to be all right. Whenever he visited her in Vial, her face would light up; and she'd come running toward him. One morning she gave him a present—a little bird she'd made out popsicle sticks.

"*Tar*," she said in Arabic. He didn't understand and consulted the app on the phone. "*Tar*," she repeated. Fly.

Then "*bar'a, bar'a*." Free, free.

Tears started in his eyes.

"Yes, *bar'a* , Dalia."

He continued to have nightmares, terrible dreams about children he couldn't reach, couldn't save. Lydia would wake him and hold him for a time; and sometimes they'd go for a walk together, splashing along the shoreline until the sun rose.

"I can't stop thinking about what was done to those kids," he told her. "I can't get past it."

"You will, Yiannis. You just need time."

"I'm thinking I should retire,"

"Quit the force?"

He nodded. "It's too much. That last case…I can't explain it. It did something to me."

"You're too hard on yourself. You did a lot of good. Remember that movie we saw, *Schindler's List*?" Remember what they said at the end? 'He who saves one life, saves the world entire.' Maybe that's all you get—a single chance —and you are lucky if you even get that."

Her eyes were shining. "You got that chance, Yiannis, and you took it. You saved Ali and those other children—maybe not all of them, but some. You saved the world entire."

• • •

The next morning Patronas left the house early and drove to the station on his moped. He wanted to call Stathis, while the station was still empty.

After he and Lydia had returned from the beach, he'd lain awake the rest of the night, thinking about what to do and near dawn, he'd decided.

Stathis would be the first stop in his new life.

He called his boss at home. A risky move always, but Patronas no longer cared.

"What is it now, Patronas?" Stathis growled, his voice heavy with sleep.

"I'm done," Patronas said. "I want to retire."

"You must be kidding."

"No, sir. I want out."

"But why?"

"I'm tired, sir. Tired of all of it."

"Take a nap."

Patronas continued as if he hadn't heard. "I will email you my resignation letter and post a hardcopy of it to you later today."

"Shit, Patronas! Who the hell am I going to get to replace you?"

"Tembelos."

"Are you out of your mind? He's a lunatic. He killed two people in the last month alone. There'll be hell to pay in the press if I appoint him."

"Both of those shootings were in defense of me."

"We haven't even begun to sort out what happened at the airport— the death of that man, that Chechen. A witness came forward and said Tembelos didn't give Khasan a chance, that he shot him to death in cold blood."

"Need I remind you of what that suspect was charged with? That he was a fugitive and there was a warrant out for his arrest for trafficking children?"

"Nevertheless…"

Stathis convinced Patronas to put off his resignation until Tembelos had been cleared, promising he would appoint him Chief Inspector in

Chios immediately after. "We are officers of the law. There are procedures which must be adhered to."

"You'll give him my job?"

"I will. I give you my word of honor."

Given Khasan's record and the horrific nature of his alleged crimes, Patronas was sure his friend would be exonerated for killing him. Still, Tembelos would be thoroughly investigated. Authorities would gather testimony and hold hearings. It would be a lengthy and tedious process.

"How long are we talking?" he asked.

"I don't know. A couple of months. Enough time for you to wrap things up and say your good-byes."

"Very well, sir. I'll wait."

Stathis didn't want to hang up and kept Patronas on the phone another fifteen minutes, hemming and hawing and talking about the paperwork Patronas had to fill out in order to get his pension.

"I shall miss you, Patronas," he said at the end. "You haven't been the easiest person to work with, but I will be sorry to see you go."

"Thank you, sir."

But Stathis wasn't done. "You are first class detective, but more importantly, you're a decent man, relentless in your pursuit of justice. A true *pallikari*." Warrior

This from a man who'd fired him twice and made his life hell for decades. Patronas was dumbfounded.

"He licks where he used to spit," he said under his breath.

• • •

Later that day, Patronas invited Papa Michalis out to dinner. They walked across the square to Hotzas, a well-known taverna. Housed in a nineteenth century distillery, it was one of the best on the island; and the old man was giddy with excitement.

"What shall we have, Yiannis?" he asked, rubbing his hands together. "What are you in the mood for?"

The waiter seated them outside in the garden and after they sat down, handed them each a menu the size of Tolstoy's opus, *War and Peace*.

"I don't know," he told the priest, flipping through the menu. "Maybe a little of everything."

Papa Michalis took him at his word and ordered *souzoukakia*—meatballs with cumin— beef with mavrodaphne—a kind of sweet wine—two portions of French fries, stewed octopus, fried shrimp and three kinds of pitas. He'd wanted to order *revithia* keftedes—meatballs made from chickpeas—but Patronas had demurred.

"No vegetables."

"A portion of suckling pig then?"

"Of course. Make it two. It's good here."

Patronas figured he better load up while he could, given his future with the crockpot which now sat out the kitchen table like an evil centerpiece. There it hummed, lights ablaze for hours on end, producing food that was the color and texture of a muddy army uniform and Patronas was sure tasted about the same.

The waiter had to bring a second table to hold all the food.

"What's going on, Yiannis?" the priest asked, surveying the dishes. "Usually you restrict my ordering, but you haven't said a word."

"It's a farewell celebration," Patronas said. "I've decided to retire."

Papa Michalis dropped his fork. "But why? You just closed the biggest case of your career. This is your moment of triumph."

"I don't care. I want out. I called Stathis this morning and asked him to appoint Giorgos Tembelos in my place. He needs to be cleared for those two shootings first, but Stathis doesn't think it will be a problem."

The old man studied him for a long time, the food growing cold on his plate. "But it's your vocation, Yiannis. Something you were meant to do. You're a genius at police work."

"I'm exhausted, Father. I haven't slept well in weeks. I keep dreaming about those kids, night after night I dream about them."

"You did your best, Yiannis."

"It wasn't enough. It's never enough anymore. When I first joined the force, there was very little crime in Greece, a few domestic assaults, some pilfering, and that was it. No one used drugs. Let alone kidnapped children and sold them. But that's all changed."

"You're just one person. You can't right every wrong in the world."

"The truth is I'm sick of people, Father. Sick of what I've seen them do, sick of what they're capable of."

Papa Michalis nodded. "I admit it's a challenge."

He reached for the pitas and piled them up on his plate. "You need to have faith, Yiannis, faith in your work, faith in the righteousness of it. A famous Hassidic leader, Rabbi Nachman of Bresov, wrote even if you have no faith, you should pray and one day faith will find you . And I think the same thing applies here. Continue to do what you do, Yiannis, and one day you will believe in yourself and your mission again."

"Does the bishop know you're going around quoting rabbis?"

The priest pursed his lips. "The church has no monopoly on the truth, Yiannis. Never has, and never will. I also quote the Koran on occasion and the *Dharma.*

Patronas raised his eyebrows. *"Dharma?"*

"The teachings of Buddha, his four noble truths: the truth of suffering, the truth of the cause of suffering, the truth of the end of the suffering and the true path that will free us from suffering."

"I'm all for the end of suffering, Father, but don't think it will happen, not while human beings walk the earth. I read somewhere that they tested our DNA; and we are ninety-six percent chimpanzee, chimpanzee, Father, chimpanzee. The only animal on the planet that wages war on its own kind. If I were God, I'd recall us."

"That's why you want to retire, isn't it? You don't think people are worth saving. I can hear it in your voice."

"Nope. Like I said. We're nothing. Just chimps, evil chimps."

"But the children, Yiannis…Without you, they would have been lost. Hold off on retiring for now. Maybe you'll change your mind." He speared a meatball and ate it off his fork, splattering himself with tomato sauce. His beard looked like it was bleeding.

"Kyria Toula spoke of you," he said, chewing thoughtfully. "She wants you to baptize one of boys she took in. Be his *νονός*." Godfather.

"I don't know, Father. I'm not much of a believer."

"Tembelos then. You think he'd do it?"

"Of course. He'd be honored."

"Now that we are on the topic, what do you intend to do with Ali? Are you going to baptize him?"

"Nope."

"What does Lydia say? As a general rule, Greek-Americans abide by the rules of the church."

"Lydia doesn't care."

"Have you asked her? We could have a big celebration after and welcome the boy into the community."

"Pass me the suckling pig."

Plate in hand, the priest hesitated. "Did you hear what I said?"

"You want to have a party."

"It would be nice."

And with that, he dumped what was left of the pig onto his plate and began to eat it.

• • •

Tembelos just laughed when Patronas told him his plans. "What are you going to do if you retire? Stay home and talk to Lydia, discuss the benefits of organic versus processed food? You'll die."

"I'll play with Ali."

"He's a kid and kids need other kids. They don't need you. I've got three. Believe me, I know."

Everyone else had left for the day and they were alone in the station, drinking ouzo out of plastic cups and smoking cigars. .

"I spoke to Father. He thinks I should stay on the job."

"You got no choice, as far as I can see. They say cowboys die with their boots on. With you, it'll be your badge. You got that hero complex going on. You can't help yourself."

"Hero complex?"

"Shit, yeah. You could teach Don Quixote a thing or two."

• • •

"I'm afraid all the time now," Melissa Costas told Patronas. "The fear, it never leaves me. I'm no good anymore as a cop."

Patronas had invited her out to lunch that day; and they'd walked down to the harbor and sat down at a table outside one of the cafes there. So far all she'd done is push the food around.

At the next table, a group of students were laughing over an image on a phone. Patronas watched them for a few minutes. He'd never been as carefree as they were, not once in his entire life. Carefree and full of laughter.

There hadn't been much to laugh about during his childhood. His mother, a destitute widow, had struggled financially and it had poisoned her spirit. Nor had there been much laughter in his years with Dimitra or during his long career as a cop.

Maybe that was something he should seek out after he retired. Laughter. It was as good a goal as any. Far better than taking up woodworking or arguing politics in the *kafenion*, coffee shop, whatever other crap old men chose to get into.

Costas continued to pick at her food. She'd lost weight and her vibrancy, that urgency he'd always sensed in her, was gone. He saw no trace of the person she'd once been, that self-righteous and prickly woman, who had lived and breathed police work.

"How can I help?" he asked.

"Don't retire. Stay on as Chief Inspector. Tembelos is a good man; and I like him, but he's not you."

"Melissa…"

"Hear me out. You watch over me. You think I don't know it, but I do. You keep me on the straight and narrow. I don't have anybody else in the world who does that for me. You're the only one."

She stared out at the water. "I'll lose my way if you go."

"You underestimate yourself."

"I mean it, sir. I won't make it."

Her words cast the deciding vote.

"Very well. I will stay on until you are on your feet again."

"It's not my feet," she said softly. "It's the rest of me."

She took a bite of her sandwich and set it down again. "I'm glad Tembelos killed Khasan. It helps to know that he's gone."

"Got a witness who says he set the whole thing in motion. Started first in Turkey and then made his way here."

"Such evil…But you know if there were a scale, you would balance him out." Her eyes were wet. "God keep you, sir."

He laughed. "Been keeping company with Father, have you?

"Yes, most nights we eat together."

"Beware of him. Before you know it, he'll have you on your knees, shouting 'hosannah, hosannah!'"

After they finished, the two of them walked back to the station together. Costas' leg hadn't completely healed; and she was limping a little.

Patronas started to take her arm, but then thought better of it. She needed to find her way, to regain her equilibrium as a cop and a woman.

He'd help as long as he could, but at some point, he'd be gone; and she would be on her own.

Maybe Papa Michalis is right; and I'll regain my passion in the coming months," he told himself. "The work itself will heal me."

• • •

Patronas and Lydia held the party for Ali one evening in early spring. The night was warm; and they lit lanterns along the beach and set up a long row of tables outside and decorated them with streamers and balloons. The house had been completely refurbished; the roof was new, the interior freshly painted. Lydia had paid a fortune to get it done on time; and a crew of workmen had worked day and night to finish on time.

The kitchen was now fully functional, the crockpot in its place of honor at the center of the table, its red eye blinking balefully.

Patronas eyed it as he set out the drinks. Who knew what Lydia had stewing in there? What sinister mess she'd concocted?

He'd enjoyed eating out, ordering whatever he pleased and gobbling it down under her disapproving eye, but those days were clearly over.

Tonight, he was roasting an entire lamb on a spit for the party—but who knew what tomorrow would bring, what gastronomical horrors Lydia would bless him with in the future.

He'd invited everyone in the police department to the party as well as the Syrians he'd gotten to know in the course of his investigation. Kyria Toula and her family had also been included, bringing the total number of people to well over fifty. In addition to the lamb, there was an assortment of mezes and salads, huge trays of moussaka and pasticcio. Lydia had hired a caterer to see to it; and he was busy now serving up the food. Everyone had brought sweets, so many they'd needed to set up a separate table for them. In addition, Tembelos had purchased a monstrous sheet cake from a bakery in town. Frosted in every color of the rainbow, it was decorated with farm animals, a donkey being the most prominent.

The Syrians kept largely to themselves, smiling shyly every so often at the other people. Patronas was learning Arabic; and he'd made a point of welcoming them into his house in their own language, explaining as well as he could who everyone was and handing them plates and urging them to fill them. *"Akel! Akel!!"* Eat! Eat!

Dimitra and her mother were also there. Lydia had insisted they be invited.

"As of three days ago, I am not sick anymore," she told Patronas when she arrived. "The doctor, he called me; and he gave me a clean bill of health."

"That's wonderful, Dimitra."

"I wanted to thank you, Yiannis. All those rides back and forth to the hospital. I couldn't have done it without you."

"I was glad I could help," he said, embarrassed.

"I'm happy it worked out with the boy." She waved a manicured hand at the crowd. "May you all live happily ever after just like in the movies."

Not convinced she was sincere, Patronas gave her a long, searching glance. There'd been something off in the way she'd said those last few words. Not malice this time it had been envy, envy he was pretty sure he'd heard in her voice. Dimitra was jealous of his happiness.

• • •

"Good on you," Lydia said when Patronas relayed what his ex-wife had told him "You were *present* in her time of need. You were *mindful.*"

This last had become a favorite theme of Lydia's, to be 'mindful' some exalted state one should constantly strive for.

Personally, Patronas didn't see it. How could a person be otherwise? Your mind was the same as your brain which was encased in your skull which, unless you'd been beheaded, always traveled with you. You couldn't go leaving your skull at home or forget about it in the front seat of your car. It was *there.*

"Mindful," he repeated.

He supposed it was better than being stupid.

The celebration lasted late into the night. Dalia and Ali ran up and down on the beach with the children of Amira Al-Bashir while Patronas played hide and seek with the rest, yelling and laughing in Arabic.

He had brought fireworks; and he set them off at the end of the party, the sudden explosions of light bright against the night sky, sparks raining down on them like falling stars.

Papa Michalis stayed on after everyone left; and he, Lydia and Patronas talked late into the night. Ali was asleep on the sofa; and they took care to whisper, not wanting to wake the boy.

They were all a little drunk and started debating justice, what it meant, if it was even possible. Around two a.m., the conversation turned to reincarnation.

"Every society tries to find a way to rectify wrongs and address injustice," Papa Michalis said. "For Christians, it's heaven and hell, for Hindus it's reincarnation."

Lydia nodded. "Coming back as something else."

"If you had the choice, what would you come back as?" Patronas asked her.

"Exactly what I am today," she replied. "Your wife and Ali's mother. What about you?"

"I'd come back as a bird. I'd master their language and sing the way they do, then I'd take to sky."

"Would you build a nest?"

"Yes. A big one with a view of the ocean for the three of us. I'd line it with silk and decorate it with ribbons and pearls."

"No worms?"

"No vegetables either."

Now is the time, he told himself. She's drunk. You're drunk. Get it said.

"Know what I don't want to come back as, Lydia? Not ever, not ever in a hundred, in a million years?"

"What?"

"A vegetarian."

She made a little sputtering noise.

Patronas blundered on. "I hate that stupid crockpot of yours."

She got up, went into the kitchen and came back out with the crockpot in her arms. Opening the front door, she walked down to the sea and heaved it into the water. It floated on its side for a moment, burped once like bullfrog, and sank beneath the waves.

"Happy?" she asked him.

Patronas smiled. "Yes."

Humming a song by Theodorakis, he grabbed her; and they danced *sitaki* together on the beach, their hands on each other's shoulders, spinning around the way Zorba had done in the movie and kicking their legs high in the air.

"*Opa!*" Patronas bellowed. "*Opa!*"

When Lydia asked him to translate, he told her he wasn't sure that he could. All he knew was it was a word you shouted when you were happy, when you could barely contain yourself for joy.

Ali had awoken and he stood on the steps of the house, watching them. A moment later, he ran down and joined them. He wanted to dance, too; and Lydia showed him the steps. He was clumsy at first, but gradually he mastered them, whooping and shouting *"opa,"* over and over.

Patronas had been practicing his Arabic and he called out, *"ebni,"* son, which made the boy laugh even harder.

"Baba!" He cried, pointing at him.

"Ebni," Patronas yelled back. *"Ebni lil'abad."* Son forever.

The temperature had dropped; and a heavy fog was rising from the water, making it difficult to tell where the sea ended; and the sky began. In front of them, the cove was bathed in moonlight, the sand luminous beneath their feet.

They were lost in it as they danced, lost in time, lost halfway between heaven and earth.

About the Author

Leta Serafim is a former journalist who worked at the Washington Post and Los Angeles Times Washington Bureau for many years. In addition to the Greek Island Mystery series, she is the author of a historical novel, To Look on Death No More, based on actual events in Greece during World War II and the children's picture book, *Molly Saw A Bear*.